Outstanding praise for the novels of Johnny Diaz!

Miami Manhunt

"Deep, poignant and a lot of fun to read."
—*Out in New Jersey*

"Extremely well written . . . with likeable charac
—*Between the Covers*

"A fun book to read."
—*AfterElton.com*

Boston Boys Club

"Breezy . . . fun . . ."
—*Edge (Miami)*

"A charming cocktail."
—*Out*

"Make way for the boys of summer! Johnny Diaz has written a sexy beach-read romp that you won't be able to put down."
—William J. Mann, author of *Object of Desire*

"Sexy, funny, you savor every page . . . a great summer read . . . all you have to do is sit back and open it and enjoy."
—*Eureka Pride*

"*Boston Boys Club* entertains, amuses and is the perfect compliment to a long, lazy day at the beach and cold tropical drink of your choice. But don't be fooled, there is a serious side to this book, which makes it all the better a slice of LGBT life. There are issues and illnesses, losses and things falling apart. But in the end, things come together and these boys will win your heart. This book is a keeper, and Johnny Diaz had better start working on a sequel."

—*La Bloga*

"*Boston Boys Club* is racy, funny and smart. With his unforgettable trio of narrators, Johnny Diaz ushers the reader through the sex-filled, weirdly skewed world of contemporary gay Boston. You're going to love this book."
—Scott Heim, author of *Mysterious Skin*

"In case you haven't heard the buzz, *Boston Boys Club* is the book to read on the beach this summer . . . fast paced and lighthearted."
—*Bay Windows*

Please turn the page for more praise for Johnny Diaz!

More outstanding praise for *Boston Boys Club*!

"A fun summer read . . . one hopes that the author will grace readers again with another story of New England's favorite city."
—*AfterElton.com*

"A bubbly beach read . . . the author clearly knows Boston inside and out, and readers from New England will appreciate the attention paid to the surroundings and the many local insider jokes."
—*Bay Area Reporter*

"A love letter to Boston."
—*The Gay and Lesbian Review*

"A winner . . . sexy, rich and charming, this one is a true page-turner."
—*OutSmart*

"Sure to make an appearance on many a beach towel this summer."
—*Here! Magazine*

"A winning book, especially for a summer read."
—*Boston Spirit*

"Johnny Diaz brings to palpable life the ins, outs, ups, and downs of gay city life and its most dangerous pasttime: dating. In chronicling the love lives—or lack thereof—of three good friends who meet weekly at a popular watering hole, Mr. Diaz gives us situations, hopes, fears, and, especially, characters, that all readers will identify with, and may even recognize as themselves. At turns comic, touching, and tragic, *Boston Boys Club* is sure to serve as a testament of American gay life in the new millennium, and the timeless search for Mister Right—or Mister Right Now. An addictive read."
J. G. Hayes, author of *This Thing Called Courage*

BEANTOWN CUBANS

Johnny Diaz

KENSINGTON BOOKS
http://www.kensingtonbooks.com

KENSINGTON BOOKS are published by

Kensington Publishing Corp.
119 West 40th Street
New York, NY 10018

All Kensington titles, imprints, and distributed lines are available at special quantity discounts for bulk purchases for sales promotion, premiums, fund-raising, educational, or institutional use.

Special book excerpts or customized printings can also be created to fit specific needs. For details, write or phone the office of the Kensington Special Sales Manager: Kensington Publishing Corp., 119 West 40th Street, New York, NY 10018. Attn. Special Sales Department. Phone: 1-800-221-2647.

Kensington and the K logo Reg. U.S. Pat. & TM Off.

ISBN-13: 978-0-7582-3425-4
ISBN-10: 0-7582-3425-2

First Kensington Trade Paperback Printing: August 2009
10 9 8 7 6 5 4 3 2 1

Printed in the United States of America

Acknowledgments

This book is dedicated to my dear friends and fellow readers who have endured the pain of losing a loved one, be it a parent, grandparent, relative, or friend. They may not be physically here with us, but their spirits continue to live on in our hearts and memories. I hope that my closest friends and my extended family of readers will relate to the fictional long-distance conversations between Carlos and his mother, Maria.

A special thank-you to Ryan Andrews for penning the song "Give You Up," which was highlighted in my previous novel.

1

Carlos

Even in death, my mother tells me what to do.

"Carlos, you look just like your father when he was your age. He was heavier though. You need to eat more, *mi amor*. You are looking thin again," Mami tells me in her Spanish-accented English. We're sitting at a corner table at Versailles restaurant, where the large glass windows face the whooshing cars on Miami's infamous Calle Ocho.

"I don't look like Papi. You always say that. Don't people have to say that a son looks like the father and that a daughter looks like the mother? I always thought I looked like you, Mami."

"*Bueno*, you have my eyes, my sense of humor. You have your Papi's short, dark brown, wavy hair, eyebrows, nose, and body. You have my quiet sense of humor, but more importantly, you have a good heart, and that comes from both your Papi and me. I think that's why you became a teacher, to help others. You always had a special gift to help people, Carlito," she says, extending her hand, softly tapping mine, and calling me by my nickname.

"Thanks, Mami. I just want to help other students adapt and learn. It was so hard for me the first few years after we came here from Cuba. The guys at school teased me because of my accent and because we came through the port of Mariel. I felt out of place and stupid."

"*Ay*, Carlos. You are better than those *estupidos*. Look at what you have become, a good-looking, hard-working professional. You took a negative from your childhood and became an honorable, respectable *hombresito. Hijo*, I am very proud of you. You need to be proud of yourself, too. Don't ever settle for less. Don't ever let anyone disrespect you. Don't ever let someone tell you you are not good enough. You are not just good enough, *mijo*. You are the best! *Te quiero*, Carlito. Whether you are in Miami or in Boston, I am always here for you."

Mami always had a way of making me feel good about myself. If I felt deflated, she knew what to say to lift my spirits. If I felt sick, like the times I had my asthma attacks, she knew how to keep me calm with her words so that I could slow down my breathing until I found my inhaler.

"Now let's eat. You need more meat on your bones. Get *la ropa vieja* and a plate of white rice and beans. This is better than the Cuban food in Boston, so eat up!" she says.

That's as much as I remember from the dream as I wait outside another Cuban restaurant, but this one is in Boston, my new home. Dreams have a way of being so short yet feeling so long. Time is of no consequence in my dreams. When Mami appears in them, I feel so loved and appreciated just as I did when she was alive. I feel at home and like I have a place in this world. I look forward to these dreams because they make me feel that Mami is still with me.

But right now, Tomas Perez should be with me at the restaurant. I dial my friend who is running late again.

"*Loco*, where are you?" I leave a message on his voicemail. I'm standing under Cuba. Well, a map of it. This Cuba is on a yellow and green sign outside our meeting place this afternoon, El Oriental de Cuba restaurant in Jamaica Plain. Tomas says it's the most Cuban neighborhood in Boston, and I believe him, since he seems to know about everything Cuban in Boston. I had no idea any Cubans existed in this lily-white town until I met Tomas, excuse me, Tommy. He likes the American nickname. He even uses it on

his byline at *The Boston Daily*. If I were him, I would proudly call
myself Tomas Perez, but then again, my name is Carlos Martin,
which doesn't scream loud and Latin as much as I wish it would.
Like Tommy, I'm proud of my Cuban roots and I don't hold back
on letting people know. (I'm wearing a T-shirt that reads HA-
VANA.) As I continue leaving Tommy a message, my finger traces
the map of Cuba emblazoned on the restaurant's front glass door.
Underneath the map, it reads "*Un pedacito de Cuba en Jamaica
Plain.*" My finger lands on a little red dot—Havana—where I was
born.

"*Chico,* hurry up! My stomach is about to eat itself. I can already taste the *media noche* sandwich, the *mamey batido* . . . *Ay mi
tierra!*" I finish the message, my mouth salivating over the mental
images of the Cuban food. I whip out a cigarette and pace back
and forth on Centre Street, which reminds me of Miami's Little
Havana. From the front window of the eatery I can see a small
plastic statue of San Lazaro watching over me and the street scene
outside. Just like Miami, Spanish peppers the air inside the barber-
shops, beauty salons, and bakeries with their seductive rows of golden
flans and crispy *pastelitos. Yum!* Bumper stickers with Puerto Rican
and Dominican flags bedeck the humping and rolling Honda and
Toyota low-riders, which blast Daddy Yankee and Celia Cruz. Wearing tank tops, Latinas with curlers in their hair saunter by in loud
flip-flops on their way to play the Mass Lotto. Men puffing cigars
with rolled up newspapers tucked under their arms pass me on
their way home or to play dominoes on someone's sagging porch.
Women with their children in tow emerge from the brick-faced
library and the mural-splashed super *mercado* named Hi-Lo across
the street. This sounds and looks like Little Havana, but it's not,
which is one of the reasons why I moved here. I glance at the classic
silver watch Mami gave me two years ago for my twenty-sixth birthday, and I smile. The inscription reads: *Carlos, feliz cumpleaños. Te quiero
mucho. Siempre, tu mama!* I trace the outline of the watch's head with
my finger, and my thoughts drift to Mami and Miami.

While I wait for my *loco* fellow Cubano to arrive, I light a cig-

arette and consider my new life and goal to be the *caballero* that my
beautiful, late mother raised me to be. I am Carlos Martin, the new
Cuban on the Boston block. I moved here last summer from
Miami, the capital of Cuban exiles. Crazy, huh? Why would a
Cubano—make that two—flock to a city known more for Pilgrims, Paul Revere, institutional racism, a disaster of a public trans-
portation project called The Big Dig, preppy Ivy League schools,
and skies that spew ice for half the year?

My reason may sound simple, but it's as complicated and layered as the history of my people who abandoned our alligator-
shaped Caribbean island to chart new lives, whether we wanted to
or not. I was one of those refugees. My parents, Aldo and Maria,
left Cuba with my sister, Lourdes, who was seven years old, and me
when I was three. We were Marielitos, although many of us do not
like that label because it came to have a negative connotation. We
fled the country when he who shall not be named opened his jails
and the port to flush out the bad Cuban seeds. (That's why
Marielitos get the bad rap. If you don't believe me, rent *Scarface*.)
But many hardworking families left too, including the Martin
clan. So unlike Tommy who is an ABC (American-bred Cuban)
born in the 33140 zip code, I am truly *Cubano*, of Havana, born at
twenty-one degrees latitude and seventy-eight degrees longitude
where the Gulf and the Caribbean winds breathe collectively. My
family boarded a rickety fishing boat named *A New Day* packed
with two hundred other Cubans. Like sardines soaked in our mojo,
we journeyed to Key West. I don't remember much about the trip.
I do remember chaos at the port and my Mami holding me tight
against her bosom as we boarded the boat. I remember her whis-
pering, singing to me in Spanish and comforting me as she always
did. *Ay, Cuba!*

Just as my family did all those years ago in 1980, I recently em-
barked on a journey of my own to Boston for a new beginning.
But this time, my mom isn't with me to share the adventure. She
passed away a year ago from colon cancer, something I still can't

seem to accept as true. I can still smell her Estée Lauder perfume and hear her in my thoughts because she seems to enjoy popping into my dreams and reminding me to eat right, fill up my gas tank before it reaches empty, and order my prescription for my asthma inhaler. (Yes, I smoke, and I have asthma.) Sometimes, I expect Mami to call me on my cell phone and advise me to change the sheets on my queen bed each week or ask me if I have taken my calcium supplement for the day. As I think about her, I pull out my cell phone again from my pocket and gaze at the photo I snapped of her as my screen saver. It's one of the last images of her smiling that I have, before the cancer raided, destroyed her body, and stole her from us. In the photo, she plants her verdant hibiscus flowers in the front garden of our Coral Gables home. She radiates the same brightness and light as the flowers and the sunlight did. The photo makes me smile. I miss her so much. I kiss the screen of my cell phone and flip it close. *Te quiero, Mami.*

The loss of my mother brought me to Boston. I had to escape my life in Miami because everything there reminded me of Mami, such as our weekly Sunday brunches at Versailles restaurant which was *our* place, *our* time together. There were the monthly shopping excursions to Costco, where we arrived with empty stomachs and left with bulging ones after sampling all the foods at the various tasting stations. I remember the *cafécito* and waffles she would whip up every morning for breakfast before I drove to work at Braddock High where I taught ninth-grade English literature.

Mami and I were a team, the same way Papi and my sister are. Without Mami in Miami, I didn't feel as moored to the city. I felt alone, an outsider in my own family and hometown. Even though Miami was where I lived, it wasn't home anymore. I didn't feel I belonged there with Papi and Lourdes, and I wanted to belong, somewhere, anywhere—again.

So here I am, in Boston, hoping for a chance at a second act. I am trying to learn to live without my mom, and God, it's hard. Her presence weighs heavily in my heart and memory. She seems to be with me everywhere I go, thanks to her cameo appearances in my dreams. I am doing my best to move forward as Mami would want me to. Slowly, Boston helps me heal. I enjoy the newness of "The Hub" as some natives like to call it. I have a new job at Dorchester High where I teach ninth graders the wonders of literature. Well, I'm trying, but they seem distracted by the Red Sox and the Patriots. In my one-bedroom rental apartment in Cambridge on the Somerville-Cambridge line, I enjoy decorating the walls and bathroom with help from nearby Pier 1 and IKEA. And I've made a new friend, Tommy. He is helping me feel at home with his infectious *Cubanity*. I didn't have many gay Hispanic friends in Miami, and Tommy is just like me in a lot of ways because of our upbringing and values.

For the past few months, Tommy has been my Cuban comfort. He brings a little of Miami to my lonely urban corner of Boston. We both grew up in Miami with super-macho fathers cut from the same cloth. We have overprotective older sisters. Tommy and I found ourselves in Boston pursuing our careers and cultivating new journeys, his as a journalist and mine as a teacher. I know if we had met in high school, we would have been instant best friends, a *cortadito*—he the cream to my Cuban coffee, a good mix. I would have been the freshman or sophomore to his senior. He is my first friend in this new city, and I like the sound of that.

Too bad we didn't know each other in Miami. With his warmth, confidence, and humor, he could have helped me a lot during my high school years at Christopher Columbus High, an all-boys private school. Tommy would have been a good guy friend to turn to when I told Papi that I was gay and infatuated with Rick on the track team. Tommy would have been great in Miami when I found out that my boyfriend Daniel cheated on me while my mother was sick. I don't want to think about those details right now. Mami always said, "It's important to listen to other people and not talk too much about ourselves."

I glance at my watch again: It's 6:30 p.m. Where is Tommy?

Speak of the *diablo* and he finally shows up. *Ay, dios mio!* Tommy is driving with the top down on his new white Jeep Wrangler. He beeps twice and waves at me, his short, dark brown, curly hair quivering in all directions in the fall breeze. He's showing off again, but it's funny to watch because he's proud of his new wheels. A few minutes later after parking the Jeep and leaving half of it sticking out on the street (he's not a great parker), Tommy hoists his *Boston Daily* messenger bag over his shoulder and crosses the street. He flashes his big happy-go-lucky smile and walks up to the restaurant with a certain bounce in his step. His black bag bounces against his thin frame the entire way.

"*Loco,* where have you been?" I ask. Tommy greets me with a big, warm strong hug. I catch a whiff of his Cool Water cologne, which is very 90s to me, but that's Tommy. He's a creature of habit who sticks to what he knows, and that includes food. He has a penchant for Boston Market turkey sandwiches, Diet Cokes with vodka, and Jeeps. (He just traded in his twelve-year-old black Jeep Wrangler for the new white one.) If I hadn't talked him into accompanying me to this restaurant, it would have been another meal of turkey carver sandwiches, corn, and sweet potatoes, and I couldn't have that again! There are only so many times I can go to Boston Market with him.

"Sorry, Carlos. I got stuck in traffic coming from the *Daily*. I had to answer some questions from my editor about my story about this famous Dominican author who just published his second book. You hungry?"

"Um, yes! Let's eat," I say, seduced by the succulent aroma of breaded steaks and fresh Cuban bread and frying *tostones* from the kitchen. The hostess with the tight ponytail and perfectly formed curlycues glued with gel to the sides of her head, greets us in Spanish. She gingerly escorts us to a corner table by the window near other customers who nibble on croquettes, beans, and rice. Tommy and I follow our noses and the hostess deeper into this small eatery. It is decorated with bright colorful photographs of Cuba's streetscapes, including a lime green 1950s' Chevrolet and a cheery group of black smiling dancers dressed in white. No matter where they are located, Latin restaurants tend to have a familiar feel. Slow-moving ceiling fans whir above customers. Infectious laughter from the waitresses echoes as they gossip about their previous night out. And, of course, the rich aroma of garlic dances through the dining room, imbuing the scene with a palpable "sabor" in everyone's mouth.

Tommy and I settle into our cushioned seats, and we immediately study the menus. It's been months since I've had Cuban food in Miami, so this place will have to do.

"So what's going on with you, *chico?* How was school today?" Tommy asks, putting down his menu, which features yet another image of my country on the cover. *Ay, Havana!* As we talk, Tommy begins to rip and twirl small pieces of his napkin over and over again into little balls, something he does often at restaurants.

"I'm still getting to know the students. They're a mix of blacks, Hispanics, and Asians, and I have to wait about fifteen minutes at the beginning of class to get them to settle down. All they want to do is talk about their online profiles and who did who over the weekend. But when I sit in front and stare at them without saying a word, they finally start to settle down and let me talk. It's all psychology, Mr. T, but sometimes I just want to start the day without them interrupting me."

"I can't imagine being a teacher here, especially in Dorchester or *Dotchestah* as the native Bostonians say. It's one of the rougher schools. It's where all those shootings take place and close to where they filmed that 2007 Ben Affleck movie, *Gone Baby Gone,* which showed the grittier side of Beantown. You get SHOT in DOT!" Tommy jokes. He tends to preface his conversations with pop culture references.

"But don't you live in Dorchester?" I break some of the warm bread the waitress brought us.

"Um yeah, that's why I know what I'm talking about. Don't leave home without your bulletproof vest! But I'm in the nice part of Dorchester, near Milton by the old Walter Baker Chocolate Factories, so I don't have to strap on my bazooka. Actually, I'm teasing. I do like living there. It's like a cute little urban hamlet. Speaking of cute, are there any cute teachers at your school?" As usual, Tommy plays reporter after hours. He flashes his big smile again. A chronic smiler, Tommy makes people wonder what he's thinking about.

"Except for that night we met at Club Café, I haven't met anyone. All the guys at Club Café are too good-looking. They're all about themselves, and they seemed snobby. They're all in their little cliques talking about everyone else like gossiping girls on a teen show. I don't know why you like that place. I was about to head home when I met you that night. Everyone else seemed really rude. Is there another bar to go to?"

"Snobby? Club Café is fun, Carlos. Loosen up," Tommy snaps back. Oops. I forgot how much he enjoys hanging out there. It's where he met his ex-boyfriend Mikey, the alcoholic. I better not go there right now. If I get Tommy wound up again about Mikey, the Ethan Hawke clone, and how much he loved him, I'll have to throw myself through this beautiful glass window, and I wouldn't want to upset the Cuban restaurant owner. In the short time that I've known Tommy, I've noticed that he repeats himself with his stories, especially those concerning Mikey. From what Tommy has shared with me, Mikey made him feel at home in Boston when he moved here from Miami, but Mikey was constantly drowning himself inside a Corona bottle. I don't know what that is like from personal experience except for Tio Augustin, my uncle who was never invited to family gatherings. We feared he would become an obnoxious drunk. From what Tommy has described, I don't want to ever experience that with a boyfriend. I'll take his word for it.

"Well, Club Café is more *your* scene, but is there another place we can go that is more laid back, more ethnic, sort of like Miami? Club Café is so white. I want to see the other side of Boston," I say, sipping my water.

"Um, white, Carlos? Have you looked at yourself in the mirror? You look like a Cuban Josh Groban except with shorter hair. You're just as white as the guys here in Boston."

"Yeah, but I'm Cuban so it's not the same thing, but I don't look like Josh Groban. I'll take that as a compliment though because he's handsome, so thank you. I just have more *café* mixed in me." I joke back. Tommy is right though. I'm pretty pale for a Cuban. People often mistake me for a European from Spain. It's the milkiness of my skin, my dark brown, wavy hair, and light brown eyes. Tommy is slightly darker with his olive skin, short, brown, curly hair, and cinnamon brown eyes. I would say that he looks like that soccer player who won *Survivor* a few years ago but with more tamed hair. (Just don't tell Tommy that because it may go to his head.) Tommy appears more Greek and Italian, which is what caught my attention when we first met. He looked, well, ethnic, and I like ethnic-looking guys, which is something this city lacks unless you're here in Jamaica Plain or in Dorchester or East Boston, Logan International Airport's neighbor. When I first met Tommy, I thought we would hit it off romantically. I was interested. Tommy is very attractive, and I immediately sensed he has a good heart. But from the get-go, he talked endlessly about Mikey and their break-up. I could tell that this ex-boyfriend resided in a large part of his heart. Besides, I needed a friend here, *un amigo,* and Tommy seemed like he would be a great one. And Mami would agree. I can picture myself introducing her to him. He would have passed the Maria Martin test with flying colors. (Oops. I am talking about Mami again. Sorry. I tend to do that a lot.) Tommy tells really cheesy goofy jokes and announces the year when movies and songs came out as if he had OCD. I call him *loco* or *loca* but as terms of endearment. I just never met anyone with all his quirks. He's a good guy, and he's taken the time to show me around the city and teach me how to navigate the subway, which is called the "T" here, and explain how some neighborhoods are stand-ins for others in Miami. (Tommy says Newton is like Boston's Coral Gables and Quincy is like North Miami Beach but with more history.)

The night we met this summer, after we talked about our families, and growing up in Miami Beach and Coral Gables, Tommy handed me his *Daily* business card with his cell phone number scribbled on the back. He said words that made me realize I had made a new friend. By the lip of Club Café's front door that night, Tommy said, "I know what it's like to be a stranger in a new city—especially one that is as cold as Boston—in more ways than one. I was where you are now, and I know what you're going through, trying to make sense of this staid and sometimes too provincial town. So if you ever need anything or you want to hang out or if you're feeling homesick and need someone to talk to, I'm here, okay? I know my way around, and I can help you figure this place out. You're not alone. Remember that! You're with a fellow Cuban. *Familia.*"

We hugged that night, and from them on, we've been chatting on the phone almost daily, our conversations spiced with stories about our families and workdays. I call him on my breaks from school or when I'm on my way home. From the beginning, we would *hang-ear*, our word for hanging out, which means anything from me going over to his condo to watch *Project Runway*, or our favorite all-time *Que Pasa USA?* episodes, a classic PBS show about a Cuban family in Miami adapting to America in the 1970s. *Hang-ear* also means that he keeps me company as I fold a load of laundry. We don't have to do anything formal. Spending time with Tommy is like being with family, a brother from another mother. And although he tends to talk about his job a lot and he becomes long-winded with his Mikey tales, I can handle that. Hey, no one is perfect. I am far from it, with my hairy arms and upper back that require monthly wax jobs. Some Cubans are as hairy as wolves. Just ask conga queen Gloria Estefan, who admitted during a concert how hairy she was as a teenager. I believe it. (She used to have a unibrow.)

"There's a place called Paradise in Cambridge next to MIT. It's a two-story bar. You've got a lot of Brazilians, Hispanics, some blacks, and Asians in there. It's a little gritty and the extreme opposite of Club Café, but it's fun if you like that sort of thing," Tommy says, gesturing for the waitress to return so she can take our order. "I like to call it *Paradise Lost* because no one from Club Café would be caught going there." Tommy laughs, which makes his brown curls shake like a shivering bush.

"*Bueno,* we should go. I want to see the other side of Boston's gay scene. I know it can't be just these twinks and yuppies at Club Café. Where's the color in these bars? I know Latinos must dance and drink somewhere around here!"

"If you want, we can go. I'll show you Paradise, but don't say I didn't warn you. The guys there aren't that great looking, but I'd be happy to take you there. It'll be fun. I can finally dance with another Cuban here," Tommy says. "If you remember that club in Miami called Ozone behind the University of Miami, then you'll know what to expect in Club Parasites, uh, I mean Paradise."

"You the man, Tommy! Paradise, here we come!" The waitress scribbles down our order on a small pad filled with shaded green sheets. I order the Cuban sandwich and a mamey shake, just as I envisioned earlier. Tommy gets a pressed turkey sandwich with fries and a Diet Coke. No big surprise there.

We sit here for the rest of the afternoon *charlando* about our work day. We laugh about the differences between Miami and Boston. Occasionally, we observe the hunky Puerto Rican construction workers as they order from the restaurant's café window during their break. The more Tommy and I hang out like this, the more at home I feel in my new city.

"So you've been christened. You ate at the one and only Cuban restaurant in Boston. You're officially the new Beantown Cuban. I pass on my tiara to you." Tommy holds up his half-empty glass of Diet Coke to toast the occasion.

"Thanks, *loco*. If it hadn't been for you, I wouldn't even know this place was here." I clink his glass with my frosty mamey shake.

"That's what new friends are for. You're not alone here. Remember that."

"I will, *loca!*" I say, raising my drink. "To Beantown Cubans!"

2

Tommy

I can't believe Carlos talked me into coming to Club Paradise. I hope no one from Club Café catches me here. I try to make a covert entry by walking quickly inside with my head down and my right hand on the side of my head, cloaking my face. Paradise isn't such a bad place. There aren't many cute guys here, that's all. It's just off the MIT campus, and looks like a former meat factory or deli. The only dance floor is in the basement and it smells like a mix of urine, club smoke, and alcohol. It's dark in here, too, something out of the *Texas Chainsaw Massacre* but with pumping music and outdated strobe lights. (Did I just hear a chainsaw?) Ah no, just some nighttime construction workers hammering into a new condo high-rise down the street.

Once inside, I notice the bar is filled with unattractive guys who look as if they came here straight from Jabba the Hutt's cantina in *Star Wars*. They seem like Club Café rejects. I'm not elitist or anything. I'm just being brutally honest. Club Café radiates more style with its cute young guys, thirtysomethings, and plasma monitors featuring the latest video mixes. But I've gone there one too many times in the last year, so a change of scenery might be good for me. Part of the reason why I want to maintain a low profile at Club Café is because it reminds me too much of Mikey, my ex-boyfriend. We met there one Thursday night, and I fell for him right then and there. I blame those piercing bright blue eyes and the way he spiked up his straight brown hair. I assign more blame to his endearing grin, which made me smile. I hold him guilty as charged for seducing me whenever he nodded his chin or bit down on his tongue when he thought he said something funny. Mikey was my first and, so far, my last boyfriend in Boston. He showed me Boston from a native's point of view. He took me on road trips to Portland, Providence, and Provincetown. He slept over at my Cambridge condo in Harvard Square, where we cuddled through the night. We were inseparable. Something—an emotional pull or magnetic force—directed my heart toward Mikey, as if Cupid had a GPS and shot me stone cold on that chilly November night. When I was around Mikey, something clicked, lighting me up from the inside like an electric spark. An unspoken magic, an invisible energy, lingered between us whenever we were together. It surfaced when we did the most mundane things such as sitting on my big blue sofa, walking on Newbury Street, or watching *Saturday Night Live*. Spending time with Mikey felt natural and right—except on our nights out at Club Café.

His drinking gradually wore me down. He was drunk almost every weekend. He'd wake up on Sunday mornings hungover, slouched on the side of my bed. It didn't matter how many times I tried to talk him into getting help, he just wouldn't listen. After a few months of watching Mikey seesaw between drunk and sober, I had to move on and let him go. I confronted him about his drinking at the Barnes & Noble in Braintree, our meeting place, since he lived on the South Shore while I lived in Cambridge at the time. And right there near the Self Help section, he dumped me because I called him on his drinking. He walked away from me because he couldn't walk away from his drinking, and that left me heartbroken. I haven't been able to fill that hole in my heart. It didn't help that I would see him sloshed at Club Café every time I dropped by with Rico, my reliable and studly Italian wingman. After a while, I stopped going to Club Café because I didn't want to see Mikey drunk in the corner of the bar flirting with some guy. It hurt too much and reminded me of what might have been, if only he had cleaned himself up and stayed sober. It never happened.

"*Loca,* are you still with me?" Carlos says as we walk deeper into Paradise. "Stop thinking about Mikey and don't deny that you are. His name is written all over your face in big bold letters." Carlos knows me pretty well.

"Um, I was, um, just thinking about my next story, that's all." Carlos's eyes roll like two light brown bowling balls at my statement.

"*Por favor,* Tommy! In the short time that we've known each other, I've learned to read you like a gay romance novel. You wear your expressions too well. Let's have fun. Leave Mikey in the past. *Comprende?*"

And with that, we venture deeper into the bar. We walk a few steps up into the main bar, where some extremely young-looking guys pole-dance á la Britney or the Pussycat Dolls. They look too boyish to be legally working. Maybe a story for the *Daily's* Metro section?

I agreed to come here with Carlos because I wanted to show him another part of Boston, well, Cambridge, since the bar is on this side of the Charles River. Carlos is the newest addition to my crew of friends in Boston. I still have Rico to hang out with, but he's been too busy with his sailor boyfriend and competing in the gay football league. That's left some room to befriend Carlos, who is extremely nice but a little bit needy at times. When I met him at Club Café, we couldn't stop talking. He reminded me so much of myself when I moved here from Miami. Carlos was lonely and adjusting to his new surroundings and trying to make sense of a city filled with icy stares from native Bostonians. But there's one major difference between us. I still have my parents (who call me every night on cue). Carlos lost his mom to cancer. Out of the goodness of my heart, I decided to show him around The Hub. We became instant friends, as if we've known each other for years. There was a familiarity there. It never ceases to amaze me how at home I feel with a stranger when I learn that he is Cuban. We're like instant oatmeal. Just add water or, in Carlos's case, a Cuba Libre, and you get something that warms your tummy. Cuban comfort.

Carlos is your typical Cuban poster boy. He punctuates his speech with whiney *Ay, Cuba* or *Ay, mi tierra* and Spanglish phrases. Carlos is proud of his roots, even more so than I am, but I have always felt more American than Cuban after growing up in mainly Jewish Miami Beach. (I speak Spanish with an American accent.) With Carlos, it's the other way around. He feels more Cuban due to his American upbringing and speaks with a true-to-Miami thick accent in both English and Spanish.

I remember what it was like to be a newcomer to Boston, so I couldn't help but want to show Carlos that Boston is a great place to be, no matter where you are from. I found a good friend in Carlos, and that's why I'm here, showing him something new even though it's an old and tired place called Paradise. Wait, was that Antonio from Club Café standing in the corner? Nah, a look-alike. *Whew.*

I direct Carlos to the dance floor located in the basement. We squeeze through a musky herd of guys as we descend the dark steps to nowhere.

"*Guao*, there are so many guys here," Carlos says, his brown eyes lighting up as much as they can in this sub-level dance arena.

"Where? I can't see a thing. I left my glasses in the Jeep, so everything looks slightly fuzzy." All I can see is Carlos's eyes glowing from our new adventure tonight.

We head to the one-man bar in the front of the dance floor, where a gay Boston Benetton ad unfolds before us. Guys are crunking, gyrating, jumping, their bodies jerking to the left and sashaying to the right like wind-up dolls. Carlos and I grab our drinks. I ordered vodka and Diet Coke, my favorite. Carlos asked for a Cuba Libre. We clink our cheap imitation plastic glasses and take big sips.

"To Beantown Cubans," we declare, using our new catchphrase and taking swigs from our drinks. We lean against the bar and watch the parade of men stream by. Carlos nods my way to point out a cute guy he sees.

"Not really my type," I say, eyeing the lean, tall, and tanned Brazilian guy with the green and yellow tight-fitting jersey and baggy blue jeans that seem to defy Cambridge gravity.

"I want to play some *fútbol*," Carlos jokes.

"Well, go and be his Tom Brady! Have fun. Say hi or *oi* to that guy. I'm sure he can teach you a thing or two about Brazilian soccer."

"Ha! You sure? I don't want to leave you here by yourself," Carlos says while eyeing the guy who is now dancing a few feet from us and staring at Carlos with seductive hazel eyes. Upon closer inspection, the guy is not bad on the eyes now that I can see him more clearly. (I need to order contacts for my night outings.) I feel like a dork wearing glasses outside of work or driving. Luckily, I am only slightly near-sighted. At work, I'm the Cuban Clark Kent with my reading glasses on.

"Don't worry about me. I like to watch. I'm a news observer. I may get a story idea just by standing here. You never know. So go and have fun. This night was about getting you out and meeting new guys and having fun. Now *go!*"

Carlos grins, takes another sip, and power walks to the dance floor where Mr. Brazil awaits. I watch Carlos introduce himself, and Cuba and Brazil begin a steamy dance. At first, Carlos moves slowly and shyly as if unsure that he really wants to do this. But then he relaxes, and they start moving in sync. Every now and then, he looks my way, making faces or cocking one of his thin, dark brown eyebrows. When he mouths to me "He's so hot!" I can't help but laugh. Carlos has found dance heaven in Paradise.

I stand alone here surrounded by the darkness of the bar. No one from Club Café has spotted me, which is a good thing. I lean against the bar counter, which curves like the letter "c." I enjoy watching the guys dance with boundless energy. I can tell most are single, lonely souls reeling from a break-up or wishing they had a boyfriend at home so they wouldn't have to be out tonight. They're here to make some of these solitary nights seem less lonely by being in a club that serves as an unofficial brotherhood of broken hearts. I know the feeling too well.

A built black guy with a red tight-fitting tank top and snug blue jeans eyes a thin Asian guy with tanned arms and a toned bum. A few minutes later, their lips brush softly together as their bodies remain entwined on the dance floor. Their kisses grow stronger and more sealed.

My mind alternates between past and present. I remember what it was like kissing Mikey. The sweetness his eyes radiated, which was eclipsed by his sweet gestures. Last year, he bought me my first Red Sox cap and welcomed me to Red Sox Nation. I wasn't even a baseball fan, but it was the thought that counted. I remember how he helped me buy my first winter coat at The Gap at Copley Place. Then there was our road trip to Providence, where we clumsily lost my Jeep in the concrete parking maze at Providence Place mall.

A gargantuan man with a drink in his hand stumbles into me, interrupting my trek down memory lane.

"Sorry, dude," he slurs in a Boston accent. He continues stumbling all the way to the dimly lit bathroom.

Two drinks and an hour or so later, I'm still standing at the bar, where I have a front-row seat to everyone else having fun. The alcohol numbs my senses and my cloaked loneliness. To my surprise, Carlos and Mr. Brazil lip-lock, swaying to the swirling beats. Carlos stumbles a bit trying to keep up with the man whose hips swivel faster than Shakira's. Carlos finally takes a break from dancing and returns to the bar, leaving his friend dancing solo for the moment.

"So what's the story?" I ask Carlos.

"He's so *guapo!* His name is Marcello. He's a waiter in town. He speaks a little Spanish but more English. We talked for a bit on the dance floor. He has this sexy Brazilian accent. He lives in East Cambridge, not far from here." Carlos's eyes widen like two saucers.

"So hit it! Teach him something new, give him a Spanish lesson," I say. Carlos laughs at my suggestion. He stands to my right and orders another drink.

"We're going to get pizza after this drink. Wanna come? That way you can tell me what you really think of him? I trust your judgment."

"Nah, you guys go on ahead. You should be talking one-on-one. You don't need a nosy reporter there asking him a hundred questions. Seriously. Have fun with him and be careful."

"Are you sure? I don't want to feel like I'm ditching you, Tommy. While I was dancing, I noticed you seem a little sad." Carlos places his free hand on the curve of my right shoulder.

"I'm cool. Sometimes when I drink, I get sad. It's the alcohol. It's supposed to do that. It makes me giddy and hyper, but then it brings me down. Don't worry about me. I think I'm going to head on home. I'm a little tired. I had a long week at the *Daily*. I wrote two stories this week, one on how Brazilians don't feel like they fit in among Boston Latinos. My other story focuses on a daytime soap opera actress who wrote a book about being raised in Boston with various foster moms. So I'm beat."

"You were thinking about Mikey, weren't you?"

"Ah, okay. You got me there. Yes, I was thinking of Mikey a little, but he's the past and I'm moving on and right now, I want to head on home, maybe stop by 7-Eleven in Central Square for a Three Musketeers and a lime Gatorade. Anyway, everything is cool. Go and hang out with Marcello before he meets another cute guy, but by the looks of this place, he's all yours. I want to hear all the dirty, juicy details tomorrow, okay?"

"Deal. Be careful driving. Text me when you get home so I know that you made it okay."

"You sound like my overprotective parents. I'll text you, I promise," I say. We give each other a tight hug and say good night.

Carlos then bounces back to the dance floor to get some more one-on-one dance time before the club closes at 2 a.m. The breezy cool fall air escorts me as I walk back to my Jeep. On Massachusetts Avenue, I drive on the bumpy bridge, which is flanked by bright light posts that resemble flickering candles on a cake. As soon as I cross the Charles River to Boston, I hear an old favorite song, "The First Cut Is the Deepest" by Sheryl Crow. The song reminds me of Mikey. I lean my head against my left wrist as I negotiate Boston's pothole-filled streets. At each light, I wonder how Mikey is doing and whether I will ever meet another guy who will capture my heart the way he did. I knew Mikey was Mr. Right, but we met at the wrong time. We were in the wrong season of our lives.

The following afternoon, I drive on Interstate 93 on my way to a hike in the Blue Hills. Hiking has become one of my favorite hobbies in Boston. The one-hour walks through the woods to the top of the old Weather Observation Tower calm my mind. I forget about my deadlines and stresses at the *Daily* as a general assignment *Living/Arts* writer, my dream job and the real reason I left Miami for a new start in Boston. Miami remains in my heart, but I felt there was something more beyond lazy afternoons *en la playa*, liquor-fueled bar nights in South Beach, and South Florida's endless supply of gritty news stories which I covered at *The Miami News*. I wanted to work for a great newspaper and learn my way around a new city. I wanted to make it on my own. I considered Anchorage, Alaska, but there weren't any direct flights to Miami. (My parents would have had a conniption.) New York City seemed too overwhelming and crazy. Boston seemed like a good place to begin anew, personally and professionally. It's a big city but one that still exudes a small hometown feel. And since I had interned at the *Daily* one summer off from the University of Miami, I felt comfortable in Boston. Boston, with its clusters of low-rise redbrick brownstones, numerous bike paths that wrap both sides of the Charles River like concrete ribbons, and historic cobblestone streets in downtown agreed with me. Boston was, and still is, an outdoor museum that never seems to close. It marries the old world established by the Pilgrims with today's ever-changing Wi-Fi culture. Today's settlers are us newcomers, students, and immigrants. This place simply fuels my brain.

When the *Daily* offered me my job, it was to cover Boston neighborhoods for the city section. I wrote colorful city tales, about things such as the popularity of a local Santeria priest and the plight of a brave, young, homeless woman in Cambridge who kept an online diary of her city travels. Over the summer, my editors promoted me to features. I always wanted to work as a features reporter in Miami, but the editors there didn't give me a chance. *Bastards!* They preferred that I cover breaking news in Fort Lauderdale, another county (and world away) from the main newsroom in Miami. I freelanced for my old paper's features section while writing full time in Fort Lauderdale, but my efforts were like messages in a bottle, floating aimlessly. So my dream of becoming a features writer for my hometown paper and owning my place along Biscayne Bay was deferred. I had to start all over again. Boston was my second chance professionally, and I gladly took the job offer. And for that, I will always be grateful to *The Boston Daily,* my new professional home, for helping Boston become my permanent home. It's also where I discovered a love of hiking. (The only hiking that happens in pancake-flat Miami involves excursions to the mall, beach, or plastic surgeons' offices.)

When I hike, I embrace the peaceful serenity that Mother Nature offers me with 4,000 acres of preserved woodlands only ten miles from my condo. The hikes are also good workouts. I benefit more from hiking up 635 feet than riding the elliptical machine at the gym with my face buried in a novel. I have to remind myself to bring Carlos here sometime, but I enjoy having all these hills to myself. Maybe one day I'll bring him and, perhaps Rico, if I can pull him away from his seafaring boyfriend.

But first, I pull into the Barnes & Noble perched on a hill off Granite Street in Braintree. I walk into the store, which is crowded with suburban mothers and older people leafing through the magazines for free as they drink their white mochas and freshly brewed teas. I approach the café counter. The friendly young Latina sales-girl greets me in Spanish. She says I'm the only customer she can chat with *en español*.

"*Hola,* Tommy! The usual, right? The chocolate brownie and bottled water?"

"Yeah, Selena. How did you guess?" I say, standing in front of the glass display of cookies, cheesecakes, and brownies.

"Oh, let me see. You order this almost every day. I guess you're OCD or something, right? Don't you get bored of eating the same thing?" With a pair of plastic tongs, she grabs my brownie from the display case.

"You're right. It's my OCD: Obsessive Chocolate Disorder. The brownies are delicious! How can anyone get bored?"

I pay Selena and use my Barnes & Noble membership card, which gives me ten percent off the total price. Since I come here daily, it pays off.

Just as Selena hands me my spare change, I hear a familiar raspy Boston accent behind me in line. The sound breaks my focus from Selena.

"Tommy Perez! Is . . . that . . . you?" the voice inquires.

I turn around, and my heart races at a million miles a minute. A flush of nervous energy fills me when I recognize the sparkling sky-blue eyes, the brown spiked hair, and freckled nose and cheeks. Mikey. My fluttery nerves temporarily paralyze my vocal chords. He's standing behind me in line at our former meeting place.

"You're still in Boston? I figured you'd be back in Miami by now after your first winter," Mikey says, looking as cute as ever. I wish I could swim inside his eyes. His skin looks more vibrant and healthier than last year. The bags under his eyes are gone.

"Hey, you!" I blurt out as I realize that he's right here in front of me. I gather my composure. I wouldn't want him to think I'm nervous or excited or anything. Internally, I am jumping up and down at the vision.

"Yeah, I decided to stick around. You Bostonians can't get rid of me that easily." I regain my composure after the words pop out of my mouth.

A smile flashes across Mikey's face.

"What are you doing around here? You're kinda far from Cambridge," he says in his Boston accent, which makes "far" sound like "fahr."

"Actually, I bought a condo in Dorchester. I'm pretty close. I hike in the Blue Hills on Saturdays. Ever been?"

"You know, I've lived here all my life and I've never been to the Blue Hills. That's very adventurous of you. Hiking alone."

"Well, there are families hiking, too, so I never feel too alone." I stand with my bagged brownie in one hand and my bottled water in the other. As we stand here, our eyes lock wordlessly as other customers mosey around and give Selena their orders. In this moment, I take a full visual inventory of Mikey. I am lust, *err,* lost in thought. He sports a dark blue hooded jacket with a brown T-shirt underneath, baggy blue jeans, and brown sneakers. He always liked matching blue with brown.

My brown eyes quickly reacquaint themselves with his blue ones, which look like portals into a bright sky. Oh, those eyes! They seem to mesmerize and seduce at the same time, just like they did when we first met a year ago. I couldn't break away from his stare then, and I certainly can't break away from it now. I'm surprised that we bumped into each other here. I always figured I would see him out at a bar drinking, as usual.

"Well, I haven't seen any mountain lions in the Blue Hills. One time I got lost and I felt like I was in a scene from *The Blair Witch Project.* It took me two hours to find my way out of the forest. I was lost in *Shrek* land."

Mikey bites down on his tongue and smiles. I could always make him laugh with my goofy jokes. His smile inspires me to smile widely. That powerful unspoken magic between us remains alive and well. It hits me with a physical force as he holds my gaze. I remember the feeling fondly. That old desire returns.

"Want to sit down and talk?" he suggests as he gently runs his hand through his hair, similar to the way Ethan Hawke has in his many films.

"Um, sure. I'll meet you at the corner table, like old times."

I walk to the corner table. The whole way, I'm floating on air just from seeing Mikey and being able to talk to him while he's sober. I wait for him as he orders from Selena, who quickly winks at me when she sees Mikey headed my way. She silently mouths to me, "He's so cute!" with her wide-eyed enthusiasm. I mouth back, "I know!" and raise my thick black eyebrows to emphasize the point. As I wait for Mikey, I run my right hand through my gelled curls.

Mikey scoots into his chair and sits across from me. He holds his steaming white mocha latte. He softly blows on the drink and takes a sip. We sit by the window facing a parking lot of SUVs. People run in and out grabbing cups of coffee or tasty desserts. The late afternoon sun holds steady, lighting up the highway and hills in the distance. If I don't leave soon, it will be too dark for me to hike, but I don't get many opportunities to hang out with Mikey. I don't want this moment to fade with the looming sunset.

"So, Tommy, what have you been up to? You look really good. I like the fact that you cut your hair shorter. Those wild curls of yours were getting out of control," he says, sticking out his tongue and biting down on it, his trademark playfulness surfacing. I have always been amused by Mikey's expressions. They are windows into his feelings. Right now, he's quite happy to see me again.

"Thanks. This is more of my clean-cut look. It's better for work. I represent *The Boston Daily* wherever I go, and having a brown curly nest for hair didn't match my professional image when I reported my stories. You like it? I still have some curls on top, but they're just more tamed."

"Yes, I like it a lot, my *Cubanito*." Mikey uses the same nickname he used for me when we dated and fell in love last year.

"Well, I'm not your *Cubanito* anymore. Remember? So what's going on with you? I haven't seen you at all," I say, leaning back in my chair. The last time I saw Mikey, he was drunk at Club Café with his boyfriend, Phil the pill. By pill, I mean that the guy always wore a constipated facial expression like he had just taken some Dulcolax. I listen raptly.

"I'm not the same guy you used to know. I've been through a lot this past year. For one, I'm sober. I stopped drinking."

The admission catches me by surprise. Last year, I hoped—I prayed—that Mikey would have said those words, but he wasn't ready. He just pushed me away when I tried to make him aware of how alcohol was affecting me and most of all, him.

"Mikey, that's wonderful." I reach out to touch his right hand, and my fingers quickly graze the top of it. "I'm so proud of you. That couldn't have been easy. I remember how much you enjoyed drinking. What made you stop?"

Mikey takes a deep breath and continues.

"I crashed my Toyota into a large tree along the side of the road on my way back home to Duxbury one night. A cop found me. I don't remember much. It's a blur. The look on my parents' faces the next morning was enough to sober me up. I almost killed myself. The car was a total wreck."

"Oh my God, Mikey. You could have died. Do you know how lucky you are?"

I sit back and listen for a few minutes. I don't interrupt because I know this can't be easy for him to share.

"I know. They gave me a DUI, but I received a hardship license so I can drive to work and buy groceries. I also have to attend mandatory AA meetings. I go once a week. They've been helpful. At first it was hard sitting in these meetings, but I've gotten used to it. I share my frustrations about not drinking and my feelings about hurting so many people that I love."

I take a few sips from my bottled water and process everything Mikey just told me. Mikey is sober and getting help. God answered my prayer.

"Tommy, I wanted to talk to you because I want to apologize for my immature and stupid behavior whenever I got drunk. You always tried to help me and make me see that drinking was slowly killing me. I wasn't ready to hear it. I'm so sorry for putting you through that hell last year. You didn't deserve it. You're a special guy." He gently grabs my hand and squeezes it in his. His touch sends a rush of tingles throughout my body.

"I just wanted you to get better, that's all, whether we were together or not. Thank God everything is okay, that you're okay."

Mikey and I sit in the corner, *our* corner of the *café,* and we carry on a conversation that is easy and casual, like we're old friends. He tells me about his AA meetings. He recounts how he came out to his parents, who completely accepted him. I always figured they would have since they're educators. He also tells me how he read one of my stories, a profile on New England's most popular and cutest soccer player. I'm surprised and flattered that he kept up with my articles. Mikey also tells me about how he ended his relationship with Phil, and that he didn't really love him.

"I needed to focus on me, so I broke up with Phil. He wasn't the right guy for me anyway." Mikey's eyes are trained on me as he cups his drink with both hands.

"I'm so happy for you. I'm glad you were able to find your way and that you're healthy. Listen, if you ever need someone to talk to or someone to go with you to an AA meeting, just let me know. I want to support you, as a friend."

I say friend, but I don't know if Mikey and I can ever be just friends. But I want to try, for his sake and mine. A friendship could heal our wounds from last year. We always had fun and enjoyed being together. Perhaps we can redefine our relationship into a meaningful friendship.

"Thanks, Tommy. I really appreciate that. I could use a sober friend. Most of my friends still go to bars and drink. I don't feel comfortable at a bar. It's not healthy for me. I come here a lot to read magazines and books. I also fill out my progress reports for my students. You can say that Barnes & Noble is my new bar and white mocha lattes are my new drinks." He smiles.

"You don't have to go to a bar to have fun. We can meet here at Barnes & Noble and talk whenever you need to," I offer.

"Thanks. You've got a deal! It's so good talking to you again. You were always a great listener." I look down, and when I glance back up again, his smile greets me.

"If you call me, I will always listen. I will always be here for you, as long as you are sober," I say. I take a big sip of my water and I get up. I momentarily take my eyes off Mikey and glance at the softening sun. As I look away, I can feel him looking at me. I really want to go hiking, but I'm enjoying this time with Mikey as well. Maybe it's time that I get going because I'm nervous, excited, and euphoric just from sitting here with him. Some of my old feelings are resurfacing. A hike right about now might be good for me, to get me grounded.

"I don't mean to be rude, but I really want to go hiking today before it gets dark."

"Oh. I don't want to hold you up. Your hiking sounds like fun." He seems like he wants to keep talking, so I make a friendly suggestion.

"Well, would you like to come?"

"Um, sure. As long as there aren't any mountain lions, right?" Mikey says, stretching his arms out to form the cutest human letter "T" I have ever seen.

"You won't have to worry about the mountain lions if the coyotes get us first," I joke. "I'll protect you."

Mikey laughs.

"What are you going to do if we come across a wild animal, whip out a pen and paper and write a newspaper article?"

"Well, I have my secret powers."

"Oh yeah, Tommy? Like what?"

"The power of positive thinking. I wished you would get sober, and my prayers have been answered. So it works."

Mikey tilts his head and grins, his eyes crinkling at each corner.

"It's so good to talk to you again, Tommy."

"Ditto."

And with that, we walk outside with our drinks in our hands, climb into my Jeep, and embark on a new adventure together, almost like old times.

3

Carlos

"Carlito, that is a beautiful new shirt. You look very *guapo!* The green brings out your beautiful, light brown eyes. I'm sure Daniel must like it, too," Mami says, sitting across from me at Versailles for our weekly brunch. When she suspects something is going on with me, she opens our talk with a compliment before she unleashes her Cuban inquisition.

"Thanks, Mami. It was a gift from Daniel. He surprised me with the Banana Republic shirt this morning," I say, trying to hide what is really bothering me.

"Carlito, *que te pasa?* You seem a little sad."

"I'm fine, Mami. I just have a lot of homework papers to grade, as usual. How is the garden? I heard there's a sale at Home Depot on rose bushes, not that we need any more. The front of the house has the most flowers on our block. Maybe you can get some more for the backyard." I sip the ice water the young waiter has brought us.

"Good idea, Carlos, but look at who you are talking to. I'm your mama. *Que te pasa?* What's going on?" She stares at me and right through me. Mami has this X-ray vision into my thoughts and feelings, which makes it hard for me to cloak my concerns. I hold up the green and white menu, which matches the décor of the restaurant, to block Mami's view of me. She pushes the menu down.

"Is this about Daniel? Did he do something to upset you and gave you the new shirt to make you feel better? *Bueno,* I never liked him. He always seemed to look at other men when you both went out, and he should only be looking at you, *mi amor.* He always finds a reason to go out with his friends and not spend time with you and your family. You deserve better than Daniel, someone who wants you and only you," she says.

"No, Mami! It's not about Daniel. He's in South Beach with his friends. We're doing okay. We should order." I hold up the menu again.

"Carlos . . . *que te pasa?* We're here, right now, talking." She taps her index finger against the table. "It's just you and me, like always. Talk to me. I'm here for you."

I momentarily put the menu down to tuck my hair behind my ears. My eyes well up with tears. I hold the menu up again, but Mami pushes it down.

"Mami, you're sick. The cancer is back. I know. Don't pretend. I overheard you on the phone with Dr. Gonzalez. What are we going to do now? I can't see you go through the chemo again and lose all your hair. This isn't fair, Mami. It's not." My throat tightens. I look down to avoid my mother's piercing green eyes. She leans over to me and grabs both my hands and squeezes.

"Carlos, I don't want you worrying about this. I am going to fight this! *We* are going to fight this. We can do this. I just need your support. Have faith, *hijo.* I beat the cancer once. I can do it again. I have too much to live for. I want to see Lourdes get married and give me some grandchildren. I want to see your Papi retire from the convenience store and take me on cruises to the Caribbean. I want to see you with your own *casita,* a child of your own, maybe even a little dog. I want to see you grow old, *mi amor,* and I will. I promise, but first, let's order. *Tengo hambre!* Order the breaded chicken steak this time, and maybe for dessert, we can share a coconut flan."

I plaster a smile on my face. Mami knows how to lighten a mood by talking about food.

"But what about your health? I don't want to lose you, Mami."

"*Ay,* Carlos, you won't lose me. I will always be watching you. We will always have our talks. But right now, let's eat and eat fast, because you have to wake up and go to school in a little. You're alarm is about to go off in one . . . two . . . three . . ."

My alarm clock thunders in my bedroom, jolts me out of my dream, and scares the hell out of me. On reflex, I press the snooze button. *Ay, Mami!* I catch myself smiling at the dream and trying to overcome my weariness. I prop myself up in my bedroom and catch my breath. My breathing is labored. I rub my fingers in my eyes and open them. I grab my asthma inhaler on my bedside table and pump some medicine into my lungs. I'm feeling better. If only it weren't a dream. Every now and then when I need to hear her or see her, she appears in my dreams like a guardian angel who steps in to give me her two cents. But why do these dreams have to feel so real? Again, we were having our weekly Sunday brunch. That was our time together to talk about my work week and my issues with my ex, Daniel. I looked forward to our weekly meetings. I didn't have Papi there talking about the Marlins or his frustrations with running the convenience store we own in Miami Springs. I didn't have Lourdes babbling about her boyfriend and whether he was serious enough to propose to her one day. It was Mami and me, the Martin team.

In this dream, she wore her favorite light-green blouse with her blue jeans that defined her big Cuban butt. Mami always liked showing off her figure, even at fifty-seven. She looked like her old self in this dream, just as she did before the cancer. In my dreams, I remember only the good things about Mami. She's radiant. Her arms are free of brown bruises from injections. She smells fresh, like the perfume she bought on discount at Macy's. She doesn't smell like the chemicals her sweat exuded from all her cancer treatments. When I dream of her, she is healthy and beaming. She is Mami.

I lie back in my full-size bed, turn on my side, and look out my bedroom window. I have a view of the other triple-deckers and brownstones in my Cambridge neighborhood near Porter Square. Red digital numbers on my alarm clock read 5:00 a.m. Soon, I have to get ready for work at the high school, which is probably what Mami meant in the dream when she rushed me to eat so I could get to work on time.

I pull my light-blue comforter up to my chin and enjoy my last hour of rest, even though now I am wide awake. *Gracias, Mami,* I can't go back to sleep.

I look forward to these dreams because they remind me in a strange way that Mami still looks out for me. I can only imagine what she must have seen on Saturday night when I was at Club Paradise with Tommy. Mami probably eavesdropped as I talked to Marcello. The lean, handsome, Brazilian guy made me laugh on the dance floor with his goofy jokes and Portuguese accent. I felt all hot and steamy whenever he brushed up against me as we danced. Every time he did, I caught a trace of his Calvin Klein cologne, which he must have doused himself with before heading to the club. It's been a while since I've had sex with a guy, a few months actually, not since I moved to Boston. I thought it would be fun to make out with Marcello until the ugly truth slapped me in the face.

I get up and turn off my alarm clock so it doesn't wake the entire building. I yawn and stretch and make way to the kitchen and brew some coffee. As I prepare it, my thoughts drift to Saturday night at Paradise with Marcello.

We danced as Tommy watched from the bar looking a little down, which is unlike him. Tommy always has this sunny optimism. It's one of the reasons that I am drawn to him and why he can be a mystery to me at times. Who can smile and laugh as much as he does? Yet that night, he was off in his own world.

After I left Tommy at the bar (with his blessing), Marcello and I headed to a pizza place in Central Square where all the other club goers gather for some late-night food. That's one thing I have learned about Boston and Cambridge. There is nowhere to eat after midnight except for a handful of places. In Miami, the possibilities are endless at any given hour. So this fine Brazilian creature of a man and I ordered two sloppy slices of cheese pizza and then sat in a corner booth surrounded by late-night revelers, mostly college students who don't have to worry about mortgage payments or teaching high school students about classic literature.

As I munched on my slice, I studied every speck in Marcello's hazel eyes, the way the yellow mixed with the caramel hues. I liked how his tight, curly, brown hair scrunched up in the front. As I scrutinized his looks, I also explained my complicated Cuban background and how I moved to Boston. *Am I Cuban? Am I American? Am I Cuban-American? Or am I just Hispanic, since my family lineage is from Spain?* He told me that he works as a waiter in Harvard Square and that he lives in Allston, where all the college students live in squalor amid the bars and thrift stores near Boston University.

"I came here two years ago to find better work and to go to school. I'm saving money to go to one of the community colleges," he said in his broken English, which I found endearing. I am biased. I have a slight Spanish accent when I speak, so I find accents comforting, familiar. "I want to be a translator and help other Brazilians find their way here. I know what they go through when they come to this country," he said between bites of drippy pizza.

I was touched by his ambitious career goals but was more impressed by his sincerity in wanting to help others. *Ay, Mr. Brazil!* As he continued talking about his job and his large family in Sao Paulo, where he has three sisters and a brother, a built older man with a salt-and-pepper crew cut and wrinkles around his eyes suddenly appeared at our side.

"It's time to come home, Marcello. Now!" he ordered him.

"But . . . I . . . was just dancing. I have a new friend," Marcello explained nervously.

"Marcello, now!" the older man barked. I suspect the man was in his mid-forties. He then began speaking in Portuguese. Because of its similarity to Spanish, I was able to make out some key words. My translation: The man was telling him that he would not put up with a cheating boyfriend. *Boyfriend?* I thought Marcello was single. Why else would he be at a bar dancing with me? *Comemierda!* I should have known better. I didn't ask if he had a boyfriend. Mami was probably watching me from the afterlife, nodding her head in disapproval with her clenched hands on her waist.

The older man then forcefully grabbed him by the arm. Marcello looked at me with pleading apologetic eyes.

"I'm sorry, Carlos. You're a very nice person. I must go," he said.

I sat there wordlessly watching this man drag my potential new friend or boyfriend away. I should have stayed with Tommy. Feeling deflated, I finished my pizza and took a taxi back to my condo, alone. I remember the wet-slicked streets as the taxi drove through Harvard Square, which reminds me of the same cobblestone streets found in the Harry Potter movies. The whole ride home, I thought of Marcello. *Ay, Marcello!* I was really hoping for something, at least a hot make-out session, but it never happened. Sometimes, I just want someone in my bed to hold and caress me throughout the night, the way Daniel did in Miami before we broke up. Loneliness envelopes me when I get home from work, the gym, or from meeting up with Tommy, but I am trying to be strong and live on my own in this new city to make myself and Mami proud. As I get ready for work, I can't help but think that my dream about Mami was related to this episode from Saturday night. In her own way, Mami was sending me a message: "Don't feel so bad about this guy. You are better than that. I believe in you, *hijo.* You must believe in yourself." The dream somehow comforted me about the whole situation.

A few hours later, I leave the academic village of Cambridge for the urban and gritty city life of Dorchester. I traverse these two different worlds on a daily basis. I stand in front of my fourth-period class, trying to teach my ninth graders the literary power of Ernest Hemingway. This week, we are discussing *The Old Man and the Sea.* It's one of my favorite Hemingway books because it is based on a Cuban fisherman looking for his great big catch. There are so many overlapping themes in the book, and I hope my students will find a connection to them in their own lives. Most of these students come from broken homes in Dorchester and Roxbury (Boston's version of Miami's Wynwood and Liberty City, according to Tommy). By reading Hemingway and other literary classics, I'm hoping they find some meaning to their lives so they can excel.

"Now class, settle down. Did everyone read the first chapter for homework, just as I asked you to on Friday?" A room full of eyes look right back at me. This is fishy, just like the tale.

"Oh c'mon now, who read the chapter?" About eight hands rise up. That means half the class didn't do the assignment. *Ay, dios!*

I have to keep the class on schedule, according to my lesson plans. They have state exams coming up at the beginning of November. I need to get them excited about literature, but they're more interested in downloading iTunes.

"Class, this is a short and beautiful story, of an aged Cuban fisherman as he goes head to head, or head to fin with a giant marlin. This is a story of fear, hope, death, and life. Imagine spending several days trying to reel a giant fish in," I tell the class. Some of the students seem more interested now that I have given them more details.

"It's man vs. nature. If any of you have grandfathers, imagine him sitting in a small boat trying to catch the prize of a lifetime and refusing to give up because he wants to win and win big."

"Have you ever been to Cuba?" asks Carol, one of my brighter students.

"I am from Cuba. I was born in Havana, but I don't remember much. This book is one of my favorites because it helps me understand my homeland and how it looked in the 1950s through Hemingway's eyes. He was considered an honorary Cuban because he often wrote from his home there. If you think about it, Hemingway is a Hispanic writer because he lived there and wrote about Hispanic characters."

The class seems intrigued so I continue trying to blend the book with my own personal experiences. I used to do this at Braddock High and it seemed to work because of the large number of Latino students there.

I pull out a map from behind the chalkboard and point to Cuba. I then explain how Hemingway lived in Key West and Cuba because he was inspired by their tropical beauty and the passionate, everyday, hardworking people found there.

"Have you been to Key West?" asks Katie, a raven-haired student who is extremely courteous but doesn't complete her assignments.

"When I was younger, I would take road trips down there with my family. It's a charming little city. Hemingway's house is now a museum and home to cats with ten toes, if you can believe that." All eyes are trained on me. Now that's how I like a classroom to behave. As I talk, I lace the conversation with talk of Hemingway and the book, to engage them. And with that, I announce, "For those of you who didn't, ahem, read the first twenty pages, I am going to give you about half an hour to do that right now. So get started. And for those of you who did the assignment, I want you to write down five things that you liked or didn't like about what you read. Be ready to discuss this."

Everyone begins their work and I take advantage of the time to step outside for a cigarette break. I ask Juanita, my fellow tenth grade English teacher next door, to keep an eye on the kids if they get too loud.

"No problem, Carlos. They won't make a peep knowing I'm next door. Go on and do your nicotine dance. I got you covered," Juanita says. She's in a perpetual good mood because she retires at the end of the year, after thirty years at Dorchester High. I can only imagine that kind of longevity for myself in the public school system. I've only been a teacher for six years.

As I walk away, I hear Juanita's tell-it-like-it-is voice booming from the hallway.

"Now you better not say a word. I may be next door, but I have super bionic hearing so you better not . . ." her voice trails off.

With Juanita's blessing, I retreat outside and light up. I dial Tommy to see how his weekend went. I haven't talked to him since our night at the bar.

"Tommy Perez, *The Boston Daily,* how may I help you?" he answers his work phone in his serious reporter tone.

"*Loco,* what are you doing?"

"Oh, hey, Carlos. What's up?" His tone softens. "It's 11 a.m. Are you on a break at school? How are your students today?"

"They're good now that I got them to read *The Old Man and the Sea.* Were you okay Saturday night? You left looking pretty distracted or something." I pace back and forth behind the school. My cigarette smoke dissipates into the air.

"Yeah, things are good. You're not going to believe who I bumped into at Barnes & Noble yesterday."

"Mike Lowell, the Red Sox player?"

"Um, no, Carlos. If I had, I would be interviewing him right now and not chatting with you. But seriously. I saw another Mike, well Mikey, at the bookstore café. He looked really cute. We started talking. He's sober now," Tommy says, telling me the whole story. "He finally stopped drinking. I couldn't believe it."

"That's great. I mean, that's great that he finally stopped drinking, not that he got a DUI. So what happened? Did you guys just talk?" I say, between puffs of my Marlboro Light.

"Yeah, we talked. I was on my way to go hiking and well, I invited him along. We had a great time, as if we picked up where we left off. I just want to be his friend."

"His friend? Hmm."

"Like us. His friends tend to go to the bars, and Mikey doesn't feel comfortable around them. Poor guy." Tommy's voice lifts as he talks about his former flame.

"*Bueno,* just be careful. I think it's great that you want to support his sobriety, but you also fell in love with this guy last year. That can't be easy, being friends with someone you still have feelings and an attraction for. This guy has a lot of issues to work out, *chico.*"

"I know. I just want to be there for him, that's all. I'm not interested in dating him. It's purely platonic. We always had a unique connection."

I hear what Tommy is saying, but I don't quite believe that he believes that he and Mikey can be just *amigos*. Their relationship sounded so unstable. I don't want to see Tommy get hurt by being nice to this guy because he has such a soft spot in his heart for him.

"*Bueno,* just know that alcoholics usually relapse in their first year. Be careful, *chico!* Maybe I can finally meet Mr. Blue Eyes. We can take him to the Cuban restaurant in Jamaica Plain and show him some good Cuban food," I offer. My cigarette is almost out. I should be getting back to the classroom.

"Good idea. He could use all the new friends he can get. I'll mention it to him the next time I talk to him. Maybe we can all meet up this weekend."

"Sounds like a plan, Tommy. I'm really happy for you. I know how much you missed hanging out with this guy. If having him around as a friend makes you happy, I am all for it."

"Thanks. Listen, I have to get back to work. I'm writing a story about Boston's first black female news anchor from the 1980s and how she just produced her first documentary about the genocide in Sudan. So I can't talk much right now."

"*No hay problema.* I need to get back to the classroom myself. We'll talk later."

"*Adios!*"

I head back to the classroom for more *The Old Man and The Sea.* As I enter through the doorway, my phone vibrates in my pocket. It's a text message from Marcello.

Oi, Carlos. Sorry about Saturday. I want 2 explain. Can we meet?

For now, my focus is my class. This gives me time to figure out whether I should respond to Mr. Brazil, even though I'm intrigued about what he has to say to me. I have a feeling that Mami wouldn't approve of him in the same way she didn't approve of Daniel. I can imagine her saying, "Carlito, he has a boyfriend, no?"

I'm not very good at picking boyfriends. I don't look for relationships. They find me, and they're usually the wrong ones.

4

Tommy

It was so good seeing you Sunday. Glad we had a chance to talk, cutie. Thanks for listening. Can't wait for dinner tonight, Mikey writes in a text message.

I'm reading this as I work out on my gym's elliptical machine. I'm one of those guys whose face is buried in a novel as I sweat and burn my calories away. (It's the sweet potato casserole at Boston Market and all those chocolate chip cookies I devour for lunch.) The reading makes forty minutes of exercise feel like ten. I put my phone away and continue reading my latest book, *We Disappear* by Scott Heim. It's a dark story about a crystal meth addict who returns to Kansas to help his mom as she battles cancer and some inner demons from her childhood. But right now, I wish the fat guy to my right with the really bad body odor would just disappear. I'm suffocating here.

As I pump up and struggle to breathe fresh air, my thoughts wander to my encounter with Mikey. I smile. He has really cleaned up his act. He seemed so at peace with himself as we talked at the bookstore. I also noticed the same serene glow during our little hiking excursion in the Blue Hills. My favorite part was when we sat at the top at the weather observatory and marveled at the city view and the scalding red sun as it began its descent.

"I can't believe I've never been up here. This is a giant forest. *Shrek*-land, cutie," Mikey said, as the view of the city unfolded before us to the north. Below, hilly acres of woodlands smeared the landscape with a sorbet of crimson and golden yellow leaves. Every now and then, the trees swayed as if waving us a greeting. The cool breeze lifted the front of Mikey's straight hair.

"This is one of my favorite places. If something is on my mind or I get the Miami blues, I climb up here and enjoy the silence. You forget your troubles up here."

"I can see why, Tommy. Thanks for letting me come with you," Mikey said. Our shoulders kissed as our heads leaned over the granite perch. He stared at me longingly with those two bright-blue orbs, which had been trained on me throughout the hike. I can recall the instances: at the base of the observatory, halfway down the hill, in the parking lot next to the museum, and on the way back to the bookstore where I dropped Mikey off at his car. If the stare was more than five seconds, I veered away and pretended to fiddle with my iPod's Gloria Estefan playlists. I looked away because I was afraid that Mikey might see the feelings that lingered in my heart.

"You're always welcome to come. I usually drive out here on Sundays. You missed out on the snakes and coyotes today, though," I said, our shoulders still touching.

"I'm sure they were hiding from you, Mr. Bad Ass Cubano, but I think I'll take you up on that offer. I had a lot of fun with you. It was an adventure. Life is always an adventure with you, cutie." Later on at the bookstore parking lot as Mikey climbed out of the Jeep, he smiled and shook my hand.

We exchanged numbers (I still had his programmed in my cell phone from the year before, but I didn't tell him that).

"I'll call ya, cutie."

"Take care and drive safely, Mikey."

"And watch out for the coyotes. I hear they hang around in Dorchester, too."

"Only if you come and visit," I teased.

And now I'm here, swaying left and right on the elliptical machine trying to stay trim for our dinner tonight. This is silly. I'm working out like a crazy mad man on the machine so that my Gap jeans will feel a little looser around the waist. This is dinner, not a date. But then why do I feel so excited, nervous, optimistic, euphoric, giddy, and fidgety at the same time? I've had this soft tingling sensation since Sunday when I first saw Mikey. I haven't been able to stop grinning. Well, I usually smile a lot. I'm just smiling twice as much as usual. I need to stop this! We're just friends or about to be friends. I know he needs a supportive sober friend. Seeing Mikey sparked feelings that were still simmering despite all that had happened.

I survive my wild cardio session and the bad-smelling gym rat (or rhino) to my right. I use my handy instant hand sanitizer to destroy any bad germs. I grab my red hoodie from the coat rack, wave good-bye to the salesgirls at the gym counter, and head back to my condo. The whole way, I'm thinking that I can't wait for tonight.

It's 7:45 p.m., and I'm at Copley Place Mall, a sprawling city shopping center that connects the Back Bay and South End neighborhoods. Shoppers stroll transparent sky bridges that connect the Prudential Tower with bustling Boylston Street and Huntington Avenue. The skywalks become a Bostonian's best friend when the weather turns to a chilly 35 degrees, as it is tonight. You can bypass several city blocks by traveling through the hotels that lead to the mall by these elevated enclosed walkways. I remember this area fondly because two years ago, I stayed at the Westin Hotel when the *Daily* flew me up for a job interview. Across the street, the mall had just opened a Cheesecake Factory, where Mikey and I plan to meet tonight. Parking is another matter, a nightmare with all the roving city meter maids. So I parked the Jeep at the Westin and sauntered like a hamster through the skywalk to get to the mall. Call me Tommy Skywalker.

I glide down the escalator to the ground floor to meet Mikey. From my moving perch, I scan the first floor for him. No sign yet.

My cell phone vibrates. It's Carlos.

"*Loco.* What are you doing tonight?"

"Hey, Carlos. I'm on my way to meet Mikey. I really can't talk."

"Are you nervous? I bet you are! I bet you are!" Carlos teases.

"Um, no. Well, okay, I am, just a little."

"But you're friends, right? You shouldn't be nervous to see a friend. I mean, you wouldn't be nervous if we were meeting up tonight, which we're not. I guess I'll stay home and rent a movie or something." Carlos sighs and continues, "Because *mi amigo* has ditched me for the night."

"I didn't ditch you. I really wanted you to hang with us, but I felt I should have some more one-on-one time with Mikey before I introduce you guys, that's all. I need to rebuild my friendship with him slowly. If we're not comfortable as friends, how am I going to be able to introduce him to another good friend?"

"Okay, I get that. But eventually, I want to meet the man you've talked about incessantly since we met."

"And you will, I promise."

As the escalator descends, I notice the crush of couples and families sitting around with restaurant pagers clenched in their hands. These hungry people fill the seating area along the glass vestibules that face Huntington.

"Carlos, I gotta go. I'm in front of the restaurant."

"Okay, *loca,* good luck! Remember, it's not a date. You're just *hanging out.* Ha! My thoughts are with you. I am really happy for you. I hope you know that, *chico.* I think you could be a really good friend to Mikey."

"Thanks, Carlos. Listen, you'll get all the details first thing tomorrow. I promise. *Adios!*"

"Bye, *loco!*"

Before I reach the restaurant's front doors, I flatten out my blue jeans. Check. I wipe the lint off my black wool coat. Check. I pull out my brown, long-sleeved shirt. Check. I apply some strawberry ChapStick. Check. I scrunch the top of my head so that my brown curls aren't too puffy like members of the '80s band Menudo.

Check. I catch a quick glance of myself in the reflective windows. I smile. Thumbs up!

"Tommy! Over heah," Mikey calls out in his sweet Boston vernacular. I forgot how thick his accent was. I hope he didn't just catch me fixing myself up at the last minute.

I turn to the right and light up at the vision. Mikey stands alone under a lush decorative plant. He wears a chambray shirt pulled out over dark blue jeans. Some scruff fills his beard, but it works. The shirt complements his eyes, making them more ocean-blue than usual.

"Hey, Mikey! You look great! Have you been waiting long?" I'm not sure whether to shake his hand or hug him. We clumsily do both.

"Hey, cutie. You look so handsome." He playfully tries to mess up my hair, but I duck quickly. I don't like it when people (even Mikey) tamper with my hair. Like clay, my hair conforms to whatever touches it. If I sleep on one side of my head, then it will be flat while the other side is wildly curly.

"I got here a little early and got us a pager. We only have about five minutes left before our table is ready, cutie."

"Great!" is all that I can muster. Here I go again with my one-word answers. Shyness suddenly envelopes me like the light fog over the city. I never used to clam up around Mikey. I could always talk about anything, a skill that helps me in my job when I interview Boston celebrities, Hispanic community leaders, and TV news anchors.

Mikey and I join the throngs of couples and families who desperately wait for their pager to vibrate. We sit side by side and talk about our work week. I tell him that I began reporting a story on a CBS crime drama actor who lived in Boston for several years before moving to California, becoming a model, and hitting it big by landing a role on *The Young and the Restless*.

"I know that guy. He is wicked handsome, half black and half white, right? It sounds like you had a really tough assignment. I feel sorry for you. Poor Tommy," Mikey teases.

"It was very hard, if you know what I mean. The guy was so painfully ugly to look at, but that's my job," I say sarcastically. "Occasionally, I get to interview some of the most beautiful people with a Boston connection."

Mikey then talks about his students. He's a guidance counselor, but his principal asked him to coach an after-school math club because Mikey wanted to have some sort of group to mentor. He's also a math fiend. I remember when we dated last year, he would calculate tax and tip in his head for each of our restaurant bills.

"I have this one student, Melvin, who always raises his hand to answer my questions about labeling decimals or fractions. Every time I ask a question, his arm shoots up. Today, I had to tell him, 'Melvin, I am impressed that you want to participate so much, but your fellow classmates deserve a chance to answer too,'" Mikey explains.

"When I met his grandmother and mother during open-house two weeks ago, I understood why Melvin is the way he is. His mother works two jobs, one at Shaw's supermarket, another at Subway, to make ends meet. His grandmother sleeps in, so Melvin has to wake himself up each morning for school and prepare his own breakfast. I suspect he doesn't get a lot of attention at home. One of his teachers told me that when the class had to write an essay about one of their heroes, he wrote about me." Mikey grins humbly.

My heart swells with affection. Mikey is a positive influence on his students, especially Melvin. And I see that Mikey is still as passionate about helping his students as he was last year.

"Well, if I had a teacher who was as kind and cute as you, I wouldn't write an essay. I'd write a book."

Mikey bites down on his tongue and laughs.

"Thanks, Tommy. That's very sweet of you. I'm just doing my job. I'd rather you write about the kids, not me. Maybe you can write an article one day about the math club. Those kids deserve some positive attention. They don't get much at home."

The restaurant's pager vibrates in Mikey's hand, alerting us that our table is ready. We rise from our perch by the mall windows and trudge through the restaurant's crowded waiting area. It looks like a typical night at Club Café as we squeeze and maneuver through the logjam of people, all waiting to sit and chow down on the super-sized portions The Cheesecake Factory is legendary for.

Our college-age hostess with the bleached blonde hair and black business suit escorts us to a corner table by a window along Huntington Avenue. She hands us our menus, and our waiter appears and greets us.

"Any drinks to get started?" he says.

"He'll have a Diet Coke," Mikey informs the waiter, "and I'll have an iced tea." Mikey looks at me. "Did I get that right, Tommy? I'm pretty sure you're still addicted to Diet Coke, right?"

Even though we haven't talked in months, Mikey still knows me pretty well. Diet Coke is my tonic. Actually, vodka with Diet Coke is, but I don't want to drink around Mikey tonight or even at all. I want to respect his sobriety.

We settle into our chairs. The waiter returns with our drinks and takes our order. I get the turkey club. Mikey orders crab cakes as an appetizer and the fish and chips for dinner.

I like this, sitting here, laughing and exchanging stories with someone who used to be a big part of my life. We are picking up where we left off as ex-boyfriends, but this time we are friends.

"Do your parents still call you every night? I remember them calling you on your cell phone or at your apartment in Cambridge whenever I was with you," Mikey says, smearing butter on the wheat rolls.

"Yeah, it's a Cuban thing. They must call me every day. If I don't call them back, they imagine that I'm in some Stephen King horror situation or that my Jeep has gone off the road and I'm just out of arm's reach from my cell phone. All this because I don't re-turn their calls. They sleep better knowing they've heard my voice, and that I'm breathing, that I'm alive in Boston."

Mikey laughs.

"My mom's the same way. She calls me four times a day, espe-

cially since the accident. My car was a total loss. May my Toyota
Matrix rest in peace. I now have a used Volkswagen Rabbit. It was
all I could afford with money from the insurance. It gets me
around. I can't complain. I'm just lucky to be alive. I did some
crazy stuff when I drank."

"You were very lucky. You could have killed yourself. I never
want to see your obituary in the *Daily*. That would kill me. Thank
God you're not drinking. Thank God you found sobriety."

Mikey reaches over and gently squeezes my right hand. "I
know, I was a crazy *wabbit* when I drank," he says, making fun of
himself with his Bugs Bunny voice.

"You were one drunk bunny, always hopping and skipping
away with a Corona, but that's the past. Let's toast to the future. To
your recovery!"

"To a new friendship." Mikey clinks my glass of Diet Coke
with his iced tea.

Throughout the dinner, we talk about all the fun things we did
together: watching a screening of the new Jane Goodall movie at
the Children's Museum in Cambridge, getting lost in the disori-
enting Providence Place mall. I tell him that I still have the Red
Sox baseball cap, the one he gave me after we first met. As we talk,
I notice every now and then how Mikey stares longingly at the
straight couple dining at the booth next to us. They each drink a
glass of wine and my eyes follow his, which are fixed on their
drinks. I can't imagine not being able to savor something I truly
enjoy. I do like to drink, but I stop after two or three because I
often have to drive myself home. (Most guys in Boston don't have
cars.) I also stop at the local 7-Eleven for water and a candy bar to
soak up the alcohol. When I notice Mikey glance at the couple
drinking, I try to distract him with another fond memory. It
works. He's focused on me again.

"I still have that big seashell you gave me on Valentine's Day
after your trip to Key West," Mikey says. "It sits in my window.
Whenever I look at it, I wonder what you're doing and if you're
okay."

"Ditto, with the Red Sox baseball cap. When I wore it, I guess you could say, 'You were always on my mind.' "

He gives me a high-five, and we burst out laughing. "Oh, Tommy, some things never change, and that's a good thing. You're still the cutie Cuban goofball. It's nice to be able to sit and talk with you."

"Same here."

After dinner, we take a stroll through the mall, passing all the merchants who sell Russian dolls; fluffy, giant, animal-themed slippers; and Red Sox T-shirts and baseball caps. We stop by Ben & Jerry's and grab two cups of ice cream. I ask for the fudge brownie flavor. Mikey gets the peanut butter and chocolate. We feed each other with our spoons. At one point, I miss and smear Mikey's face with a glop of fudge brownie.

"Oops, sorry about that."

"I can't take you anywhere, can I?" says Mikey, cleaning his face with a napkin.

Around 9 p.m., we walk into the Prudential Tower corridor of the mall, which abuts the convention center. There's a sign that reads "Observatory Deck Open." We take a closer look. The sign states that the observatory is on the fiftieth floor and offers a 360-degree view of the city. I look at my watch.

"It's only open for one more hour. Wanna go up?"

"Sure, I've never been up there. It will be safe, right? That's kind of high. I'm scared of heights. I haven't flown in ten years," Mikey says nervously.

"Well, if you can tackle the Blue Hills, you can ride in an elevator. You have nothing to worry about. Besides, I'll be right there."

We cram into an elevator with ten other people. Mikey and I are sandwiched together, but I don't mind. I smell his Dolce & Gabbana cologne, the same one he wore when we first met. Wherever I was, in town or in Miami, and I caught a whiff of that cologne, my heart would flutter because I thought Mikey was nearby. And here I am, squeezed in an elevator with him riding to the top of one of the city's highest skyscrapers. A few months ago, I never would have imagined us doing this. We exchange smiles in the elevator until it pings at the fiftieth floor.

Inside, we pay the cover and move with the crowd of people dispersing to see their own personal slice of Boston despite the light fog, which appears as a transparent white curtain. Directly ahead, we see the John Hancock Building, which juts into the sky like a gleaming Rolex watch. Behind that is the tiny forest of skyscrapers that make up the financial district. Behind that, the harbor beckons with ships and sailboats dotting the horizon. Immediately below, Mikey and I marvel at the sea of red and brown buildings that line the South End and Back Bay neighborhoods.

"Who knew there were so many trees in Boston? Look at how the brownstones create the letter 'U' with trees in the middle. This is such an amazing view. I've never seen Boston this way, and I'm from here," Mikey says, cupping his face against the glass with his hands.

"See the big gas tank with the vibrant rainbow design along the Southeast expressway? The *Daily* is to the left of that. And wow, look at the Blue Hills in the distance, lighted by the artificial glow of the city. During the day, it's like looking at a colorful mountainscape because of the changing leaves. It's hard to believe we were just there the other day. It's like a beautiful Monet painting." I turn to Mikey.

"You're a beautiful painting, Tommy."

I feel the warmth of a blush. "*Gracias*, Mikey!"

He winks.

"So where's your condo? Isn't it near the *Daily*?"

"Somewhere over there," I point out ahead of me, "in the smattering of homes near the Neponset River. Look for the run-down four-story brick building surrounded by beautiful charming Victorian and Cape homes and renovated triple-deckers, and that's where I live. It's the eyesore of the neighborhood."

"Don't denigrate your home, cutie. I'm sure it's a nice building. Your studio in Cambridge was very cute. I practically lived there every weekend. You could have charged me rent for passing out on your sofa so much," says Mikey, standing two inches from me. I smell the minty gum he softly chews.

"My new place isn't too bad. I bought it because I got a good deal. It's a two-bedroom condo. It's not the most beautiful building, but it's my home. I've been happy there. I wish it looked like the building that I rented in West Cambridge. That looked more like a piece of Harvard University, but I was outpriced. All I could afford to buy in Cambridge was a tiny studio. So I looked in Dorchester where other gay guys have been migrating to, the pink gentrification. My building looks like it was a former housing development. Actually, it was before it went into foreclosure and the bank sold it off. But I do love my sliver of Dorchester. Despite the bad rap the neighborhood gets because of all the shootings, I can cycle to work along a bike path, and I'm a block from the Neponset River and a few minutes from Quincy and Milton. This is my home," I say.

Mikey puts his hand on my shoulder.

"Tommy, you should be proud. You write for a big newspaper. You write about people trying to make a difference. You own your own home. You're a good guy. That's why I never stopped thinking about you."

"Ditto," is the only thing that comes to my mind because once again Mikey has my tongue and heart all twisted. Repeat to myself: *Mikey is a friend. Mikey is just a friend. Un amigo, a friend, a cute comrade.*

We take in the city from all vantage points. We gaze at the cluster of MIT buildings on the Cambridge side of the Charles River. On the other side, we point at the minions walking along the Esplanade, which lights up the Boston side of the Charles. At the rear of the observatory, we laugh at how tiny Fenway Park appears. It resembles a green cooking bowl. There's the celebrated Citgo sign, rotating and aglow in red, blue, and white lights. Thousands of twinkling lights fill Beantown the same way that Mikey lights up my heart right now as we share this moment. It reminds me of our times together last year when alcohol wasn't a third wheel in our relationship.

We spend the rest of the closing hour scrutinizing innumerable details from our bird's-eye view of the city. As Mikey finds something familiar in a new light, I, too, adjust my own personal viewfinder of him. The freckles and scruff on his face. The way he furrows his thin, light brown eyebrows as he squints at another point in the distance. Watching him compounds my feelings of warmth toward him. But most of all, he seems centered, comforted by his own peace of mind. Mikey seems like a different person, someone unanchored by the weight of alcohol. He hasn't brought up going to Club Café or ordering a drink, which is what I always dreaded him asking on the weekends. Right now, he seems completely content to be here with me. I wouldn't want to be anywhere else, with my, ahem, friend. I can just imagine what Carlos would say to me now if I shared these thoughts with him. *Ay, loco!* And maybe I am crazy to think that I can just be friends with Mikey. Well, I'm trying.

5

Carlos

Ay, fall! I'm in the Cambridge Common, a lush park near Harvard Square, strolling in a sea of yellow leaves. Bright yellow leaves. Golden ones. Sun-kissed leaves. Some are soft and mushy on the brick sidewalk. Other leaves appear dry and crisp as they pile up against the edges of the park. I kick them up with my feet. I grab a handful of leaves and toss them in the breezy air. I've never seen this before. In Miami, the closest we get to fall is when a hurricane threatens or passes through and plucks the leaves off all the coconut and palm trees. But these leaves in Boston aren't shredded and damaged. They are intact, gently falling and floating like butterflies until they settle and rest on the ground. I wonder if heaven is like this, if Mami has her own fall there. She always loved her garden, manicuring her rose bushes, tending to her hibiscus trees, and slicing thorny pieces of her aloe vera plant to extract its soothing cream for her skin. I remember one time when I came home from work, I caught Mami talking to her lush gardenia tree. She called it "Nena."

"Nena, how are you today, *preciosa?* You are growing fast and you look very healthy, *mija*," Mami said, barefoot and wearing a farmer's hat, her favorite light-green blouse, and denim blue shorts that hid her varicose veins. With the garden hose in hand, she gently sprayed water on the tree's roots and the sprouting white flowers above. Mami's back was turned to the front of our house as I walked up and briefly watched this endearing scene unfold. I quietly laughed at her affection for her flowers. She treated them like another set of children. She didn't just shower them with water but with care, attention, and most of all love.

"Aldo is working all today, Carlos is teaching, and Lourdes is at her real estate office. So it's just you and me, Nena, and all your beautiful *amiguitas. Ay,* you have a bad leaf! Don't worry. I will take care of that, Nena," she said, as she snipped off the bad leaf with her scissors. Mami then cut off one of the fragrant white flowers. She sniffed it and then tucked it behind her right ear.

After watering the gardenia, which was now beaded with droplets, Mami whirled around and caught me laughing. I surprised her.

"Oye, Carlos, you scared me!" she said, playfully nudging my arm.

"Sorry, Mami. You looked really sweet talking to, ahem, Nena. Mami, she's a bush—a plant—not a real person."

"She's a beautiful being. She may not talk, but she listens to us, *hijo.* I talk to all my flowers and plants. And you know how I know they listen? They make themselves look *bonita.* I take care of them, and *tu sabes,* they take care of me. They give us beautiful flowers. Where do you think I get all the flowers to decorate the inside of the house?" Mami was always proud of her garden. The front of our house in Coral Gables looked like a colorful collection of Georgia O'Keeffe paintings. After Mami died, the garden slowly began to wither away. Papi hired a gardener to maintain Mami's work but to no avail. It didn't matter the number of times he visited each month or how much fertilizer and mulch he used—the garden wasn't the same. It lost something when we lost Mami. Three of the six hibiscus flowers died. The trio of aloe vera plants? Down to one. The plants still standing were the gardenia and red, pink, and white rose bushes. They all stood proud and strong as if

Nena and her friends were hanging on for Mami and for us. The best thing that came out of the garden wasn't the rows of roses or the gardenia tree but my mother. This was her personal Garden of Eden, something she looked forward to every day. I think she truly would have appreciated the burst of colors in Boston. I could imagine her picking up and talking to the leaves and making a mosaic for a frame out of them.

I grab a few of the leaves and put them away in my backpack, between my students' papers and Tommy's most recent *Daily* articles. (He quizzes me on his most recent stories to make sure that I read them.) I want to send these leaves to Lourdes and Papi. I want them to see a slice of Boston. A teacher at the high school mentioned that you can preserve these leaves with wax paper and use them for decoration. Maybe I'll put some of them in a frame for my apartment. It would serve as a reminder of my first year and my first fall in my new life in Boston.

I'm on my way to meet Marcello. Yes, *that* Marcello. The handsome Brazilian man from Club Paradise who forgot to mention that he had a *novio*. He text-messaged me the other day at school and asked to meet me so he could better explain his situation. After I finally triumphed in teaching *The Old Man and the Sea,* I called Marcello on my drive to Cambridge. He profusely apologized and explained.

"I am sorry for not explaining my situation. Richard isn't my real boyfriend. He just thinks he is. I dated him in Brazil for a few months years ago. He is an ex-boyfriend, and he has helped me get settled here. He rents me a room in his house. But I don't love him. He is still in love with me," Marcello said over the phone as I crossed the Charles River into Harvard Square.

"So he is an ex-boyfriend who is still in love with you and you live with him? *Chico,* that is weird and awkward. How can you meet other guys with him around?"

"I care about him, but I am only staying with him until I can afford my own apartment. Rent is very expensive. You have to

have a month's deposit, first month's rent, and last month's. I only
have a few more months to save, maybe until April. Then I can be
on my own. I was going to explain my situation when Richard
showed up at the restaurant. Can we talk in person? I enjoyed
spending time with you. I have not been able to stop thinking
about you. When can I see you?" he said. My heart softened at
those words. I haven't been able to stop thinking about Marcello
either. He seemed so kind and fun when we met. He's the first guy
I've met in Boston, besides Tommy, who has intrigued me. He
seemed *real*, a hard worker. He didn't offer any pretenses of who
he was or where he was from.

"*Bueno*, I am headed home to take a nap. Maybe we can meet
this weekend. I like to walk around Cambridge and look at the
leaves. Do you know where the Starbucks in Harvard Square is?
Maybe we can meet there Sunday afternoon."

"Thank you, Carlos. That would be nice. I look forward to it."

And so here I am, taking the scenic route to Harvard Square by
cutting through the Cambridge Common where hunky guys play
football in the center of the park. My eyes focus on some of the
shirtless guys. No matter where you go in Cambridge, you can't
help but run into some taut collegiate bodies, especially along the
Charles River. But instead of the tanned, hairless bodies I marveled
at (and fantasized about) in South Beach, the guys here are pasty-
white, hairy, and lean. But nonetheless, hot in a Matt Damon sort
of way.

I saunter down Massachusetts Avenue, as the bright red sign of
the Sheraton Commander Hotel beckons down the street. I pass
the centuries-old cemetery on my right, the crimson gates of Harvard on my left, and the cosmopolitan crowds of students and resi-
dents making their way to and from the square, a city circus. I
notice the Starbucks straight ahead when my phone vibrates. I
glance at the caller ID. It's Papi calling from his store. I haven't spoken to him in a few days. Mami used to call me every night even
though I lived only a few miles from our house in Coral Gables.

She would tell me the latest gossip in the family or (surprise!) talk about her flowers. Papi, however, isn't much of a phone person. He calls me every now and then to check up on me. I guess I can chat briefly. Our conversations are typically short since we don't have a lot to talk about. Just mundane everyday things like the weather, my job, or my car. He'll talk about the Red Sox and the Marlins, even though I'm not a sports fan. He doesn't ask me about my personal life except for friends and co-workers. We don't talk about Mami either.

"*Hola,* Carlos, how are you? Are you cold yet?" he says in his accented English, which was always better than Mami's. His proficiency in English helped him open his business, Martin Mercado, as soon as we arrived in Miami from Mariel.

"Hey, Papi. Not yet. The weather has been in the sixties like Miami in the winter. I'm doing okay. Busy with the students and learning my way around Boston. All the leaves are changing colors. It's very pretty here."

"How is your car doing there? On television, I see that the roads are very old. Ten *cuidado, hijo.* A friend of your *tia's* told me that people are super *loco* drivers up there."

"Papi, my Toyota Camry is still in good condition, even though it's eight years old. I drove up here, didn't I? It's still in one piece. I'm just happy it's paid off. How is the store? Has it been busy this month?"

"*Sí, hijo.* I had to lay off one of my cashiers. She was stealing from me. *Carajo!* So I am working extra behind the counter. But business is good. Did you see the Red Sox game from last weekend? They are winning again. Watch them head back to the World Series this season. The Marlins are doing horrible, Carlos. Horrible! *Son tremenda mierda.*"

I don't know why I never shared the same passion for football and baseball as Papi has. When I was younger, he tried to teach me to catch a ball and enlist me in Coral Gables' little league team. I resisted. I preferred to hang out with Mami as she window-shopped on Miracle Mile while waiting for Lourdes to come out of her Barbizon modeling classes when she was in middle school. (Most Cuban women enrolled their daughters in modeling classes to teach them how to walk and apply make-up. Cuban mothers all believe their daughters are undiscovered models.) Thank God Mami was around and talked Papi out of forcing me to play baseball with my uncles at Tropical Park every Sunday. To make up for my lack of interest in sports, Mami urged me to help Papi at the store when we had three-day weekends off from school or during the summers. I know the price of every Chef Boyardee can, bag of Doritos, pack of Marlboro cigarettes, and candy bar that stock his shelves. Even then, Papi and I didn't have much to say to each other besides shop talk. So I can understand how he is trying to fill today's conversation with the sports talk.

"Yeah, the Red Sox are big here, Papi. Everyone wears their baseball caps and jerseys. The stadium is near Cambridge, over the Charles River. When you visit, I'll show you. There's a big Citgo sign that revolves during game nights."

"I would love to see that, Carlos. So you're okay? I worry about you, being there all alone and not knowing anyone."

"Papi, *estoy bien!* I am making new friends. I even have a fellow Cuban friend from Miami, Tommy Perez. He grew up in Miami Beach. Remember? I told you about him a few weeks ago."

"Ah, *sí. El cubanito de Miami. El reportero* with the Jeep, no? If he's Cuban, you're in good company. *Bueno,* I just wanted to say *hola* and see if you were okay. Remember, *hijo,* wear a coat. The Latina on The Weather Channel says it will be colder there in a month."

"*Gracias,* Papi. I gotta go. Say hi to Lourdes for me."

"Okay, *hijo, cuidate.*"

I press "end" on my cell, tuck it away in my backpack, and continue towards the Starbucks. I walk in, and I spot Marcello sitting at one of the tables, with two mocha lattes. *Ay, Marcello.* He looks so handsome with his snug green hoodie sweatshirt, which makes his hazel eyes more luminous. The hoodie also defines his tight, lean, and naturally tan body. Our eyes meet once again when something suddenly comes up. A boner mushrooms in my jeans. I quickly use my backpack to cover my groin. *Que pena!* It's been a while since I've had sex. (The last time was right before I broke up with Daniel because he gave me crabs. The bastard cheated on me.) So when I am near a handsome man such as Marcello, my body can't help but gladly react.

Marcello rises to greet me although I've already risen (in my pants) upon seeing him.

"Carlos, so good to see you again," he says, with a hug. His warm embrace and grassy cologne soothe me.

"Same here. Is your boyfriend here?" I shoot back.

Marcello smirks.

"He's not my boyfriend."

"But he thinks you're his." I settle into my chair and place my backpack on my lap to hide how happy my body is to see Marcello.

"I don't love him."

"But he loves you, no?"

We continue going back and forth, a verbal tennis match. I enjoy taunting him.

"It's complicated, Carlos. I asked you to meet me so I can explain."

"Oye, what's there to explain? You live with an older man who loves you but isn't your boyfriend, but you need to live with him because you can't afford to be on your own here in Boston. Did I get that right?"

"He is an old friend from Brazil. Nothing more. We don't have sex."

"You don't need to explain anything to me. I'm not your boyfriend."

"I just wanted you to know the truth. Richard likes my company. He doesn't charge me a lot of money to live with him, as long as I spend time with him."

"Like a boyfriend?"

"We are friends, or *amigos,* as you Cubans would say. As I said, it's complicated, Carlos. But I like you. You are so smart, sweet, and extremely handsome. You are a good person. I can tell."

Ay, he likes me. I like him too. But I don't quite understand what he wants from me. This can't go anywhere. I won't date a guy who is living with his ex-boyfriend. Too complicated. I moved here to start fresh. I left complicated in Miami.

We sip our mocha lattes. Our feet accidentally tap one another's. My throbbing boner remains intact. So maybe Marcello isn't boyfriend material. Maybe he will never be. He's obviously taken in some way, shape, or form. But having a play buddy/friend wouldn't hurt because I know we can't seriously date as long as he's with Dick or Richard or *el viejo,* whatever his name is. I know what Tommy would say if he were here, "Just hook up with the guy! Live a little, Carlos. Let loose. You're the new, cute, gay guy in town. You can have any guy you want here. Have fun, *chico,* just be safe."

Marcello and I spend the rest of the hour at Starbucks, exchanging stories about our childhoods. I tell him about my brunches with Mami at Versailles and how much I miss her. He tells me about how much he enjoyed surfing in Brazil in high school and how much he misses his family and friends. I tell him how I worked at Papi's convenience store in Miami Springs when I was in high school as a stock boy and cashier to buy my first car, a used red Dodge Neon. Marcello describes the beaches of Brazil, the annual carnival festivities, and why he enjoys being in Boston.

"You have more opportunities in the United States," he says. "I want to be a teacher, like you, Carlos."

The conversation grows deeper as we talk about our desires to make a difference through education.

"Some days are good. Some days are hard, Marcello, but I know in my heart I was meant to be a teacher. If you focus on those good days, when you feel the class actually listened and learned, then the days when the students won't behave or listen aren't so bad. I still have the letters from my former students in Miami who thanked me for being their teacher and for being so enthusiastic about their progress. I keep those letters and their pictures in a folder at home. They remind me of why I keep teaching."

"And that's what I want: to help other people learn Portuguese so they can communicate and understand us better. I start community college next fall. But for now, I am saving money by working as a waiter."

"Where do you work now, Marcello?" He smiles and points across the street to the Border Café, the happening and cheap Tex-Mex restaurant that all the college students go to. On weekends, a line spills out the door. Tommy and I went there once, and we waited thirty minutes for a table. It was worth it though. The chicken burrito was delicious. I also devoured two bowls of nachos.

"Well, maybe I'll have to stop by sometime."

"You and your friends can stop by anytime."

"*Bueno,* I only have one close friend here—Tommy. He was at Club Paradise."

"Well, now you have another friend, Carlos." Marcello winks and finishes up his drink.

Maybe Marcello can be a new friend. Although he didn't tell me about Richard immediately, he was honest and thoughtful enough to take the time to call and then come here to explain everything. He obviously wants to get to know me better, and for that, I may just give him the benefit of the doubt. Mami always taught me to see the best in people, but also, not to be taken advantage of. And so far, Marcello has scored some points with me.

Now if only I can get make my boner go away. Being friends with Marcello will literally be hard. I'm extremely attracted to him. I can't wait to tell Tommy about him when we have dinner. I know he wants to tell me about his night with Mikey. Just as the leaves slowly fall over the city, Tommy may be falling for Mikey all over again. And that concerns me.

6

Tommy

"*Loco,* so what happened Saturday night with Mikey?" Carlos's Cuban Inquistion begins as he peels off his Army-green windbreaker and settles into his chair.

"Nothing. We had dinner at The Cheesecake Factory, walked around Copley Mall, and took an elevator to the top of the Prudential. You should do that sometime, by the way. It will help you better understand Boston. And we walked around some more and talked, a lot."

"Nothing else? *Por favor,* Tommy. As you reporters say, I smell a story. Spill it, *ahora!*"

"Dude, nothing happened. As I said before, Mikey and I are just friends. Got it?" I demur. I don't know if I am trying to convince Carlos or myself, but nothing physical happened. Friends are platonic.

Carlos and I are here at El Oriental de Cuba for an early Sunday dinner. Since Carlos liked the restaurant so much the first time around, I thought he might appreciate an encore. Maybe it could be our meeting place since Carlos isn't a huge fan of Club Café, and I'm still not a fan of Club Paradise.

I glance out the restaurant's window, and I notice the sun has already faded at 5 p.m. Damn it! Winter is on its way, which means

I will have to readjust to driving my Jeep on the snow-caked roads. Last year, I slid the Jeep into a mound of snow that some genius had piled next to the Boston Market drive-thru. Another time, I rear-ended a Canadian couple's Mazda on Memorial Drive when the Jeep slid on black ice. Carlos's voice snaps me out of my mental winter collisions.

"He didn't try to kiss you or anything? How did you leave things? I don't have much man action or romance in my life, Tommy, so I have to live vicariously through you. So, *que paso?*" Carlos says, his eyes wide and animated. He also sips his mango shake, something my dad would make for me and my sister Mary when we were kids.

"No, no, and no! You're making more of this than it really is. Mikey didn't make a move on me. That's not what dinner was all about. We had a fun, sober night out. No bars. No clubs. We explored Back Bay from fifty stories high. Seriously, you need to see the city view from up there."

"Okay, if you say so. I just don't think you guys are going to be just *amigos* no matter what you say, *chico*. So when am I going to meet this guy? I really want to see how much he looks like Ethan Hawke and what made him so special that you've been obsessed with him for over a year. I doubt he looks like Ethan Hawke because you're—no offense, Tommy—terrible with comparing people to their celebrity look-alikes. You say I look like Josh Groban. *Por favor!*"

"Obsessed? Nah-uh. Mikey's just a sweet guy who had some issues, that's all. We may hang out again at the end of the week, maybe meet up at the Barnes & Noble in Braintree for coffee. I would get the hot chocolate though. I'm not a big fan of coffee."

"Tommy, how can you be a true Cubano, excuse me, Cuban-American, if you don't drink *café*. I find that so strange. It's in our blood. We were born to whip up *café cubano* and savor the creamy drink. It's our crack, *chico.*"

"I know. My parents say the same thing. Pepe and Gladys Perez can't go a day without at least two cups of *cafécito*. Well, my mom prefers *un cortadito*. They would tell me, '*Por que no tomas café, Tomasito?*', and I would shrug my shoulders. I can't help it. I prefer Gatorade and Diet Coke. I guess in that aspect, I'm more American."

"And then there's your gringo accent. You're funny, Tommy. You speak Spanish like an Anglo who is learning it for the first time at school whose parents don't speak a lick of English. I don't get that. No *c-o-m-p-r-e-n-d-o?*" Carlos says, embellishing my accent. I toss a piece of bread at him and twitch my nose.

"Ha, very funny, *meng*," I mimic his accent. He hurls the same bread roll back at me and sticks out his tongue. We laugh.

As we wait for the young waitress to return with our orders, Carlos tells me that he spent Saturday night at home with a Blockbuster rental. (Carlos lives a short walk from the Porter Square shopping plaza, home to Blockbuster, CVS, Dunkin' Donuts, and McDonald's. Basically, your typical Boston area square.) He then starts talking about Marcello and their afternoon together. He looks up and down, smiles here and there, as he recounts the story. I can tell right away that Carlos likes the guy. I think it would be good for him to have someone else to focus on in Boston besides me and his students. Maybe it will distract from dwelling too much on his mother and Miami. When I hang out with Carlos, I try not to babble too much about my parents. I don't want to rub it in his face that I have two healthy but elderly parents in Miami and he has only one, who seems distant with him. When Mami calls me too much, I keep the complaints to myself and count my blessings. I know one day, I will miss those calls from home as Carlos does. I hope that Carlos finds strength, comfort, but most of all, fun from our friendship. But I also want him to go out, live, and enjoy himself in this town without me. He can be the new kid on the block for only so long, so he better live it up. After a year of living in

Boston, I pretty much know most of the gay guys. I'm old news. Carlos is the newest headline.

"So the guy's roommate is a sugar-daddy-ex-boyfriend-friend? What's the deal with that, Carlos? From what you've told me, Marcello sounds like a nice guy, and from what I remember, he's pretty sexy. Why not just have fun with him, you know, get a little something-something, have a little—or a lot—of Brazil in you, if you know what I mean? Just don't get involved romantically. Who knows, he could be someone else to hang with. You'll never find out unless you get to know him better."

The waitress with the curly cues and expertly painted red nails arrives with our dishes. She serves me my usual: a turkey sandwich on Cuban bread and a side of *tostones,* which I madly salt. Carlos ordered the breaded chicken steak and rice and beans. Both smells mix with the aroma of garlic that fills the restaurant. As much as I enjoy devouring the food here, I don't enjoy smelling like the restaurant when I leave. The last time I was here, my clothes wore the eatery's perfume as if we had just walked out of the kitchen.

"I have a good feeling about him, Tommy. He's just—there's no other way to describe him but—*guao!* I can't help but feel excited when I'm around him or when I think about him. Just looking at him gives me a boner. Those soothing hazel eyes, the taut tanned skin. The veins that bulge in his arms. The whole time we were talking, I mentally ripped off his clothes, jumped him, and went down on him. *Ay, Marcello!* When we hugged good-bye at Starbucks this afternoon, I rushed home and jerked off—twice. He makes me so horny. It's driving me crazy."

"So give him a chance—as a friend, like I am with Mikey. You'll never know what can be unless you try." As I listen, I bite into the scrumptious sandwich which rains crumbs on my plate. "So what's next for you and Marcello?"

"*Bueno,* I don't know. We didn't make plans, but I know that he works at the Border Café."

"Uh oh, you know what that means, don't you? We're going

to have to run to the Border sometime soon. I haven't eaten there in a few months, so it would be nice to visit again and have the chicken quesadillas. I would order a turkey quesadilla, but they haven't added that yet to the menu."

"Tommy, I don't think they will anytime soon, but let's go sometime this week or next."

"Deal."

After Carlos and I finish our meal, we grab our windbreakers and say our good-byes at the restaurant's entrance, which is lined with small stacks of Spanish weekly newspapers, the source of news for the majority of Latinos here. I walk back to my Jeep on Centre Street and begin to think about my long week ahead of me. I am writing a story on the lack of televised community programs aimed at Hispanics in Massachusetts. Only two shows exist, and they air at odd hours, 6 a.m. once a month and 8 a.m. each Saturday. In Miami, no question about it, there are a slew of shows on English and Spanish news outlets. In Boston, we don't even have a full-time radio station. When I need my fix of Gloria Estefan, Shakira, or Juanes, I turn to my iPod. You'd think in a historic and cosmopolitan city such as Boston, the country's seventh largest TV news market, there would be more programming tailored to the growing Hispanic population here. We are sixteen percent of the city. But then again, I'm the only Latino writer in the Features section. If the newspaper and online newsrooms aren't diverse, then they can't cover their cities fully. The same goes for radio and TV stations. Boston is old school in more ways than one, but I am trying to change that perception one story at a time and with my presence in the newsroom.

As I pop my Gloria Estefan CD in the player in my Jeep, my phone vibrates. It's a text message from Mikey. I smile as I read the text.

Hey, cutie. I had a lot of fun last night. Thank you for hanging out with me. Coffee Friday night? Maybe dinner on Saturday? I know a good place on the South Shore. Don't take this the wrong way, but it's so good to hang out with you again.

I reread the messages a few times and then read it out loud. I punch back an answer. I say yes to both invites and end the text with a smiley face. I then begin my drive back home. I pass the grand Victorian and colonial homes along the pond side of Jamaic-away and urban park, Arnold Aboretum. I drive by the rows of run-down pastel tripledeckers in Mattapan off Blue Hill Avenue where several panhandlers carry cardboard signs and bombard me with requests for spare change. I check that my windows are closed and my doors locked. A few minutes later, I pass a clutster of Cape homes, manicured tripledeckers, and the brick former chocolate candy factory that was turned into condos until I reach Adams Street, my block. Home.

As much as I would like to see Mikey this weekend, I also wouldn't mind having a drink with Carlos on Thursday or maybe even Rico, who I haven't seen in weeks. I would invite Mikey, but he said he's uncomfortable hanging out in a bar with people drinking their apple martinis, Coronas, and cranberry vodkas. Plus, I know he has to get up early for school.

I haven't had a drink since that night at Club Paradise with Carlos, and I'd like to have a vodka and Diet Coke or two. I want to be out and about and see who is doing what and what all the club boys are up to. I like how the alcohol loosens me up after a hard week at work and how it unleashes my spirit. When I occasionally drink, I temporarily forget about my problems and stresses at work where I am the resident Latino everything.

When I drink, something within me is freed. I let loose, and I'm just me, this fun and optimistic guy who enjoys having a good time and cruising. I don't know how I am going to be able to balance that side of my personality with my new alcohol-free friendship with Mikey. I don't want to disrespect his sobriety, but I'm not the alcoholic. He is. If I want to go out and drink, why should that be any of his business, even though I care about him immensely. He's my friend, an ex-boyfriend. These thoughts fill my head as I pull up to my condo and put the Jeep in park. As I head inside, I wonder why am I so worried about what he may think of me drinking at a bar.

7

Carlos

The addictive aroma of *café* commands me to wake up. When I open my eyes, I see Mami sitting at the edge of my bed in Coral Gables with a nice steaming cup of *café,* her secret weapon. No matter how tired I am, Mami can summon me awake by brewing her special blend. It always works.

"Carlito, wake up! It's time for you to get up."

"*Ay, Mami.* I'm really sleepy. Give me five more minutes." I hide my face under my pillow, but even there, I cannot escape the seductive coffee as it permeates throughout my room.

Mami grabs the pillow and starts tickling me.

"Okay, okay, you win," I say in between giggles. I am very ticklish, and Mami uses that as her other secret weapon to get me to do what she wants. "I'm up! I'll be ready in ten minutes. Where are we going again?" My brain is still asleep.

"*Gracias, Carlito.* Here's your *café.* I need you to take me to the doctor. Remember?" Sometimes, I forget that she's sick again except for little reminders such as these weekly appointments.

She kisses me on the forehead and sets the coffee on my nightstand. I notice her bottle-green eyes try to hide her fear, but then she smiles and looks away, as she always does. She always has that look when we go to the doctor's office for her chemo treatments. Papi had too much to do at the convenience store today, so it was my turn to take Mami this week. She slowly gets up from the bed and adjusts the light pink handkerchief she wears to hide her hair loss. I dread going to the doctor's with Mami. I can't escape the sterile smells of the room as an IV slowly pumps poison into her body. The monitors beep every so often and flash her heart rate. When I go with Mami, I sit with her, hold her hand, and watch *The Bold and The Beautiful,* my mother's favorite soap opera, to keep her distracted. On days like this, I ask for a personal day from school so I can accompany her to the appointments. My principal, Mrs. Avila, always understands. Lying in the chair, Mami looks so vulnerable, but she makes the best of the situation by remaining positive and talking about everyday things.

"Carlos, *tu sabes que* your birthday is coming up. Is there anything you want? I was thinking of inviting the family over and your friends or co-workers from the high school and of course, Daniel. We can have *un* big barbecue *en el patio* and dance to Celia Cruz and Ricky Martin. I want to have a big celebration."

"*Ay, Mami!* I hate those big parties. All everyone does is gossip about everyone else. Who lost their job? How much does he make? Where did they get the money to finance that house? What was Tia Christina wearing? I want something simple and low-key, maybe just a dinner out."

"I know, I know, Carlos. You don't like big productions, but it's been a while since we've had the family over for a big celebration. I want to celebrate your birthday in a big way. I want to celebrate life."

Coño! Now I feel bad. Mami wants to coordinate a big family gathering, and I'm being selfish about the whole thing. The party seems more important to her than to me, and who knows, it may be good for her, having the family around and keeping her mind off her cancer treatments. It will give Mami an excuse to dress up and be *la grand dama* in Coral Gables. I cave in. Although it's my party, I want it to be about her.

"Mami, you win again today. I think that's a great idea! It would be great to see my cousins. We're all so much older these days that we don't see each other like we used to whenever someone had a birthday. Go wild!"

"Trust me, Carlito, you will love this *fiesta*. No one can plan a party like your mama. Remember, I will always be there for your birthday. Always remember that no matter what bad things happen to us, celebrate the life that God has given you and not just on your birthday but every day, *hijo*. Appreciate what you have. *Te quiero, Carlito,*" she says, her eyes lighting up at the thought of organizing another Martin party.

I hold her hand. "I promise, Mami. Just get better. You have to."

My cell phone vibrates like a jackhammer on my night table and stirs me from my dream, which felt more like a vivid memory, a reenactment of all the times I accompanied Mami to the hospital. Next to the phone is a big photograph of me with Mami. Papi took the photo on my twenty-sixth birthday, my last birthday with Mami. She didn't seem sick at all that day even though we all knew better. In the photo, Mami's arms caress me tightly from behind as she plops a kiss on my right cheek. Papi snapped the candid photo as I looked away, laughing. I smile whenever I see that photo. It captured Mami living life and not suffering. It's the only way I want to remember Mami.

"Mami, why are you doing this to me? You are not really helping me by showing up in my dreams," I say to the photograph. I can imagine her response being, "Don't talk to your Mami like that. If I want to talk to visit *mi hijo,* my only son, in his dreams, *pues* I will." Again, she always wins.

There were so many times I had to take Mami to her appointments. With each trip, she grew weaker as the treatments intensified. The cancer persisted and made her frail, but Mami continued fighting back until she no longer could. She slowly wasted away, yet her spirit never waned (as evidenced by my dreams). She managed to keep the focus on me, Lourdes, and Papi, always pelting us questions about our days and what was on our minds. Mami wouldn't allow us to keep her at the hospital. She wanted to be home with a view of her garden from the bedroom as hospice workers rotated in and out of their shifts. As we neared the end, when she was too sick to travel a few miles to Versailles restaurant, we managed to keep our Sunday brunches going. Mami would order from a menu, and I would pick up the food. In her room, we would sit down and eat our brunch and have our talks. I always brought her the coconut flan, and she always finished it despite her lack of appetite.

I grab my cell phone, and I notice a missed call from Lourdes. I'll call her in a few. I want to lie here on my side as tears gradually dampen my pillow. My hands are tucked under the pillow just as they were in the dream.

The slanting rays of sunshine fill my bedroom, announcing the start of a new day in Cambridge. Lourdes always woke up early, so I'm not surprised by the 8 a.m. phone call. I slowly climb out of bed and straighten out my pajamas, which are decorated with little Red Sox bats and balls. Lourdes bought them for me when she and Papi helped me settle into Cambridge over the summer. I amble toward the kitchen where I start brewing some Cuban coffee the way Mami would. Somehow, it doesn't taste the same, and I don't know what I am doing wrong. Too much sugar? Too many coffee grounds? Not enough water? *No se.*

I dial Lourdes, who by now has already gone to the gym and spent an hour on the treadmill with her latest Alisa Valdes-Rodriguez novel and cleaned the house. She has one of those type A personalities. Lourdes always thinks she knows best. She always believes she is right. Most of all, she tries to mother me, which I find annoying. We're siblings, yet she gets into this disciplinarian mode with me. I remember how she would argue with Mami about what classes I should have taken in middle and high school. Lourdes pushed for me to take the honors and Advanced Placement classes. Mami always asked me what I wanted, while Papi was smart enough to stay out of the whole thing. To Mami, my being in a regular class where I had high B's or low A's was just as good as being in an Honors class where I often received low B's and high C's. I was your average B student, but Lourdes wanted me to be something more, to excel more. I never understood why she pushed me so hard. My plans were to go to Miami-Dade Community College like she did and then transfer to FIU like the rest of Miami.

"Hey, little brother, how are you?" she says as she answers the phone.

"Doing well. Just woke up or am trying to wake up."

"Did you try making Mom's coffee? That always worked."

"I've tried, but it never tastes the way she made it."

"Carlos, you have to use Bustelo *café*. Don't use the other brands. How many times do I have to tell you this," Lourdes scolds me.

"I do, Lourdes, but it doesn't work. Oh well, coffee is coffee. This stuff wakes me up anyway."

"So how are you really doing? How do you like teaching in Boston compared to Miami? Are you getting lost in Boston?" she asks. I sprinkle some brown sugar into my coffee and sip it.

"Doing okay, Lou. You don't have to worry about me. I'm fine on my own. I'm not a little kid anymore. School is good. I'm still adjusting to the various students. I think their accents are so cute. And I've lost count as to how many times I've been lost in this city, but Cambridge is pretty easy to figure out. I pretty much walk everywhere here."

"Well, good, little brother. I was checking in. You know, we worry about you being there all alone. I still don't understand why you had to move so far away. At least you could have stayed in Florida and closer to home. Papi wonders how you're really doing."

Here we go again. The Lourdes speech. Just because she can't imagine herself moving away to another city doesn't mean that it wasn't the right decision for me. Between her mothering or smothering me and her personality, we never seem to get along. The stripes in our personalities don't match. Lourdes is one small part of the reason I wanted to start anew in Boston and be on my own.

"*Ay, Lourdes*, I'm doing fine. Seriously. Listen, I gotta get going. I'm headed to the gym in a few."

"Well, *fine!* I was going to talk to you about visiting you up there for Thanksgiving with Papi, but I guess you're not so inter-ested in seeing us so soon," she says, using her manipulative guilt trip.

"We can talk later and figure something out. Say hi to Papi for me. Bye."

"But I . . ." I hear her say before I hang up the phone. I con-tinue sipping my somewhat tasty, yet bitter coffee. I glance over to the refrigerator and stare at the family photo of all of us standing in front of Mami's garden. *Ay, Mami.*

I don't want to start my day being a poster boy for a pity party. It's Sunday and a little chilly from the draft that is seeping in through the kitchen window. I wonder what my *loco amigo* Tommy is doing. It's too early to call him. One time, I called him at ten in the morning on a Saturday, and he pretty much put me in my place by saying, "Carlos, please don't *ever* call me this early on a weekend. Wait until noon. I like to sleep in on the weekends. I'm tired from our night out last night." Okay. From then on, I wait until noon.

I jump in the tub and take a nice hot bath. I dry myself off and gel my wavy hair and tuck the longer loose strands behind my ears. I get dressed in my favorite blue jeans and long-sleeved white shirt and head outside. *Que frio!* I dash back into the apartment and grab a coat. It must be thirty-five degrees outside. I notice the sidewalks are strewn with dead leaves, their colors faded. The cold weather has stripped the trees of their leaves and I see puffs of cold air as I breathe. This must be winter. I decide to run back inside again and grab some gloves and a scarf, which I haven't had to use so far.

I walk down to the Starbucks in Davis Square, order a double espresso to really wake me up, and grab a copy of the *Daily* to read Tommy's latest article. I sit at the counter on a bar stool surrounded by other young people tapping away on their laptops or gabbing with friends about their night out. The rising sun continues to warm up the coffee house. I browse the headlines, which sound like the same old stories. Economy is down. Housing market is slumping. The Patriots win again. Another student scandal at a suburban private school. My eyes stop when I come across an article about an increase in local Brazilians applying to college to become educators. The story goes on to explain how Brazilians represent the largest number of newcomers to Massachusetts. I read the article, and I think of Marcello and his interest in education. I carefully tear the story from the paper, fold it up, and store it in my pea coat's pocket. I'm planning on giving it to Marcello the next time I see him, which may be today at the Border Café.

8

Tommy

"Tommy Boy? No, it can't be. You remembered your old pal Rico, your Italian brother, your first friend in Boston, your hot friend in Beantown, your—?"

"Yes, Rico!" I interrupt him. "Of course I remember you. I'm the one calling you after all. How are you doing?"

"Just great! David left today on his boat for Newport for a few days so I have some downtime. What are you up to, Mr. Cuban Clark Kent?"

"Doing well. Too much to get into it on the phone, but it's all good. Want to hit Club Café, for a drink? We haven't done that in a while. It's long overdue." I fiddle with my phone at work. *The Miami News* online version appears on my screen. Some habits are hard to break. I like to keep tabs on what's happening down there.

"Just like old times. Meet me there at 11 p.m. I'll have your vodka and Diet Coke ready if I get there first. It will be great to catch up. I've missed you, bro."

"Same here. See you tonight," I say before hanging up my phone at my desk at the *Daily* where Post-its decorate the top rim of my computer like yellow flags. I finish transcribing my interview with a Cuban high school history teacher who has his own radio show in Boston. On air, he shares his own sarcastic brand of satire with Spanish-speaking listeners. Whenever I'm scrambling to find a new story, a story somehow finds me. Through the Cuban/Latino Boston grapevine, a steady flow of stories and news tips head my way. I know what the headline and my lead will be, but I can worry about the rest tomorrow morning. I usually find that I write better in the morning when I disappear into my creative writing zone and lose track of time.

It's 6:30, and the majority of the newsroom employees stampede out of the building to their suburban lives on the South Shore or even Rhode Island. Not me. My commute is five miles. I want to head to the gym, grab some dinner at Boston Market, and get ready to meet up with Rico. Although I have had Carlos to hang out with lately, Rico was my first Boston wingman, my chum, when I moved here. We were inseparable. He was there through all my Mikey drama. (It was Rico who first pointed Mikey out to me at Club Café.) I miss our nights at Club Café, our brunches at McKenna's in Savin Hill, and our walks and talks along the Charles River and in P-town during warmer months. Part of the reason we haven't spent as much time together is because he has a boyfriend, David the seaman. He really is a sailor as in the Popeye mold. David lives on a sailboat in an East Boston marina, home to a community of live-aboards like himself.

For some time, Rico resisted David's charms. Rico didn't see himself dating anyone seriously after his ex-boyfriend cheated on him and scarred his heart. But eventually (with my urging), Rico realized he had to take a chance with David and open up the brick wall around his heart. They've been a couple ever since. I've noticed that couples hang out with other couples, and single people hang out with other bachelors and bachelorettes. It makes things easier. The couples meet up for dinner and do couple things such as rent movies or bowl. More often than not, they'd rather not be at a bar or going away on trips with their single counterparts. Perhaps that is why I've gravitated toward Carlos. It's easy for me to call him on a moment's notice to meet up and not worry about him breaking his plans with a boyfriend. I can't really talk about things with Rico when David is around because I find that I censor myself. Although he is Rico's boyfriend, he's not really my friend. But he makes Rico happy, and that makes me content. As a couple, they'd rather do their own thing on the weekends, from sailing to the Cape or playing on the gay football league in South Boston. So it's been a few weeks since Rico and I spent quality time together like we used to. I understand and respect his desires to spend time with his man. Sometimes, friendships have their seasons, but that doesn't always mean that they fade and die. True friendships are unconditional. I know that if I really need to talk to Rico, he will be there for me, no questions asked, at a moment's notice—unless he's having some hot sex with David on his boat. Then I would have to wait a little bit or a few hours.

At 10:30 p.m., I'm halfway to the South End from Dorchester. Mikey calls to say hi, and I tell him about my plans with Rico.

"Oh yeah, I remember that guy with the green eyes, black crew cut, and big arms. I always thought he had a crush on you, Tommy, but then again, who wouldn't, cutie?" Mikey says.

"We're just friends. He has a boyfriend now. We're going to catch up. I haven't seen him in a few weeks." I hop on Interstate 93, passing the newspaper building on my right. The city's small skyline unfolds before me and rises in the distance like a pop-up book. I slow down as I approach the upcoming South End/Back Bay exit.

"Well, be careful driving. We're still on for tomorrow night at Barnes & Noble, right?"

"Yeah, it's a . . . um. Mikey, I've confirmed this with you twice this week. I'll be there. Don't worry." I avoid the word "date" because I don't want to think of it as that, but what else do I call it? A coffee meet-up?

"I'm not worried. I just wanted to make sure you remembered."

"I do, and I will. Anyway, I gotta jump off here. I'm almost there."

"See you tomorrow, cutie."

"*Hasta luego!*"

I manage to find a parking space outside of Club Café, which is a miracle on a Thursday night because of all the guys pumping, sweating, and cruising in the gym downstairs from the bar. (All those work-outs will prepare them for another kind of pumping, sweating, and cruising later on upstairs.) I called Carlos earlier to see if he wanted to join us, but he's pooped out from his workday and wants to rent the newest Almodóvar movie or watch another movie on Lifetime: *Television for Women, Their Gay Friends, and Carlos Martin*. He wants to take it easy. I have a feeling that he's going to call Marcello or make an excuse to see him or something.

As soon as I walk into Club Café, a wave of music hits me. Memories of my nights return in flashes. Couples or first dates eat in the dinner salon that faces Columbus Avenue. I venture deeper into the bar and there's a line of twinks at the ATM machine. Along the hallway walls, posters of cute young men entice patrons to return on Wednesdays for karaoke night and Sundays for eighties retro night. I hang up my jacket at the coat check and begin to walk into the main video bar where a pack of gay skinny and built Italian guys in snug T-shirts with over-gelled spiked up black hair and eyebrows that have been plucked to near extinction slurp their drinks. Near them: a trio of gay Asians (or gaysians) with copper highlights in their perfectly straight, flowing, black hair. That's Boston for you. Everyone lingers in their little social circle defined by ethnicity. As I try and count how many Latinos are here (that's easy, none!) someone suddenly hugs me from behind and lifts me off my feet. I know this embrace well.

"Tommy Boy!" Rico announces, while holding me up.

"H–i, R–i–c–o. I c–a–n't b–r–e–a–t–h–e. P–u–t m–e d–o–w–n!" I manage to squeak out.

"Oops, sorry, man. Sometimes I don't know my own strength," Rico says as I fix my red hoodie and straighten out my blue jeans. To emphasize his point, he flexes his big biceps in his black V-neck shirt. I raise my thick eyebrows, and we laugh.

"So good to see you, Tommy!"

"Same here, Rico. I see that we're as modest, as usual. If I had a pin, I would pop your bicep. It's like you have a balloon under each arm."

He flexes again with macho pride. "They look bigger? I've been trying to bulk them up by an inch. You just made my day, Tommy!"

He puts his arm around me, and we walk to our corner of the bar and stand along the wood-paneled wall. We order our drinks. Rico gets the low carb beer. (He has to maintain those tight abs somehow.) I get, well, the usual.

"Where's your fellow Cuban friend?" Rico asks.

"Carlos is staying in for the night."

"If I wasn't with David, I wouldn't mind, you know, hanging out with Carlos."

"Don't you mean, letting it all hang out, Rico?"

Some quick background on Rico and Carlos. I introduced them one night in the late summer hoping that we could be the three *amigos* in Boston. But sometimes, a friendship with one friend doesn't automatically translate to an instant friendship with another. When they met, Carlos was immediately attracted to Rico. (Who isn't? Geez, I still am!) And Rico thought Carlos was super cute and adorable. We all had drinks that night at Club Café. Later on, after we all went our separate ways, Carlos began joking to me that Rico was tacky, talking about money and his lack of it. Yet Carlos thought he was hot nonetheless. (Rico has always reminded me of the gorgeous, green-eyed, Italian guy who Diane Lane falls for in the 2003 movie *Under the Tuscan Sun*.) As much as I'm attracted to Rico, I've always mentally labeled him as a friend the same way I categorized Carlos. Anyway, I defended Rico, but Carlos did have a point. Rico is my friend, but sometimes he can act like a dork when he talks about doing anything to cut corners financially, even collecting all his Canada Dry cans to recycle for nickels or taking Metamucil to save on toilet paper, which he swears works. On the other hand, Rico thought Carlos's accent was a bit thick. In our private conversations, he mimicked Carlos's accent and kept referring to him as Mexican or Puerto Rican or simply Juan Valdez. I defended my Cuban friend to my Italian one, but there seemed to be a little tension between them. Probably sexual tension. I was the common denominator, and I had to realize, these two wouldn't be friends on their own terms. A hook-up, possibly if Rico were single. But *amigos,* nah! I also have a hard time giving both of them attention at the same time. I am better one-on-one with people. Maybe it's my OCD. So, I will always invite the other to hang out, but so far, it hasn't happened since that night.

The bartender returns with our order, and we immediately start sipping.

"So . . . what's going on? Is this about one of your stories?" Rico says, talking to me but eye-fucking every single, young, cute guy who walks into the main bar. Even though Rico is off the market, he still browses and flirts every now and then. He has told me that he memorizes each guy's features so that when he's home alone, he can jerk off to them. Even in coupledom, Rico needs his bag of eye candy.

"Remember Mikey?" I look down at my drink as I smirk.

"You mean, your alcoholic-ex-boyfriend-who-treated-you-like-shit-for-six-months-and-you-kept-on-putting-up-with-it-until-I-snapped-you-out-of-your-denial? If it's that Mikey, shit yeah, I remember him. Is the dude calling you again?"

"Well . . ." I take another gulp.

"Oh no! You're hanging out with him again. I don't believe it."

"Hold on, Rico. Let me finish—or begin."

"Let me guess, bro. He's sober and he apologized and misses his Cuban ex-boyfriend and wants to hang out with you as friends?" Wow, how did Rico guess all this?

"Something like that. Actually, you're right on, Rico."

"And you're talking to him and being supportive?"

"Did you wiretap my phone? How do you know all this, Rico?"

"Because I know *you.* So did you guys do the do yet?"

"Rico!"

"Don't Rico me, Tommy Boy. He's sucking you back in. Don't you get it? You're falling for this all over again. Tommy and Mikey, part two, the sober season."

"He stopped drinking after he got a DUI. He seems really sincere. He's put his life back together. He's going to AA meetings. He dumped Phil the pill. He's a different guy. He's the sober Mikey I fell in love with, the one I hoped could emerge from the drinking."

"You're my friend so I am going to tell it to you like it is. The guy is an alcoholic. Once is, always is. Let him find his own path. I know you're trying to be the supportive friend, the nice guy, but you are so much happier without him. Why hang out with him and possibly start your old relationship up again? Why not find someone new and fresh, without any baggage? Look," Rico points to the crowd of guys mingling and cruising and dancing in place to the latest pop music. "You can have any guy here. Why go back to Mr. Corona!"

"Because people deserve second chances. I always said that if he ever got sober, I would try and be supportive. Wouldn't you want someone to give you a second chance, Rico?"

"Not if I was a total jerk to a great guy like you. You deserve better, my friend. That's all I'm saying." Rico pats my shoulder.

"We're just friends. He hasn't had a drink in months."

"Tommy, Tommy, Tommy. You're too nice sometimes. You gave this guy second, third, and fourth chances. Why go back to him, even as a friend? Besides, new dicks are always more fun."

"Because I believe in my heart that he has changed, and I will always make room for new friends or people trying to better themselves."

"That's just it. With your history together, I don't think you guys can be *just* friends. Do you?"

"I can try. I have nothing to lose but so much to gain."

"Tommy, I have a theory about dating. If it didn't work out the first time, it won't work out the second or third time, or tenth time."

"We're not dating!"

"But you will!"

"No we won't!"

"Um, yes you will. Let's make a bet on it. If you end up dating the guy, you have to let me borrow your new Jeep for a weekend. Shit, it's hard getting around the city when it snows. It would be nice to have a car to run my errands one weekend."

"Fine! You have a deal. But if we stay just friends, then you have to cook Mikey, Carlos, and myself one of your fabulous Italian dinners. *Comprende?* It would be nice to have all my close friends in Boston under one roof."

"*Capisce,* Tommy! Deal." Rico shakes my hand and pulverizes it with his strength, but he gives me one of his skeptical looks that says that he doesn't buy any of this for one second and that I should stay away from Mikey for my own good.

"Dude, watch it with your grip. Remember, I'm fragile goods."

"You should get some meat on your bones, Tommy Boy. Focus on the weights and not the cardio. I know you like to read your cheesy romance novels on those cardio machines, but if you spent as much time on the weights as you do on the cardio, you could be big and brawny like me," he says, flexing those biceps again like a body builder.

We spend the rest of the night hanging out at the bar. We rotate from room to room, maneuvering through various batches of guys, from the older men wearing their Hollister and Abercrombie & Fitch shirts to look younger to the real young guys with spiked hair and T-shirts that are size "t" for twink. Three drinks later, Rico and I are pretty buzzed. We laugh and playfully punch each other on the arms. (Rico's punches bowl me over.) We scan the crowd just as we did when we first met here over a year ago or so. I like this feeling. The alcohol makes me feel light and loose. I also enjoy feeling young and spending time with my friend. Every now and then, a cute guy catches my eye, and I smile, laugh, and turn to

Rico, who nods for me to talk to him. But as much fun as I am having, my mind flashes to Mikey. I keep thinking about him and wondering where he is tonight. I bet he misses going out to the bars.

When a thin guy with short, dirty blonde, spiked up hair, á la Matt Damon, walks by me and says hi, our eyes lock, and I smile back. Rico suddenly shoves me and sends me right into the guy.

"Oops, my bad. Sorry about that. I must have slipped," I say to the guy while narrowing my eyes at Rico.

"Hey, this is my friend Tommy and you are . . . ?" Rico sandwiches himself between me and the guy.

"I'm Noah. You're cute, Tommy," Mr. Matt Damon says.

"Thanks, Noah. Nice to meet you."

We stand there staring when Rico announces, "Hey, I gotta get going. Tommy, great seeing you tonight. I'll call you tomorrow. Noah, will you keep my friend company?" Rico pats the guy's back.

"Sure, I'd be happy to," Noah says.

I'm left speechless, my mouth forming the giant letter "o" as Rico makes his exit and leaves me with this cute guy. Tonight was about Rico and me catching up, not about me looking for a hookup, but this guy is cute and seems to radiate good energy. Rico waves good-bye, winks at me, and sticks out his tongue. He silently mouths to me, "Have fun. He's cute. Forget about Mikey."

It's just past midnight, and Noah and I sit and talk in the corner of the bar as the monitors flash the latest videos and dance remixes, which make me want to groove in my bar stool. Noah offers to buy me another drink, and I gladly accept.

"Vodka with Diet Coke," I tell him.

"Huh? Are you sure you don't mean rum and Coke, handsome?" he says.

"Nope. Vodka with Diet. It's my own concoction. Try it, you might like it. It's strong but not heavy on the calories." I smile, which makes him smile.

"You got it. Be right back, Tommy."

As I sit alone at the bar table, I watch the flow of guys stream in and out of the main bar under a cloud of noise and cheap cologne. I look over at the bar counter and I see Noah waiting to order our drinks. I'm tickled by how cute and mellow he is. He looks over at me to make sure I'm okay. I grin. As he orders the drinks, I notice a guy with light brown hair and big blue eyes. For a moment, I believe it's Mikey. My heart pounds into my stomach. Why would Mikey be in a bar if he doesn't drink? But as the image becomes clearer, I notice it's a Mikey look-alike. Once again, my thoughts drift back to Mikey, even as this cute *Good Will Hunting* guy returns with a big smile on his face as he carefully walks with our drinks.

For the next half hour, we talk about our jobs. (Noah works as an assistant in the media relations department at Channel 3, the breaking news in-your-face station with all the cute young reporters.)

"I know your byline. You've written some stories about our anchor, Ryan Rudat, and about local TV news. Is that your beat?" Noah asks, eyes trained on me as he sips his drink.

"I write about anything going on in Boston, but I watch a lot of local TV news and sometimes, I get ideas from my viewing. So every now and then, I pitch a story. You guys are number one again at eleven o'clock, and you win in the key demographics." Noah seems impressed by my knowledge about his job and his industry. A warm alcohol flurry fills me as we talk.

"Tommy, you shouldn't be writing about the news. You should be on the news. Have you ever thought about being a TV reporter?" The lighting in the bar causes Noah's eyes to change from blue to green or a mix of both. A smattering of freckles, like grains of Cape Cod sand, sprinkle his nose and cheeks.

"You are too kind. Not with this bush of curly hair," I say, twirling one of my brown curls. "Anyway, how did you end up in media relations? Why aren't you on camera? You've got the looks, and I bet you can talk to just about anyone. You're definitely not shy," I say, leaning in closer.

"Why thank you, Mr. Perez. I enjoy what I do. I help coordinate interviews with local media. I help orchestrate local community events such as our annual health expo. I don't need to be on camera. I enjoy being the puppeteer behind the scenes. Someone has to help our reporters look good," he says, leaning closer my way. We stand in the corner of the bar, my buzz beginning to hijack my judgment. We lean in closer and kiss long, wet, and open. I forget about the guys at the bar. I forget about work. I forget that my new Jeep is killing me in gas mileage. I'm in the moment, kissing this guy and feeling the stubble from his chin gently brush against mine. A boner mushrooms in my jeans, and we rub against one another. I'm having trouble standing, so I lean more on him.

"Wow, great kisser," Noah says, recovering.

"That's what my sister says," I joke. We start to laugh.

We continue kissing, and I start to purr and pant a little. He starts kissing my neck, slipping his tongue in a certain spot behind my right ear, which sends a rush of tingles racing throughout my body. I halfway close my eyes and through the veil of eyelashes, I barely see Noah. I surrender to the feeling when Mikey's sweet face pops into my mind. Huh? I open my eyes again and I'm face to face with Noah.

"Are you okay, Tommy?"

"Yeah, totally fine."

We keep kissing. I close my eyes again, but Mikey invades my thoughts. I picture him at Barnes & Noble or hiking along the trail with me. I see his sweet smile. I feel confused and disoriented.

"Whoa, hold on. I gotta drink some water. I'm a little dizzy," I say to Noah as I balance myself against the bar table.

"Sure, no problem. I'll get you some water. I'll be right back," he says, softly squeezing my shoulder.

I sit back on the stool and the reality of the situation begins to sober me up somewhat. I made out with a guy I barely know (but wouldn't mind getting to know) in the corner of a bar while I'm wobbly. And why is Mikey stuck in my head? This doesn't feel right.

Noah returns with the bottled water, and I immediately start nursing it. All I want to do is go home and hit the sack—alone. What do I do with Noah, who seems so nice? The alcohol got the better of me. I notice some chest hairs poking out of his green shirt, and my boner returns.

"Do you need a ride home? My car is just outside." Noah offers, being a gentleman.

I decline. It's better that I call it a night before I become a sloppy and slutty drunk.

"Thanks, but I drove. My Jeep is on Berkeley by the 7-Eleven. Listen, Noah, I think I'm gonna get going. I have an early day tomorrow, and I need to get something to eat at the store before I drive."

"You sure?" he offers again, his aqua eyes pleading with me to go home with him.

"Yeah, maybe another time. I have to get going." He takes out his business card with the big Channel 3 logo and the rainbow-colored peacock. He scribbles down his personal e-mail and cell number. I do the same, but I'm not sure I'm going to be calling him.

We kiss again, hug, and say our goodnights. As he disappears back in the bar, I grab my jacket from the coat check and descend outside into the South End. I take a long walk along Berkeley and Clarendon, under the twinkling constellation of stars, with Mikey on my mind and in my heart. With each step along the bricked sidewalks, I reflect on the entire night and last few days. Perhaps Rico was right. What am I getting myself into again?

9

Carlos

Ay, Marcello. He dashes back and forth in his white long-sleeved shirt and black jeans as he caters to the whims of his customers at the Border Café. I'm peeking through the glass windows that face Church Street in Harvard Square. I can stare at him all afternoon. I hope no one inside the restaurant thinks I'm some sort of weirdo for peeking the same way kids gaze into the shark tank at the Miami Seaquarium. I can imagine what the pack of preppy smokers down the street must think I'm doing here. It's called spying, and I'm guilty as charged as my eyes are trained on this sexy Brazilian man. His biceps curl under his snug shirt when he carries a plate of quesadillas, sizzling fajitas, overweight burritos, or those crunchy fresh-baked nachos that I can never have enough of. Too bad I can't have Marcello on a plate. I'd feast on that beautiful, dark, lean body hidden underneath those clothes.

Ay, what am I doing? This is ridiculous. I'm spying on a guy I barely know. This is the kind of thing that you see on those NBC *Dateline* predator specials. I should get out of here, head home, watch Lifetime or PBS, grade some papers, and enjoy my day off because Mondays are usually a headache for me at school. Just as I'm about to turn away, Marcello turns my way. He looks surprised, but then a gentle smile forms. He nods at me because his hands are occupied with the dishes. *Que pena!* He is probably wondering what I'm doing here. Luckily, I have a good excuse this time. I invited Tommy to meet me here for a late lunch.

Ay no, Marcello is coming outside. What do I say? What do I do? Tommy, *donde estas?*

"Carlos! What are you doing outside in the cold? Come in, Cubano!" he says, hugging me. He smells like today's special (maybe beef fajitas), but I don't mind. My nose digs deeper into his neck, under his curls, where I catch a trace of his musky cologne, the one that makes me want to rip off his clothes and eat him right here. The scent is masculine, grassy, and raw, calling to mind those sleeveless, muscular Latin gardeners who would manicure my neighbors' lawns in Coral Gables. I would spy on them as well.

"Hey, Marcello. I was just in the neighborhood. Actually, *mi amigo* Tommy is meeting me here. We were thinking of getting something to eat. Tommy is—should be—on his way. He's probably running late, as usual."

"Well, come inside. It's cold out here. You have to sit at one of my tables, handsome. But I need to get back to work. Tell the hostess that you are a friend of mine and she'll take care of you," he says in his Portuguese-accented English.

"Okay, *chico*. I'll be right inside."

Marcello winks and heads back in.

I stand in the cold, early November afternoon, my hands thrust into the pockets of my wool coat to keep warm. Cold puffs of my breath mark the air. *Que frio!* Channel 3 said it was thirty-five degrees today, so I wore my blue corduroy pants and a sage green cardigan. Mami always told me that green best complemented my eyes and hair, so I think I look pretty *guapo* for Marcello, if I may say so myself. I ask one of the preppy smokers for a light, and the cigarette begins to warm me from within. A plume of smoke rises before me, clouding my view of the small Starbucks across the street. As I puff, I hear a grinding, rumbling sound coming from my left. I turn and see a bouncy white Jeep Wrangler trudging this way. Tommy's driving and waving to me at the same time. He abruptly pulls over and swings the passenger door open.

"I'm looking for parking. Hang on! I'll be back in twelve minutes," he declares. I wonder how he came up with that exact figure.

"Are you sure you don't mean thirteen minutes and ten seconds, or ten minutes and forty seconds?"

"Because of that, make it thirteen minutes and thirty seconds," Tommy says, sticking out his tongue and closing the Jeep's passenger door. He hangs a right on the side street of unleveled cobblestones, which make his Jeep (and his head of curls) bounce like a toy bobblehead. *Que loco!*

Exactly twelve minutes later (how did he do that?) Tommy reappears. We hug in front of the Border Café, its logo marked by hand-painted, light blue letters on red wood.

"Tommy, you're right on time! You're so funny, *chico.*"

"Why thank you, Carlos. Has Marcello seen you lurking outside? It's not like you're inconspicuous. I noticed you peeking into the windows from up the street. He's going to think you're a stalker."

"I was looking for you!" I demur.

"Bullshit! You were looking all right, but it wasn't for me. You were looking for some Brazilian beef." I playfully punch Tommy on the arm. We open the screen door of the restaurant, and a smiling young hostess with black-framed glasses seats us in Marcello's work area. I peel off my coat, and Tommy unwraps himself from his scarf. We scoot into our chairs which screech against the weathered wooden floors. Marcello comes around with large glasses of ice water and a bowl of fresh nachos. He puts his arm behind my back as he introduces himself to Tommy.

"Nice to see you again." Tommy shakes Marcello's hand.

"Same here. Welcome to the Border Café. We have some specials tonight," Marcello continues and hands us our menus. For a brief second, our fingers graze each other's in the exchange and the touch instantly transports me to the night we met and danced at Paradise. As Tommy and I scan the menu, we give Marcello our drink orders. I get a Sprite. Tommy gets his must-have diet soda.

As Marcello walks away, Tommy leans and says, "Wow, he is

better looking in the daytime. Usually it's the other way around. You lucked out! Guys you meet at night look twice as bad in the day. They're trolls."

"Did you notice how the light brings out the yellow flecks in his hazel eyes? They remind me of shards of old Coca-Cola bottles," I tell Tommy, leaning in with my menu. He whips out his portable hand sanitizer and cleans his hands.

"Now I can see why you wanted to play *Spy Games* with this guy." As Tommy browses the menu, I notice he's wearing that same red hoodie that he always wears. I haven't been able to pinpoint the label. Come to think of it, Tommy doesn't wear any designer brands. His blue jeans are pretty generic.

"Tommy, can I ask you something?"

"Sure, *Papo,* go ahead, I'm an open book," Tommy says, repeatedly curling the white straw wrapper around his fingers.

"Where did you get that hoodie? Actually, where do you buy your clothes? I can't really tell."

A Cheshire cat grin unfolds on Tommy's face.

"Really? You can't tell?" He beams proudly.

"Yeah, I can't. I mean, your clothes are cute, but I can't figure out where you bought them. Sears? JCPenney?"

Tommy laughs, with his head flinging back and his hands on his stomach.

"It's my secret. Shhh! You'll never guess, Mr. Urban Outfitters and Abercrombie."

"Just tell me. I won't tell anyone. *Ay no!* Don't tell me you go to the Salvation Army clothes store in Central Square?"

Tommy laughs some more. He's clearly enjoying this game.

"Guess?" he says.

"Okay, you buy your clothes at Guess. That's a great store. Macy's carries their line."

Tommy can't stop laughing.

"No, no, Carlos, not Guess the store. I mean, guess as in try again."

"*Chico,* I give up. Where is this place?"

"Okay, but you promise you won't tell anyone? I've been teased about this especially by my sister and my parents. They think I should wear nice clothes being a reporter and all."

"I promise. Just spit it out."

"Costco!" Tommy blurts out.

"Que cosa?"

"Costco, you know, as in the grocery warehouse. They sell clothes there. I buy my jeans there for $12. This hoodie," he flips the hood over his head, which makes him look like a Cuban red riding hood, "was $15. I buy most of my clothes there. And I know the clothes look cute because people always ask me where I buy my stuff. It's a great deal. Just don't tell anyone, okay? It's my *shhh* secret."

"I regret to inform you that the Gay Fashion Mafia has suspended your lifetime membership. You must surrender your membership, now! The Gap and Abercrombie will post a Most Wanted Fashion Felon sign with your *Daily* press photo in their stores. The fashion tribe has spoken," I say, as Tommy throws a nacho at me. "You're too funny, Tommy, and cheap! I've never met anyone quite like you."

"And you probably never will," Tommy says, now twirling my straw's white paper wrapper into small little snakes.

I pick up the nacho and Tommy's paper designs and neatly place them near the bowl. I wouldn't want to make a mess in front of Marcello. He returns with our drinks and takes our orders. Unfortunately, there's no turkey fajita here, so Tommy settles on the chicken fajitas. I order the beef burrito. When Marcello walks away, he gradually grazes the back of my upper shoulder with his fingers, which send pebbles of goosebumps along my neck.

"Carlos, you're blushing. You're like Rudolf, the red-nosed gaydeer."

"Wouldn't you? Look at him, but more importantly, doesn't he seem like a nice guy?"

"Yeah, he does, and I bet his boyfriend would agree with you on that," Tommy snaps back, sipping his towering glass of Diet

Coke. If he could, Tommy would dive into it and playfully swim in it and drink it all day like it was a whimsical concoction from *Charlie and the Chocolate Factory.* "Remember, Carlos, the dude has a guy at home. Don't get too caught up with him. Just enjoy the, ahem, ride."

"Trust me, *chico,* I know. There's nothing wrong getting to know him—in bed. I need me some. . . ." I lean in and whisper "dick!"

"Well, it's right there for your taking. Maybe you can order it from the to-go menu."

We slouch into our seats, and I notice that white flecks begin to dot the windows. I narrow my eyes to focus. It's snowing. Quilts of white flakes sail over Harvard Square, making it look like a snow globe that has been rattled.

"Oh my gosh, look! It's snowing!"

"Yeah, it's official. Winter is here. Get ready, Carlos," Tommy says before beginning one of his monologues. "You see, the snow is beautifully deceiving. It's cute at first, softly falling like it is now. You fall in love with it. You want to capture and treasure the moment with photographs. But then, it keeps falling and falling. It piles up. It gets mushy. The armies of snowplows come out and sweep the streets and pile it on every corner. Cars get stuck on the road, spinning in place. Three days later, you're stuck in your apartment wondering if it will ever end. You wonder, can I leave the apartment without looking like an astronaut? So enjoy this light snowfall for now, because it's going to get worse. Thanksgiving is two weeks away."

"Um, okay. I get your point, but this is so pretty. After we eat, let's walk in the snow. This is why I moved to Boston, to discover something new and different. I'll take some photos with my cell phone and e-mail them to Papi and Lourdes."

"Maybe you can mail the snow too! I hear FedEx has a special on snow deliveries!"

"Maybe I can FedEx you back to Miami!" I tease. Tommy responds by throwing back the nacho I had tossed at him earlier.

As we wait for our food to arrive under the soothing tropical sounds of Jimmy Buffett's *Margaritaville*, I bring up something that I've been wanting to talk to someone, anyone, about: my dreams with Mami. I haven't mentioned this because I don't want Tommy to think I'm some weirdo who dreams of dead people. But I think he might be able to explain what's going on. If anything, it would be nice to actually talk about it for once. I've been keeping this bottled up inside. I dare not bring it up to Papi or Lourdes because what if they're not having the same visits from Mami? I wouldn't want to rub it in their faces, yet I don't want to appear that I am making this stuff up either. I don't want them to think I am desperately mourning Mami and need to see a psychiatrist. So here I go.

"Have you ever dreamt of someone you were close to who had passed away?" I ask, munching on the nachos.

"Do you mean, do I dream about my dead grandparents or friends?"

"Yeah. Exactly."

Tommy furrows his thick black eyebrows and scratches his head. "Um, no. It hasn't happened to me yet. Carlos, I think I would freak out if my Abuela Marie popped into my dream and started chatting with me as if we were at her house in Little Havana. I don't think I could handle it. I'd wake up screaming and lock the doors, but that's just me. I have heard of what you're talking about on *20/20* and *Dateline*. Why do you ask? Are you being visited from the other side?"

"Well . . . sort of."

"Is it Celia Cruz?"

"Um, no. That's not funny."

"Okay. Bad joke. Hmm. It's your mom, right?"

"Yeah. Good guess. Ever since I moved to Boston, she appears in my dreams. It's like she's still with me. I don't understand it."

Tommy leans over and listens more intently.

"What does she say? Are they nightmares? I've heard that souls or ghosts stick around sometimes until they feel that they can truly leave, like on that CBS show *Ghost Whisperer.* Maybe your mom is just watching over you, making sure that you're okay, and when she feels that you've healed or moved on from her death or adjusted to Boston, maybe she'll go on to the afterlife or something," Tommy says, putting his hand over my right hand and gently squeezing it. He looks at me with a gentle half smirk.

"I don't know what's going on. In the dreams, we're having our weekly brunches at Versailles like we used to. She tells me things, gives me advice about what's going on in my life."

"Really?" Tommy's eyes widen.

"Yeah. After I met Marcello at Paradise, she basically told me not to settle for less. In another dream, after I felt drained from teaching, she reminded me why I wanted to be a teacher."

"Has she mentioned me at all?" Tommy inquires.

"Yeah, she said, '*Tu amigo* is a little *loco.* Watch out!' Just kidding, Tommy. This is about me, not about you or one of your stories. But since you asked, she seems to like you. She says you seem like a good guy and a good friend."

"Well, your mom has good taste then," Tommy says with a smile and a cheesy wink. "Wow, this is so weird but in a sweet way. She's keeping an eye on you. Maybe she senses that you're still trying to figure out what you want in Boston or in life. I think it's wonderful that she's talking to you in your dreams. It's her way of communicating with you. Appreciate this. Not many people have this kind of experience."

"Thanks. The thing is, I wake up so sad or I don't want to wake up at all. I miss her so much," I say, my eyes brimming with tears.

"Hey there . . . it's okay," Tommy says, reassuringly. "That's natural. I don't know what I would do if I lost my mom or dad. I would be a complete wreck and probably move back to Miami for good to help Mary. I know you've had a hard time dealing with the loss of your mom, which is why I never bring it up because I don't want to get you down. But I think she would be really proud of you, Carlos. It sounds like she's told you so. Not anyone can just relocate to a new city and not know anyone and start all over again. That's really brave of you. Why don't you start writing down your dreams? Keep a journal next to your bed and as soon as you wake up from one of these dreams, write down what she says. Maybe she's trying to tell you something. You might feel better getting this out on paper. Writing can be like therapy."

"That's a good idea. Maybe I'll do that." I already feel better about sharing this with someone.

"Carlos, listen. I know I can be goofy at times and cheesy with my jokes and my quirky habits, but if you need me to be serious and listen, I will, okay? If I act silly sometimes, I do so because I want you to have fun in Boston. I want to bring some jolly into your life."

"I know and *gracias.*" Just as we high-five one another, Marcello returns with our food on teardrop-shaped dishes. Tommy's fajitas sizzle and crackle. Marcello warns him not to touch the plate. He then swings over to my side and gently places my burrito before me on the worn wooden table.

Marcello leans over. "Enjoy, Carlos!"

Over the rest of our late lunch, Tommy and I chow down and talk about the next few weeks. I tell him that Papi and Lourdes have decided to fly up and spend Thanksgiving with me in Cambridge.

"Hey, that'll be nice, having your family up here. If I could ever get my mom on a plane, I'd invite her up here too. She never leaves Miami Beach, if you can believe that. I'll be in Boston for *Sanguiven.*"

"Having you here for Thanksgiving would help take the edge off of entertaining them. I bet you can keep my dad talking on just about anything."

"I'd love to meet your dad and sister, so count me in."

When Marcello comes back to pick up the check, Tommy suggests we split the bill.

"But put more on his check," I joke. "He makes more than I do."

After we pay the bill, I say good-bye to Marcello, who gives me a hug. Again, that musky smell, the tingling arousal stirs in my pants.

"I'll call you later," he says by the restaurant's entrance.

"Yeah, that would be nice."

Tommy shakes Marcello's hand. We venture outside into the winter wonderland.

"*Bueno, chico,* I think this is my stop for today. I'm gonna head on home and do laundry. Need a ride? My Jeep is two blocks away." Tommy zips up his black coat and pulls out his red hood over it.

"Thanks for coming out this afternoon. Who knows, maybe Marcello will call me later and want to hang out for a bit. I could use the company. Don't worry about me. I just want to walk under the snow back to the apartment. I want to experience this weather."

"Okay, be careful. The snow can get slippery. We'll talk later in the week. Take it easy," Tommy says, hugging me and patting me on the back.

"You too, *loco!*" A few minutes later, I spot Tommy hanging a right on Massachusetts Avenue and disappearing into the curtain of snow, which makes Harvard Square look like a holiday postcard. I hang a left on the busy street and begin my walk back home to Porter Square. I pass the Cambridge Common on my left and Harvard Law School on my right as the lumbering, white, city buses circle the rotary around the park. As I walk, I take in all the snowy wonders as if I were an explorer on a newfound land. I feel snowflakes freckle my face where they coolly dissolve upon impact. I stick my tongue out and taste the fresh white droplets. I look back and see a trail of my footprints along the sidewalk.

At the light outside the Starbucks on Shepherd Street, I hold out my gloved hands and watch the snow transform my brown gloves into white ones. I pass beauty shops, clothing stores, and real estate offices along the way. In each of their glass windows, I see my brown wavy hair soaked in white. I shake the snow off and watch it fall from my head to the ground. At each intersection, the snow quickly accumulates on each corner, replacing the leaves that were there a few weeks ago. I step on the mounds, and my feet slightly sink into the newly formed powdery piles. Approaching Porter Square, I bend down and pack some of the snow into a small ball, but it crumbles when I try to lift it. I still manage to hurl some of it like a Red Sox pitcher. Papi would be so proud. *Not!* I love this place. Optimism and happiness bubble up within me as I enjoy Mother Nature's snowy exhibition. I whip out my cell phone and snap the images of the snow salting the rotating sign at the Porter Square subway stop. I hold my cell up and photograph myself (as best as I can) surrounded by the snow in the background.

By the time I reach the front of my three-story tripledecker, my black wool coat is completely white. I smile as I brush off the excess snow and it sprinkles to the ground. I climb the three flights to my one-bedroom apartment, soaking the wooden steps with my wet shoes, when my phone vibrates. It's a text message from Marcello.

I leave work in an hour. Can I come and see you?

I stand midway between the second and third floors and type back: Sure, followed by my address. This has been a one-night stand that has been waiting one too many nights to happen. Maybe I'll finally be able to see Marcello in the flesh, once and for all. Maybe I will have a nice warm body to cuddle with tonight. Finally!

It's 8 p.m., and the buzzer goes off. It must be him. *Ay, Marcello!* When I press the intercom, I hear his Brazilian accent. I am instantly aroused. I've had an erection since he text-messaged me that he was going to stop by after work.

"I'm on the third floor!" I instruct over the intercom. I bounce up and down out of pure excitement.

His footsteps grow louder in the stairwell. I open the door and wait as he comes toward me. He changed shirts from work. He's wearing a tight black T-shirt under his green coat. His dark blue jeans are snug in all the right places. Our eyes lock the entire time he ascends.

At the door, we hug tightly. We start to kiss. I taste the salt on his lips from . . . who knows. I don't care. I lick his lips and shut the door. I place one hand on Marcello and the other on his bum. We kiss repeatedly, an exchange of tongues and moans. He drops his coat on my wood floor. My hands creep underneath his T-shirt. I feel the tautness of his stomach. I massage his shoulders. I press his biceps as my tongue wiggles all around his mouth and rubs against the inside of his teeth. I haven't felt this alive in so long. It's intoxicating. With our eyes closed, we manage to kiss and walk over to the sofa where he collapses on top of me. My tongue explores his nape, which smells of his grassy cologne. He must have sprayed enough on to cloak the restaurant stench. My hands burrow into his hair, and I play with it. I pull off his T-shirt fast and hard. I press his lean, tan body against mine and squeeze his hard butt. I repeat *Ay, Marcello!* several times as I slip my hands under his jeans to squeeze his hairless, tight butt. It feels so good to be touched, to be desired.

"Carlos, you are super *bello!*" he says. "I have not been able to stop thinking about you," he says in his broken English. His hazel eyes peer into mine, piercing my mind and penetrating my soul.

Marcello pulls off my sweatpants, and my dick pokes out from my underwear. He pulls me forward and takes off my T-shirt. My hands explore his hairless tight chest and tickle his small, dark nipples. I slink my hands into the front of his jeans and feel his hard cock. It's a little wet. I get up and forcefully lead him to my bedroom. We throw each other on the bed and continue this sexual dance. When I look to my right, I see the framed photo of me and my mom. The image starts to weaken my impulses.

"Hold on a second!" I lean over Marcello and place the photo inside my nightstand drawer.

"Sorry, Mami! You can't see this."

Marcello grins. For the next two hours, we kiss, suck, grab, lick, massage. Name the action verb, and we performed it. Our bodies engage in a rhythmic cadence, flowing and pumping as one. At one moment, he sits up on top of me and grinds his smooth ass against my throbbing, uncircumsized, Cuban cock.

"I want you inside me, *guapo,*" Marcello says, his eyes half opened and closed as if he were in a lustful trance.

"I want you so much," he continues. Hearing those words, I grab an ultra sensitive ribbed condom and some lubricant stashed under my bed. Within a few minutes, I'm inside him, feeling the warmth and wetness of his core. A delicious, forceful, tingly feeling fills my entire body, a stimulation I have longed for. I don't want to be anywhere else right now. As he rides me, I keep my hands on his chest, squeezing his muscles and pulling on his nipples. Our bodies move, fluidly entwined. When Marcello and I come, it is with a barbaric and primal intensity. He collapses on top of me in a sweaty stupor. Breathless, we lay in my bed in a sweet lulling state of ecstasy. I carefully remove the limp and wet condom filled with my creamy liquid and toss it into the waste basket near my desk.

I turn to my side and spoon with Marcello. I lick the sweat off his neck as his breathing slows. God, I want this guy so much. I want him to stay the night and hold me. I want to wake up with him in the morning and prepare him breakfast. I want to show him how I whip up *café Cubano,* just as Mami taught me. I want him to be with me and take away all the loneliness that invades me when I'm alone at night. In the brief moments I have shared with Marcello, I have felt good about myself. I don't want the feeling to be fleeting.

After half an hour of relaxing, Marcello yawns and slowly rises. He takes his clothing and goes to the bathroom and washes up. I lay in bed and wait for him to return. Maybe another sexual romp? *Ay, Marcello.* I want to do this again and again until my skin is raw.

When he reappears, he is already dressed. He tucks in his shirt and sits on the edge of my bed. He begins to slip on his socks.

"You're not staying?" I ask meekly and confused.

"I'm sorry, Carlos. Or as you say in español, *lo siento.* I must go." I lean closer to him and rub his back to get another feel of it.

"But why? Stay the night. We can have so much more fun. There are more things I want to do with you. I want to make you breakfast. Do you have to work in the morning or something?" I embrace him tightly from the back and feel the hard edges of his deltoids.

"I work later in the afternoon, Carlos, but I must go. Remember, I have a roommate." I suddenly deflate. I know he has that older guy roommate-boyfriend, but I know Marcello is not in love with him. The guy just gives him a place to stay. I just want Marcello to stay at least the night and keep me company.

"But you said he's not your boyfriend?"

Marcello gets up and pops his back. "He is not, but we have some rules. I just need to stay with him until I move out next spring. I don't want any problems," Marcello explains.

"So if you like a guy and want to be with him and spend the night, you can't? That's one of your rules?"

I get up and stand before Marcello, face to face. His curly hair is all messed up from our sexual encounter. He notices me looking at it so he tries to fix it.

"Carlos," he says, brushing the side of my face with the back of his hand. "I want to stay but I can't. Please understand. I am in a complicated situation," he says, using the same tone an employer would use to reject an employee for a promotion. He tries to sound reassuring, but he's not. My heart sinks. Tommy was right. He suggested that I mess around with Marcello but expect nothing more. What was I thinking? I'm such an idiot. Here I am, standing naked with my penis flacid and pleading with a guy to stay with me. I'm pathetic. I'm the same loser-dork I was in private school where everyone made fun of me because of my accent and wiry frame.

"Okay. I guess I understand." I slowly put on my underwear and my sweatpants as if my internal batteries were running on low.

Marcello gives me another long kiss, but somehow, I'm not

feeling it. I was just a Cuban conquest to him. I hoped for something more. A new friend perhaps? I walk him to the door because that is where he obviously wants to go.

"You are so handsome, *guapo.* Thank you for coming to the restaurant and for tonight, but I need to go. The subway stops at midnight. Maybe I can come over again another night?" He puts his coat on and weakly smiles at me.

"I don't know. You should get going before your boyfriend, roommate, or sugar daddy gets upset," I say.

Marcello waves, and I shut the door. I look around my small apartment. Despite my sofa and desk and bar stools, this place feels empty. I feel empty. I walk to the bathroom, gargle, and brush my teeth. After I'm done, I stare at my reflection in the mirror. Tears creep down my face. I wipe them away, but more form. I blow my nose. I wish things were the way they used to be in Miami. If they had been, Mami would be alive. I would still be teaching at Braddock High. I'd feel more complete. Maybe moving to Boston was a big mistake. I remain a stranger in this city even though Tommy has done his best to inject some fun into my life. And he has. Yet, I don't necessarily feel all that happy and complete. I don't know where home is. I just know that I can't shake this depression, this loneliness. The last few weeks since winter arrived, I have wanted to stay under the covers and not go to Dorchester High and deal with reality. Sometimes, I cry for no reason. An unexplainable void lingers inside me. I want to be my old self again, but Mami was a big influence, and she's gone. Her death showed me how things can change in an instant even though I saw her slowly fade away over the last few months she was alive. Sometimes, I feel weak, scared, depressed, and confused. A heavy depression pins me down no matter how hard I try and get up.

I want to be more like Tommy, so optimistic, confident, and happy. Tommy is a mystery to me. I don't know his secret to his joie de vivre. I am hoping that by hanging out with him, I can catch some of it, because I desperately need it.

I grab my cell phone and text him. Maybe he can talk now and cheer me up.

Hey Carlos, que pasa? I'm out with Mikey, Tommy messages back.

Nada. Just wanted to talk. We can talk later. Have fun with Mikey.

Are you sure? If you need to talk, I can go outside for a second.

It's late, loco. Let's talk later in the week.

Okay, we'll go to El Oriental or something and chat. Take it easy!

I place the cell on my bar stool in the kitchen as I dry my tears and amble back to my bedroom. I lie on the bed and stare at my popcorn ceiling. My arms cushion the back of my head. I remember that I left my favorite photo of Mami and me in the drawer. She wouldn't like that. So I take it out and place it back on my nightstand. I roll over on my stomach and rest my head against my pillow, facing the photograph and the bedroom window. I hold the photo and say, "I miss you Mami, so much." I caress the glass cover and kiss her on the cheek. As the snow falls outside over Cambridge, I fall asleep, holding the picture, hoping that I may see her in a dream. Alive or dead, Mami knows how to make me feel better. I just want to feel good again.

10

Tommy

"The chocolate brownie, Tommy?" Selena greets me at the Barnes & Noble café.

"Yeah, plus the hot chocolate. I need to warm up."

"I'll add some whip and chocolate shavings. You'll be set to go," she says, as the machine hisses with bursts of steam that warm up my drink. As I wait by the lip of the counter, I take a 180-degree inventory of the store. The café is packed! College students bury their heads deep into their textbooks. A group of suburban women gab about their book club pick of the month. A teacher mentors a frustrated high school student in trigonometry. Other coffee drinkers browse *People, Time,* and *Consumer Reports.* I like the quiet frenzied rhythm of this place. It reminds me of the *Daily* newsroom where everyone is ensconced in his or her own world. It suits me. When my eyes return to Selena, she says, "Psst! There's your cute, blue-eyed friend coming in," and winks.

"Oh yeah?" I turn around and see Mikey at the front entrance, dusting off the snow from his jacket and tucking his light brown hair behind his ears. "Thanks for the heads-up." A smile spreads across my face.

Mikey spots me and nods up my way. We hold each other's gaze. It's Friday night, and we're meeting up for another coffee chat.

Selena sets my drink at the counter. I turn around and grab it, feeling the heat penetrate the cup and my hands. Mikey heads my way and peels off his brown scarf.

"Hey, you!" he greets me with a hug.

"Hey, yourself! Good to see you. Do you want some coffee to warm up?" I return the embrace.

"Yeah, but I'll get it. Why don't you grab us a table, cutie. I'll meet you over there."

With my brownie and drink in hand, I gingerly walk over to the green table in the corner, which has become our meeting spot in the last few weeks. Instead of Club Café where we used to meet up once upon a time, we've been meeting at Barnes & Noble. Instead of Diet Cokes and vodka and Coronas, we drink coffee and hot chocolate. I kind of like this, the casualness of the place and easy conversation that flows between us. I look forward to our meet-ups. They remind me of what could have been.

After Mikey grabs his regular house brew coffee, he scans the café area until his eyes meet mine again. He heads to the sugar table and grabs some cream and sweetener. He then twirls his caffeine concoction, takes a sip, and tops it off. He casually walks toward me.

"So . . . how was your night at Club Café last night, cutie?" he says, inquisitively.

"It was fun. Rico and I had a good time catching up, like old times."

"Ya know, I don't miss that place at all, Tommy. Too many bad memories or at least the ones that I remember. Most of my nights there are blackouts. I was such a mess. No more Club Café for me. Those days are over," Mikey says with relief. His thick Boston accent treats "over" like "ovah." Although he doesn't remember some of his nights there, I certainly do. There was his sloppiness whenever he walked with a beer in each hand. I recall the nights after our breakup when I would see him with Phil the pill, who had to carry him out of the bar. I think of the times Mikey and his friends Patrick and Will stumbled over guys and nearly started a brawl with other patrons. On second thought, I'd rather not remember. I'd rather have one of Mikey's blackouts to block those memories. I prefer to see him the way he is tonight.

"Well, maybe when you're ready, you can go there and have a Coke or a Sprite. You don't have to drink alcohol at a bar. It could be like being here at the bookstore. We're drinking and talking but with coffee," I hold up my cup.

"Cheers," he toasts back. "So, Tommy, tell me, did *you* drink last night?"

I take a bite out of my chunky brownie before I answer. How do I tell an alcoholic that I drink and really enjoy it? I'm not sure what the protocol on this is. I don't want to come off insensitive.

"Um, yeah. I had my regular drink, but I wasn't drunk or anything. I usually stop after two or three drinks. Remember, I have to drive home. I'm not the world's biggest drinker. I'm a lightweight."

"And the cutest lightweight," Mikey says, sticking out his tongue and playfully biting down on it. "So, Mr. Cute Lightweight, did you meet anyone?"

I'm a little puzzled by the question. Does he really want to know that I made out with a cute publicist named Noah? Should I even tell him? It's not really his business, and it's not something I normally do—suck face in public. I take another bite out of the brownie and slowly chew to buy some time to come up with an answer. Friends confide in one another, but Mikey and I aren't just friends. There's a level of fondness between us that delves deeper than friendship, yet I don't feel comfortable spilling the beans about my public display of sluttiness. Mikey stares at me and waits for an answer. I start to laugh.

"What? You think just because I had a few drinks that I hooked up? Give me some credit, Mikey. I was there with Rico, and we had a good time." I wonder why I'm explaining myself.

"And yeah, I met plenty of guys. I get story ideas by talking to people. I'm a reporter. We have to be social to get information about what's going on. Most of my ideas come from either people suggesting stories to me or from my own local observations as a Latino in Boston." Mikey gives me a suspicious I'm-not-buying-your-story look. I don't know what's worse, telling Mikey that I did make out with a guy or that I stopped kissing a guy because he kept appearing in my head while doing it. When in doubt, change the topic. Deflect. I take another long sip and do a topic switcheroo.

"How was your day at school, Mikey?"

He twirls his coffee and takes a nice big swig, which leaves some coffee on his lip.

Mikey lights up as he explains his day at work.

"School was great. I had some productive counseling sessions today. I love my kids. I know their quirks, their personalities. I can read them pretty well. Today, I met with Melvin again, and he showed me some improvements from our last session. He's a low B student now, up from a D average. And I found a bilingual math tutor for Vanessa to help her improve her grades. Her mother signed off on twice-a-week after-school tutoring sessions. My heart goes out to Vanessa and her mom, who's here from Honduras and never finished school. Vanessa felt embarrassed asking her mother for help on her math homework because she knew she couldn't read the word problems in English. Tommy, I tell you—these kids are wonderful. They just need a little direction, and I'm glad that I can do that for them."

Listening to Mikey talk about his students makes me say "awww" internally. I enjoy hearing his school stories. Something fills inside me when I see his passion for his work. He enjoys what he does. Counseling centers him. His work is a positive arena in his life. It's a turn-on for me that goes beyond the physical.

"Well, if I ever have a problem with math, I'll be sure to make an appointment with you at your school."

"Hey, you got my number. Call whenever!" he says in a flirtatious tone.

We spend the next two hours at the bookstore. We browse the magazines and compare the various music and movie rankings. We stroll up and down the fiction section, talking about our favorite authors.

"Are you still a Nicholas Sparks fan?" Mikey asks, as we stand in the "S" section of the aisle.

"Yeah, I've read all his books back to back. I'm waiting for the next release. For now, I'm reading Danielle Steel. She's addictive."

"Tommy, you're so cute. You're such a romantic. Most guys wouldn't admit they read romance novels."

"I'm not like most guys, Mikey. I wear my heart on my sleeve," I say, flexing my tiny bicep.

"And that's one of the things I always . . . liked about you," he suddenly stammers. "You're your own person with quirks, ticks, beautiful qualities, and small biceps."

"You must check your vision. They're not *that* small. I work out. Me muscle man. Me lift weights. Ooga ooga."

Mikey rolls his eyes at me. "Ok, Mr. Ooga Ogga. I get the point. You have huge biceps. Oh my gosh, you should enter a bodybuilding contest. You'd beat everyone," he says, flexing his thin arms to humor me. "And now back to reality, have you ever thought about writing your own book? You write for the *Daily,* and your writing has a nice conversational rhythm to it. How different can it be from writing a novel?"

"I've written short stories about growing up in Miami but never a book. I don't think I'm that good of a writer. I don't even know where I would start. I can write 1,000-word or 1,400-word articles but a book? Mikey, that's like 90,000 words, 300 pages, months and months of writing and rewriting. In a nutshell, *mucho trabajo!*"

Mikey puts an assuring hand on my shoulder.

"I think you should write about your experiences in Boston. It's a fish-out-of-water story. It would be great. I'd read that book. I just wouldn't write a book about building muscles or anything. I'm kidding, cutie."

"Um, thanks, Mikey. I think. I'll take most of that as a compliment. But if I did write a book, you'd probably be my only reader."

"Nah . . . I really believe you can add something new and fresh to all the tired Boston authors. I've read my share of Irish-Italian Boston books in school. This would be different, cutie."

"I'll take that to heart, Mikey, and think about it, but I don't think books are in my future."

We saunter to the biography section where I notice a new book on primatologist Jane Goodall. Mikey was always a big fan of hers. I remember when he took me to see a documentary of her lifelong dedication to chimpanzees at the Children's Museum in Cambridge. Sitting in the angled seats gave me vertigo, but Mikey held my hand throughout the show and surprised me with a Diet Sprite to calm my tummy.

"I completely forgot about the new book. I'll have to come back this weekend and buy it. I didn't bring my debit card with me. I just have a few bucks. I can't wait to read it," Mikey says before excusing himself to go to the bathroom. "I'll be right back, Tommy."

"Take your time! I'm not going anywhere."

As he heads to the back of the store, I grab the Jane Goodall book from its display table. I power walk to the cashier register and pay. I look back toward the bathroom and realize that Mikey is still inside. I dash outside to my Jeep, toss the bag in the trunk and then head back inside the store all within three minutes. Just as I walk back to the biography section, Mikey reappears and smiles as he walks back my way.

It's just past eleven, and the store manager has announced over the store speakers that it's closing time.

"I can't believe we've shut down the store, Mikey."

"I know, wild night, huh? We're some of the last few in the house."

We walk outside. A light snow falls over the South Shore. Mikey lights up a cigarette to warm up. We lean against the side of my Jeep and talk some more as the store's front lights begin to shut off one by one like a flickering line of Christmas lights.

"What are you doing tomorrow, Tommy?"

"I don't know. I hadn't thought about the weekend. I was thinking of going hiking or coming back here to the store to read some of the news magazines. Actually, not a lot. What about you?"

"I was thinking we can have dinner or go to the movies. They're replaying the U2 concert in 3-D at the IMAX theater. I've always been a big fan of theirs. I was thinking we can go to the theater at Providence Place. Remember the last time we were there, we lost your Jeep in the garage?"

"Yeah, how could I forget. We had the mall security guard drive us around in the little golf cart until we found my old Jeep on the other side of the parking garage. How embarrassing. Yeah, that sounds like fun. It'll be nice to visit Providence again."

"Okay, so it's a plan. Do you think we can meet up here at the bookstore and drive in your car, Tommy? I'm not supposed to drive beyond work and groceries, according to my hardship license. The bookstore is sort of in the middle."

"No worries, Mikey. I don't mind driving."

As we stand there and talk, Mikey's eyes twinkle like the constellation of stars over Braintree. We smile and look away. We're both quiet. I decide this is the moment to surprise him.

"Hey, wait right here. I got something for you." I turn around, swing open my Jeep's driver side door, and pull out a green bag.

"What are you talking about, Tommy?

I hand him the plastic bag and he looks puzzled. He opens it up and then he laughs.

"When did you . . . ?"

"When you were in the bathroom," I abruptly interrupt. "I thought you'd want it."

"You're so sweet, cutie. Thank you very much. I'll start reading it tonight as soon as I get home," he says, giving me a hug.

I return a hearty pat on the back even though every part of my body wants to grab him, kiss him, and not let go.

"I'll see you tomorrow, and thanks again, Tommy, for meeting up and the book."

"No problema."

I hop into my Jeep and adjust my rearview mirror to watch Mikey walk back to his white Volkswagen Rabbit. Once inside the car, he flips through the pages of the book. I crank up the Wrangler, back up, and pull away. Tomorrow should be fun.

It's Saturday afternoon, and I'm back here at Barnes & Noble to meet Mikey. As soon as he pulls up, he hops into my Jeep and we embark on our short trip to Providence. Along the way, he fiddles with my CD player, which is playing Gloria Estefan.

"You're still a fan of Gloria Estefan?" he says, looking perplexed as he sits shotgun.

"Um, of course! She's my homegirl!" I shift gears as we pull onto Interstate 95, passing the Blue Hills on the right.

"Well, I brought some U2 CDs to get us in the mood for the movie. Do you mind, Tommy? I wouldn't want to cut off Gloria in the middle of a "Conga" megamix."

"No worries. Gloria won't be offended. Go ahead and pop in some Bono."

Mikey slides the band's greatest hits into my CD player and the sounds of Bono, The Edge, and the two other guys whose names I never seem to remember blast inside the Jeep. Mikey uses his right hand to groove to "Mysterious Ways" as traffic whooshes by us.

Half an hour later, we pull off exit 22C into Providence Place, the grand city mall that looks like a stacked Lego architectural feat come to life but with a cement facade. We enter the garage and make our way inside the mall. We pass all the stores on the second floor as shoppers stroll on the carpeted walkways. When we pass the Abercrombie store, pounding music and an intoxicating men's fragrance spill into the walkway. Midway through the mall, we stand in front of a wall of glass windows where the city unfolds before us. We notice the grand high-rises near the lip of the river. The afternoon sun reflects against them and the small houses in the distant residential neighborhood on the hilly side of town, home to Brown University. Mikey and I stand and point to all the little homes that are blue, yellow, white, or pink with snow-caked roofs. To the left, we see the lighted grand white Statehouse looming over the city like a watchful guardian. As we take in the view, Mikey puts his hand on my shoulder, and I smile at him. Being here with Mikey feels so right and natural. I take a mental snapshot of the moment to appreciate later on when I'm home alone.

We walk around some more and browse in some of the stores before we settle in at The Cheesecake Factory downstairs and chow down. After a twenty-five-minute wait, we find ourselves feasting. Mikey has the fish and chips and I eat my usual turkey club. We compare Providence to Boston.

"It's like a mini Boston," I say, sipping my Diet Coke at our table near the front of the restaurant where a mob of hungry people wait for their pagers to vibrate.

"It's really cute here. It's not as crazy as Boston, but then you don't have as much to do here. It's quieter."

"Would you ever live here, Mikey?"

"I've always wondered what it would be like to live here. I've never lived anywhere outside the South Shore. I'm not as brave as you, Tommy, moving from your hometown for Boston. I don't think I could ever do that. But I love coming to this mall and walking around—when it's warmer. During the summer, they have those fire nights when they light up the river with fire and soothing music. It's a cute little city and cheaper to live in. You can buy a new condo here and not pay Boston prices. Why? Are you thinking of moving here, cutie?"

"Nah. I've just always been drawn to this town. I don't know why. I know a lot of *Daily* reporters who commute to Boston from here. It's about a forty-five-minute drive. I'm happy in Dorchester, but I wouldn't rule out buying something newer down the road. My condo has its share of warts because of its age, and as you know, crime keeps going up in Boston, especially in Dorchester. Two cars were broken into in my parking lot last month, so it's spreading to

Lower Mills. I keep seeing ads for new condos in Providence, and the prices aren't that astronomical."

"Well, maybe when you grow tired of Dorchester, Providence will be waiting for you. It's not going anywhere," Mikey says with a wink. "I would visit you here."

"You better! I think Carlos would get lost coming here. He's not very good with directions. He's pretty much a Cambridge and Somerville guy."

We finish our dinner and maneuver through the restaurant's crowd and in between the waiters dashing with huge plates of food. We ride up three floors on the escalators to the IMAX theater. There's a small crowd of young people, mostly college students and teenagers, in line. As Mikey grabs the tickets, I venture inside to buy us some Reese's Peanut Butter Cups and M&M's. Theater employees hand us our funky 3-D glasses as we head deeper into the auditorium. We plop ourselves in the rear seats and prop our feet up and relax. Our heads lean together as the lights dim.

"You look so funny, Tommy!" Mikey turns to me, wearing the weird glasses.

"Yeah, tell me about it. I look as weird as you!" We laugh.

The lights dim, and Bono and company start rocking. Bono looks like he's about to leap off the screen and land in our laps while singing "Even Better Than the Real Thing." The Edge appears as if he will strike us in the face with his guitar. I feel I can reach out and touch the crowds rising and swaying in the film's concert. This is pretty trippy. When I take off my glasses for a brief moment, I see a kaleidoscope of blue, green, and yellow hues outlining each of the band members like a halo. I begin to feel disoriented, so I put the glasses back on.

Throughout the concert, Mikey bobs his head and softly pounds his fist against his knee to the rhythm of the beat. He's clearly enjoying himself. He sings along to the lyrics. As each song passes, I make a mental count and hope the concert doesn't have more than thirteen songs, because then that would mean it's more than ninety minutes long. I'm not the biggest U2 fan, but I am a fan of Mikey's so I agreed to come here as a way of spending quality time with him. No bar. No drinking. Just Mikey and me, as I always envisioned us. At some point, I doze off. Mikey awakens me by playfully punching me in the arm.

"Oops, sorry. Must have been the digestion, Mikey."

"Yeah, all that turkey. I bet if this was Gloria Estefan in 3-D, you'd be up on the stage doing the conga or the rumba or whatever you Cubans call it and dancing the night away."

"You're probably right, but hey, I'm here and I actually know the words to every song," I say and sing the words to "One" to emphasize my point.

"Okay, okay, Tommy. You proved your point, but hush now. You sound like a howling dog, and the people in the front row are looking back at us and are going to demand their money back if you don't stop," Mikey whispers. I playfully hit him back.

At the end of the concert (Thank God!), we take off these dorky glasses, and we walk down the steps of the theater and back into the mall area. It's nighttime, so the same view we marveled at earlier is now filled with the sparse and silent flickering nights of the city. We stroll around some more, past the Food Court where teenagers stand in line at Johnny Rockets, Ben & Jerry's and Subway. We glide down the escalators as throngs of other shoppers and visitors exit this gargantuan mall. We actually find my Jeep on the first try.

On the drive back home, Mikey and I enjoy the silence of the night. I gaze out the window where I see the blur of the oncoming lights from southbound traffic. To my right, Mikey passes out, his head pressing against my Jeep's glass window. A sliver of moonlight lands on his forehead. I pull down the sunviser to block the light so he can sleep peacefully. I like watching him sleep.

Forty minutes later, I pull into our regular meeting spot, the Barnes & Noble parking lot. Mikey finally wakes up.

"We're here?" he yawns.

"Yep, this is your stop. You slept the whole way."

He rubs his eyes with his knuckles and stretches like a cat in the car. He turns toward me, shakes my hand, and moves in closer for a quick hug, and we linger in the embrace.

"Thanks for hanging out with me tonight. I had a lot of fun, Tommy."

"Me too, sleepyhead."

He closes the door, looks my way again, and bites down on his tongue. He slowly walks back to his little Rabbit, which is parked a few spaces down. We have the only cars in the lot. The store is closed and cloaked in darkness. Mikey waves good-bye as he hops into his car. I stand by until he starts his engine. Once his headlights flash, I pull away.

About ten minutes later, as I drive on Granite Street in Braintree, my cell phone rings. The caller ID reads Mikey. I pick it up. Maybe he wants to wish me a sweet dream.

"Tommy! Tommy! Where are you? I need you." He sounds frantic, alarmed.

"Hey . . . what's wrong?"

"I just got into an accident. This woman hit my car outside the bookstore. I can't move my car."

Panic and adrenaline fill me. I imagine Mikey hurt and bleeding at the steering wheel. I immediately make a U-turn, almost tipping my Jeep over in the process, and floor my Wrangler. I grind my gears, rev the engine, and force my 200 horsepower into warp speed. My speedometer reads eighty-five mph.

"Mikey! Stay right there, I'm on my way. I'll be there in a few minutes." I gun my Jeep to the scene and pray that Mikey is okay.

11

Carlos

Mami snips the leaves from her gardenias. Her back is turned to me as I sit on the cement decorative garden bench along her verdant green lawns. Behind me is a row of Mami's radiant red hibiscus flowers and yellow daffodils that throb with life in our backyard. The sun casts an almost ethereal, buttery light over Coral Gables and Mami. I have to squint and cover the rim of my forehead with my hand to look at her.

"*Carlito,* can you pass me the plastic bag for the leaves?" she asks. "You know, gardening is very healing. Maybe one day, you will have your own *casita* full of beautiful flowers like these," she says, snipping the bad leaves.

"Mami, you're not helping. I don't want my own garden. I don't have the touch that you do. I don't think I can afford a house with a yard in Boston on my teacher's salary. I don't even know if I want to stay there," I blurt out, sitting with my hand touching the right side of my chin as I watch her in action.

"*Carlito, que te pasa hijo?* Why are you so sad?"

"*Ay,* I'm fine, Mami. The gardenias are getting bigger. They look like white dangling bulbs." Mami turns around with her scissors in one hand and her other hand on her waist, and she gently scolds me.

"Carlito, you are talking to your Mami. *Que te pasa?* Why were you crying so much last night? That's not like you."

"*Ay,* Mami. I thought Boston would be different. I thought things would be better if I left Miami. I'm still depressed. I want to make things the way they were, when you were here, when we were still a family, when things felt right." My voice trails off, and I look down at the grass, which looks like saturated paint strokes of green coming to life. Mami's garden is still lush and healthy like she is at this moment.

Mami slowly walks toward me. As she moves closer, a white glow laces her body and highlights the grass and all the flowers and plants and everything in this garden, our garden. She scoots by my side and puts the scissors down. She then loops her arm around my shoulder and gives me a reassuring embrace followed by a sweet kiss on my cheek.

"Now listen to me," she points at me with her index finger. "You are doing so well in Boston. You have a new friend, *el loco* with his Diet Cokes and his Jeep. He's a good person, a little weird but *buena gente.* I like him. He makes you laugh and I believe he is *un bueno amigo para ti.* You also have an amazing job and your students respect you. You have to walk in life, *Carlito,* not crawl. You have been crawling too much and crying. I want you to walk with *confianza,*" she says, standing up to show me how it's done. She paces back and forth like a soldier to emphasize her point. "Stand up tall with your chest out like a proud Martin man. Life is not over because I am not in Miami. I am here," she says, leaning over me and grabbing my right hand to pat my heart with it. "Remember that, always. You are young, and I see a beautiful future for you, *hijo. Tu sabes que tu* Papi needs you. He misses you at the house. Without you, *nuestra casa* is not the same."

She scoots next to me and points below at the grass. With her index finger, she outlines a square in the grass. The square opens up to a bird's-eye view of our living room. Papi sits in his reclining chair and watches a baseball game by himself. He looks serious and sad. Mami then outlines another invisible square against the grass and that opens up to another view. This one features Lourdes sitting in her closet picking out clothes for a suitcase. The house does seem empty and lifeless.

"Carlos, look at their faces." She points to each of them in their own individual squares. I feel like I am peeking into a dollhouse of our house.

"What is missing *en la casa?*" Mami looks back at me.

"You!" I fire back.

"Not just me . . . who else?"

"Me?" I ask, feeling stupid for not having followed her train of thought.

Mami simply nods.

"They need you, Carlos."

"Well, Papi and Lourdes are coming to Boston for Thanksgiving, so it will be nice to have them around, I think."

Mami smiles.

"Just because you do not have a lot to talk about with your Papi doesn't mean he doesn't love you. Lourdes is taking care of him, but he needs you too. I need you to be good to him in Boston. Show him all the beautiful parks, the Boston Common. Take him to *ese* Cuban restaurant that *tu amigo* Tommy takes you to. Show him *el estadio de los* Red Sox. He would like that, Carlos. Take Lourdes shopping. Make this Thanksgiving a new tradition for the three of you. I won't be there but I will be watching in my own way, *mijo.*"

I lean my head against Mami's, and I hold her soft freckled hand, as it rests on my shoulder. Mami's Estée Lauder perfume mixes with the raw smell of the just-mowed grass and the gardenias' sweet intoxicating fragrance. The scene reminds me of an image Monet or Van Gogh painted depicting a lovely garden with a little bit of heaven and home.

"And one more thing, believe in yourself. I do. Papi does. Lourdes does. *Hasta tu amigo tambien.* Do not fall for these *muchachos* who have boyfriends and want to get to know you just because you are a cute *Cubanito* from Miami. Don't settle for *porqueria.*

You are better than that. When you least expect it, something good will happen," she says, with a sonic clap to underscore her point. "*Te lo prometo*. Now, I must get back to my gardenias. They don't like it when I ignore them," she says, getting up and walking back to her bountiful tree, which is also surrounded by a glowing white light as if it had its own aura.

"But Mami . . . don't go . . . Wait . . . I want to . . ." I run and call out to her, but she slowly fades away into the garden's ethereal white light. She waves good-bye to me before she finally disappears. My cell phone rings, and I'm abruptly summoned back to reality and awaken from my dream.

I look at my cell phone, and it's Papi.

"*Hola, chico,* did I wake you up?" I turn on my side in my bed with my cell phone pressed to my right ear. I stretch my legs and several yawns escape. My alarm clock reads 10 a.m.

"It's okay," I yawn loudly. "My dream was ending anyway. How are you, Papi?"

"Everything is good here. Lourdes and I made our flight reservations. We will be there in seven days. Lourdes says she will cook the turkey. Are you ready for our visit, *hijo?*"

"*Sí,* Papi. More than you know. I think you and Lourdes are going to have a nice time up here. *Preparate!* It's already snowing."

"We are looking forward to it, Carlos. *Bueno,* I will let you sleep. We will talk later."

"Okay, Papi. Bye." I hang up my phone. I stretch myself like the letter "T" in my bed and moan loudly.

I actually feel better after last night. Mami was right. She's no longer alive, but her dreams feel as real as if she is. Using the past tense to describe her state of being somehow feels wrong because I feel she is still with me although it's in the realm of my dreams or in the depths of my heart. Her pep talk rekindles my enthusiasm for my newfound life. Standing in my living room, I declare to myself: No more pity parties and no more lusting after men with boyfriends. I need to focus on the good things I have. My family. New friends. My new city. My job. I am tired of being the sorry and depressed Carlos. I want to be happy again. I want to feel like I used to, but I know I can't completely with Mami gone. But I have to learn to forge ahead. I will away the negative thoughts, the constant depressing track that spins in my mind relentlessly. This is Carlos Martin 2.0, the Cuban in Boston who will embrace life instead of lamenting of what was or could have been. Marcello lost out on a great guy. Perhaps there is a future husband for me running around Boston or somewhere in Massachusetts looking for me. *I'm here and waiting!* I want to be with someone again to share my thoughts, stories about my family and my students, someone who will nurture me as I nurture him. I smile to myself as I get up and think these inspirational thoughts with renewed energy and put it to good use. I decide I am going to clean this place and start decorating. I want to make this place look and feel like home. A stack of unopened boxes still remain in my closet, and today feels like a good day to tackle them. After making some *cafécito* (I still cannot replicate Mami's magic formula) I go to the closet, squat down, and start opening the boxes I dreaded rummaging through.

I remove some framed photos of Papi, Mami, and Lourdes with me. There is one from our Carnival cruise to Conzumel when I was fifteen. I remember how much Papi and Mami acted like honeymooners and how that embarassed Lourdes and me. There's another photo of all of us standing in front of the house with our arms around each other. I remember that day so clearly. I was twenty-two and had just graduated from FIU. I didn't care to attend the graduation ceremony under the sweltering ninety-degree heat in early May, but Papi insisted on seeing his only son accept his college diploma. As I dig deeper into the box, I find my framed education degree from FIU.

I whip out the photographs and good-bye cards that my former students at Braddock High made for me. I gather all these things, and I begin to hang them up around my living room and my bedroom. I fill my noteboard above my desk with my former students' cards. There is one from Miguel, one of my freshman students who came to the United States three years before. He thanked me in a beautiful essay for being his role model and for letting him know it's okay to speak with a thick Spanish accent. He is now a senior and preparing to go to Harvard. (I credit myself with helping make that happen. I wrote him a recommendation a few months ago.) He's exactly why I wanted to become a teacher. To show that no matter where you are from, you can always reinvent yourself in Miami and in this country. Life is limitless if you put forth some effort. And, like him, I am going to try harder to be the person I know I can be and was meant to be. The guy Mami believes in.

I stand in the middle of my bedroom and study all the frames, photographs, and cards that fill my home. I hope that Papi and Lourdes feel as comfortable as they do in Miami when they visit Boston.

12

Tommy

When I pull up to the scene, Mikey is standing alongside his Volkswagen Rabbit or something that resembles what it used to look like. He looks dazed, disoriented, and pained as he walks around with his hand kneading his forehead. His front tire is flattened, and his front fender is folded back, crushed, and mangled as if two giant hands squeezed the front of the car into metal mush. Black liquid spews from the car and onto the street. The bunny is disabled.

"Mikey, are you okay?" I climb out of the Jeep and dash toward him. The lights of a police car flare and spin, illuminating the street with blue and red hues.

"Oh, Tommy. I'm so glad you're here," he smiles, rubbing his forehead. "Yeah, I was just scared. This woman hit me as I pulled out of the Barnes & Noble parking lot. She ran a red light." When he removes his hand from his forehand, I notice a red bruise marks the spot above his thin light brown eyebrows. I want to kiss it and make him feel better.

"Well, it looks like you'll survive." I closely examine the bruise. "You just got banged up a little. Look at it this way, Mikey, at least you don't look like your car. The bunny is banged up!" I say, holding up my two index fingers on each side of my head like a rabbit. Mikey warmly smiles back.

"Thanks for coming. I guess I freaked out and called you. The crash happened so fast." I put my arm around him and wait as the Braintree police officer finishes speaking to the other driver, who looks worried. The cop then walks over to us. He talks to Mikey, who recounts his version of the story: He was pulling out of the bookstore's parking lot at the bottom of the hill when a driver ran a red light and clipped the front of his car. After examining both cars for about twenty minutes, the officer hands the woman a ticket for running the light and reckless driving. Mikey looks relieved.

"Whew! With my DUI from earlier this year, I thought I'd get arrested." Mikey leans against the police cruiser.

"But you weren't drinking. It was an accident, Mikey. It can happen to anyone," I reassure him.

"I know, but I was just scared. Thank you for keeping me company." Mikey looks at me with those beautiful blue orbs of his. He continues to rub his head and his temples.

"Mr. Williams, you might want to go to the emergency room and have that bruise checked out, and just to make sure nothing's broken. But first, one of you has to move the car. It's blocking some traffic." I volunteer and grab Mikey's keys. I slowly park the limping car on the side of the road and out of traffic's way. When I emerge from the car, I notice the headlights of a Ford Taurus quickly pulling up with its hazards on. A middle-aged couple steps out.

"Oh, Mikey!" the woman wails in a Boston accent while rushing over to him.

"Ma, I'm okay. Really. I just hit my head against my sun visor," Mikey explains, looking all embarrassed. His mother cradles his face with her hands and examines his head.

His father grabs a handkerchief from his pocket and dabs the bruise.

"You have to be careful with those sun visors. You never know when one can smack you in the face," his father says.

And I just stand there smiling awkwardly, feeling a bit out of place during this family reunion. Why am I here again?

"I think he should go to the hospital, just to be sure that everything is all right," I suggest as his parents study me, probably wondering who I am.

Mikey picks up on my discomfort and realizes that his parents don't know who I am or what I'm doing there. He makes a pleasant introduction.

"Ma, Pa, this is Tommy, a good friend of mine. He's the one who writes for the *Daily*, the one I've told you about. I called him too."

I notice how much his mother, Susan, looks like Mikey. The same sky-blue eyes but instead of light brown straight hair, hers is curly. A perm I suspect. She's also pasty white. Small freckles dot her nose, just like Mikey's. His father, Ron, looks like a tall school principal with white, bushy, straight hair. Both have kind, caring eyes.

"Oh, nice to meet you, Tommy. Mikey has mentioned you before. We read your articles. We've never met a real reporter," his mother warms up to me. "Thank you for being here for our son," Susan says with a familiar Boston accent.

"I saw your story on the soccer player. Good stuff," Ron adds, shaking my hand firmly.

Mikey's mother decides to take him to a nearby hospital and invites me along. I explain to her that I don't want to impose, but she insists.

"Mikey gets all nervous around doctors and hospitals. Having a friend there might take the edge off him. Do you want to ride with us or follow us?" she asks.

"I couldn't. I don't want to intrude."

"Not at all! Just follow me. We're going to South Shore Medical," she says.

I cave in. I have trouble saying no at times. I look over at the Ford's passenger seat, and Mikey smiles impishly, embarrassed that his ma is making such a fuss over him. I wave good-bye to him, hop into my Jeep, and tail his mother's Ford. His father stays behind with the crippled Volkswagen and waits for a tow truck to haul it back to their house in Duxbury.

About fifteen minutes later, Mikey, his mother, and I are in the emergency room at the hospital. A nurse has escorted Mikey into an examination room. It's just me and Susan in the lobby. An easy, nice conversation takes place.

"I think he'll be okay. The bruise didn't look too bad," I say, sitting in an uncomfortable chair as Channel 3 rebroadcasts its 11 p.m. newscast on a small TV set in the waiting room. Susan holds a women's magazine in her hand as we chat.

"I know. It's just better to make sure that everything is still in place. How did you know about the accident?" she asks.

"We had gone to Providence for dinner and to see the U2 in 3-D concert at the IMAX theater. We had a lot of fun. We had met up at the bookstore earlier so I had to drop him off. When I left, he called me about the accident so I turned around and came back. I think I broke some traffic rules to get back here."

"Well, that's sweet of you, being here. I'm sure Mikey appreciates it. He doesn't have a lot of close friends. Most of them were his drinking buddies and don't hang out with him anymore because he doesn't drink. So I want to thank you, Tommy, for being there for my son, for supporting him."

"Anytime," I grin.

Susan and I exchange stories about our jobs. She's a middle school teacher with a sixth grade class. Ron works as a principal at another school in the South Shore. They are a family of educators.

"My sister Mary is a teacher in Miami Beach, where I grew up," I say. "I feel like I'm always surrounded by teachers. It's always been my second career choice if I ever get bored with writing and journalism. But for the last year and a half or so, I've been enjoying Boston. In a way, journalism is like teaching. We're informing people on what's going on in the community, and in some ways, I feel like I'm a teacher."

"That's very sweet. I learn something new whenever I read the paper, Tommy. I grew up in Dedham reading the *Daily*. Your parents must be so proud." She smiles with the warm friendliness of a caring teacher. "What brought you up here? Your whole family is in Miami, right?"

"Yes, which makes it hard sometimes. I miss being able to drop by my parents' house every Sunday for lunch or to do laundry. I came here to write for the *Daily,* which is like an institution in New England, as you know. It's such a great newspaper, and I couldn't say no when they offered me my job. Being in Boston has been like a new chapter in my life. I'm enjoying this city and all it has to offer. I still visit my parents, but it's hard. I miss them. They call me every night at eight o'clock on the dot."

Susan laughs as if she knows the feeling.

"My mom always calls me too, and she's eighty-five and lives with me!" she chuckles. "I do that to Mikey. It sounds like you have a wonderful family and a nice job. I'm glad you and Mikey are friends."

"Me too," I say.

After talking about our hair products (Susan says she wishes she had natural curly hair like I do), she suggests, "Why don't you go inside the examining room and keep him company. If I know my son, he's probably all nervous hearing the beeps and other sounds from the machines, wondering what is going on. He probably wouldn't want me in there anyway, fussing over him and treating him like a baby."

"Sure, I'll go and check on him." I rise from my seat and head into the examining room area. I poke my head into each of the examining rooms until I spot Mikey, sitting hunched over with a bandage on his forehead. He looks like a sad plush toy doll, but he lights up when I walk into the sterile-smelling room.

"I heard the doctors talking in the hallway. They say they're going to have to amputate both your legs," I joke.

"If they do, I'll amputate you, cutie."

I shake his hand, and I sit by the edge of his examining bed to keep him company.

"Tommy, you don't have to be here. Go home. I know it's late and you must be tired from our drive to and from Providence. Besides, isn't there a *Providence* rerun on Channel 4 or Lifetime right about now that you're missing?"

"Nah, I'd rather watch this. It's like the real *ER* or *Grey's Anatomy*."

Mikey gently holds my hand and squeezes it. He rubs each of my fingers. I'm instantly excited; a rush of sensation tingles my spine and heart. I have to adjust my sitting position to make room for my boner, but it's more than that. My feelings for Mikey are blooming strongly like the tulips in Boston during spring.

"Thank you for coming to the crash scene and for being here. Seriously, that was nice of you."

"I wouldn't be anywhere else," I say with a wink.

As we hold hands, the doctor comes in, and we quickly separate. He tells Mikey that the tests and X-rays came back fine and that Mikey has a slight concussion. He releases him but urges Mikey to call him if he feels dizzy or light-headed.

I walk out with Mikey and return to the area where Susan and Ron are waiting.

"They say Mikey has a bad case of sun-visor bruising. There's no cure!" I announce. Mikey, Susan, and Ron burst out laughing.

"Maybe there is a chiropractor who specializes in that," his father says, laughing loudly at his own corny joke. We're all laughing, but I secretly smile, inwardly happy that I've bonded with the Williams family.

Mikey explains to them that he has a slight concussion and that it's not too serious.

"But you know what I could really use right now?" he announces as we stand outside the hospital under the starry night.

"What?" we all answer.

"Food! I'm starving," he says, making "starving" sound like "stah-ving."

"Now I know for sure that my little boy is going to be okay. Despite his skinny frame, you'd never know that Mikey eats like a horse. At night, I hear him scraping the fork against the plate, all the way downstairs. It's Mikey eating his late night snacks," Susan explains with a certain loving gleam in her eye.

"Well, we can get something to eat. There's an IHOP nearby in Quincy that's open late," I offer.

"Mikey, why don't you get something to eat with Tommy as long as he doesn't keep you out too late and drops you off at home? Can you do that for us, Tommy?" Susan says.

"Sure. As long as Mikey gives me directions, I'll get him home safely and with a full stomach."

"What about my car?" Mikey asks.

"It's already back at the house. Don't worry about it for now. We'll take it to the repair shop on Monday. You probably have about $1,000 in damages. Once we swap the front tire, it should be drivable, if you don't mind the dents in the front," Ron says, patting Mikey on the shoulder.

"Thanks, Dad!"

His parents hug him and kiss him. We say our good-byes, and I give Susan a hug and a kiss on the cheek and shake Ron's hand.

"It was great meeting you, Tommy. Maybe we can have you over for dinner sometime. I make a mean lasagna," Susan says.

"That's why I have this belly." Ron pats his stomach. She playfully punches him, and they head back to their car.

After Mikey and I each eat a stack of pancakes topped with blueberries, strawberries, and banana slices at the IHOP, I drive him back to his parents' house on the Marshfield-Duxbury border. The whole way, we talk about the accident, and I tell him how fun his parents are.

"I can see why you became an educator. Your parents seem to love what they do. How could you not be a teacher?" I say, driving on desolate Route 3 South.

"I used to visit my mom at her school and help her clean the chalkboard and decorate her room. It grew on me. And she'd let me help grade her papers. I felt like I was being groomed to pursue education from an early age, but instead of teaching, I went into counseling. I prefer to have small groups of kids or to be one-on-one," he says, as the blur of the highway's lightposts flash by behind his face in the passenger seat.

When we pull up to the colonial two-story house, I turn off the lights, and we sit inside the car. We both look at each other and look away. I grin with my mouth closed, even though a big old smile wants to break out.

"Tommy, I know I've thanked you about a dozen times, but I wanted to thank you again for tonight, for Providence and for everything." His blue eyes glisten in the faint moonlight. I quickly look up through my Jeep's front window, and I notice that the night sky is sequined with stars.

"Stop it! I would have done that for anyone!" I say, slouching in my Jeep's bucket seat. I feel myself blushing.

"I know you would have done that for anyone who needed help. It's the person that you are, but you did it for me, and that means the world to me right now."

We sit there in silence, our eyes dancing with each other's. And slowly, we lean toward each other. And then it happens. A sweet gentle kiss on the lips that makes my heart and spine tingle. Several more kisses follow until we pull away.

"Mikey . . . we shouldn't."

"Why? My feelings for you never went away," he says, coming in for another kiss. I surrender to it.

"But . . . you shouldn't be dating anyone. It's your first year of recovery."

"I know," he whispers. "But my heart is telling me something else. I've got my drinking under control. My heart is another matter."

We continue kissing. I taste remnants of the maple syrup on his lips.

I pull away again and create some distance on my side of the Jeep.

"I just want to support you, Mikey, and be your friend. I've read that alcoholics shouldn't be dating someone in the first year of recovery because they have so much to deal with, and being emotionally involved with someone can only complicate matters. It's not that I don't care about you. You know that. I'm just trying to be the best supportive friend I can be."

Mikey tilts his head and smiles.

"Tommy, I know you're looking out for me, but I'm a big boy. I know what I can and cannot do. You came back to me for a reason, and that has to mean something. Whether we're friends or more, I want you in my life. But I am not going to stop feeling the way I feel or have always felt toward you."

"But . . ." I say, and he interrupts me with a kiss. "Look . . . let's just take things slow. I think you got banged up in the head more than you realize," I joke.

"Okay, cutie. We'll see how things go, but I know and you know what's going to happen."

"And what's that?"

"You're going to have to drive more often to see me until my car gets fixed." We start laughing.

"Just go to bed before your parents give you a detention!" I tease.

He kisses me one more time and climbs out of the Jeep. As he walks up to the steps to his front door, he sticks out his tongue and bites down.

I wave good-bye and drive back to Dorchester, thinking about what just happened. I feel like I am transported back to the year before when Mikey and I met and the magic between us kindled.

I don't know what this all means. Who am I kidding? It means that Mikey and I have found our way back to each other. It's nice. No, it's wonderful. Okay, it's incredible having Mikey's presence—his sober presence—back in my life as if it were meant to be. I blast some Gloria Estefan in the Jeep and wildly sing along to "Everlasting Love" like the *loco* that Carlos and the other drivers on Route 3 think I am.

13

Carlos

"Class . . . class . . . *class!* Settle down." *Ay, Mondays!* My students are so wired on Monday mornings, it's as if they chugged down cans of Red Bull before walking in. They mumble and chatter about their weekend as if they hadn't seen each other in weeks when it's only been since Friday. I stand in front of the class where I have a perfect view of my twenty-three students, the peeling paint on the classroom's south wall, and the cracked linoleum below on the green tiled floor. Through the eastern windows, I also have a perfect view of some shady characters—Latinos and blacks sitting on their porches and running out to the occasional car to trade something under a gloomy gray winter sky. It's an odd juxtaposition: students learning a few hundred feet from drug dealers, but perhaps the view may motivate these kids to keep studying as well. What better incentive to excel than your own dicey neighborhood?

A few months before I arrived, a stray bullet was shot through one of the windows at a nearby public library, sending parents and kids into a panic, according to Tommy who wrote a story on the impact that bullet had on the library and its patrons. Since then, security and police patrols have been beefed up. The school security guards keep the thugs off our property, but sometimes the realities of urban life happen. We've had two lockdowns since September and Channel 3 reported the story with the urgency of Columbine. This neighborhood reminds me of Liberty City back in Miami, which was always featured on Channel 7 News. Despite this rougher part of Dorchester, which borders Mattapan and Roxbury, this school remains a safe zone, a place where students can and should be at ease to learn. I make the best of my situation here for the sake of my students. I see a little of myself in them. They don't think they quite fit into mainstream Boston, but they do because they are mainstream Boston, today.

The radiator hisses and clanks, and the students continue gabbing. I prop myself on my stool and stare at them with a steely gaze. After five minutes, they finally shut their mouths and focus on me. *Ay, finally!* This secret weapon works every time—silence from a superior or authority figure. It makes the students wonder what you're wondering about because you're not losing your cool, which is what they want—to push your buttons. I know better. They stop talking so they can solve the mystery of my silence.

"Thank you. Finally! And now we can begin. Open your copies of *Finding Mañana* by Mirta Ojito." I hold up my own copy, which Ms. Ojito signed at Books & Books back in Coral Gables after a reading. The students rummage through their backpacks and messenger bags and pull out the used copies I found at various used book stores, craigslist, and eBay. I used my own money to purchase these books because I thought my students, most of whom have immigrant parents, might appreciate the story, even though it's not part of the curriculum. It never hurts to deviate from the rules if it benefits a good education. (I got that from the movies *Freedom Writers* and *Dead Poets Society* a few years ago.) But I received permission from my department head to discuss this book as part of diversity month, so I'm not straying too far from the rules.

"Okay, class. In this memoir, the author is literally looking for *Mañana,* a boat that ferried her and her family to Key West from Cuba during the 1980 Mariel boatlift. But she's also looking for answers that will help her come to terms with her past and the political catalysts that led to one of the biggest mass migrations in

U.S. and Cuban histories. This story is close to my heart, because I'm *un Marielito.*"

For the most part, the class is quiet and listening. I hear some scattered whispers of *"un Marielito?"* from the back the room.

"If it wasn't for Mariel, I wouldn't be here today with you. I would probably still be living in Cuba with my parents and sister. I can't even imagine that because I love my Dunkin' Donuts coffee during lunch." The students laugh. "Anyway, how many of you have parents born in another country?"

Several hands shoot up. I'm engaging them. Good.

"How many are from the Dominican Republic?" Six hands are raised.

"And how many are from Vietnam?" Four hands pop up.

I ask the other students to name the places their parents are from.

"Puerto Rico!" three students announce.

"Ireland," another two shout out.

"And what about Cape Verde?" I ask. Three students raise their hands.

"So we're all from somewhere else, more or less, like this author who used this book to trace the events that caused her and her family to flee their native country. That's why I want you to read this book because it illustrates how political and historical events in one place affect people in other parts of the world. It's history and literature in one."

As I explain further, I make the lesson local by peppering some facts and figures that I gleaned from Tommy's news articles. How Boston is a minority-majority city or what the mayor and community advocates refer to as The New Boston. How Dorchester is the largest and most diverse neighborhood in Boston and how it was settled three months before Boston was in the 1630s. How one in every four Bostonians is foreign born just as the early British explorers were. How we can make a difference by talking, connecting, and exchanging our stories from where we are, how we got here and what we want to do with our lives. I love diversity. It makes us richer. In Miami, the most diverse place is Miami International Airport. Like Boston, most people self-segregate, which I don't understand. How can we enrich our lives by living in silos? But then again, Mami and Papi raised us in uppity Coral Gables, and our family and friends lived there or in Kendall, the sprawling Cuban suburbia. That is why I chose to teach here in Dorchester—to learn about other people and cultures in another city.

When I met a recruiter from Boston Public Schools at a job fair in downtown Miami a year ago, she asked me if I would be interested in coming to Boston to join its small but growing pool of bilingual Hispanic teachers. The pay was considerably more than in Miami, and they had a list of schools I could choose from if I got hired. Also, Mami had just died, and I didn't want to be in Miami. I wanted to escape and start fresh somewhere else. The house and the city in general carried too many memories of her. So when I told the recruiter I would be interested in teaching in an urban school to gain more experience, her mouth widened and she almost fell over her chair. I told her, "I want to make a big difference. Those are the kids who need to see more professional minorities in their daily lives unlike here in Miami where we're a dime a dozen." I was pretty much hired on the spot.

For the rest of the class, I have the students share stories about their parents' or grandparents' struggles to come to the United States. I also lace the lesson with my own experiences, something they seem to enjoy hearing about. Teaching is a give and take process, an educational exchange. The more I share about myself, the more they want to reciprocate by listening and actually doing what I ask of them. Speaking of homework, I need to give them their new assignment.

"I want you to talk to one of your relatives who lived in another country and write an essay on how and why they came to the United States and Boston. I want you to trace that family history in the essay from their point of view and I want you to write some of those similarities you found in the Mirta Ojito book.

Comprende?" The class starts to chatter again about the assignment. Most of my students seem somewhat enthusiastic. When you learn something new about yourself and connect that to a larger global picture, your knowledge base deepens. It makes learning personal and fun. If I had them write an essay solely on Mirta Ojito's book, I bet they would be bored and uninterested. A teacher has to tailor the lesson to the student and the setting.

By 8:45, the second bell rings, and I use the brief break to walk outside and smoke a cigarette. I dial Tommy with one hand and wave with the other to Juan, the school's friendly janitor. Juan is hauling away some trash from the school's breakfast session. *El pobre!* With budget cutbacks, he and Luis are the only two custodial workers left at the school. I can see small chocolate milk boxes and candy wrappers topping the trash can from where I stand in my own cloud of smoke.

"Why, Carlos, why?" Tommy answers the phone with a yawn.

"*Loco,* it's almost nine. Shouldn't you be up already?"

He yawns and groans some more.

"I don't have to be at work until ten-thirty. I live ten minutes away."

"You're so lazy, Tommy. Knowing you, you probably get up, roll out of bed, drink your Gatorade and slice of wheat bread, grab your Diet Coke, and you're out of the door all within fifteen minutes. Right?"

He simply yawns, which means I'm right.

"*Bueno,* I'll let you get back to sleep. I'm on my cigarette break at school. I just wanted to know if we're still meeting up later at El Oriental to catch up. I'm planning to stay here at school to grade my ever-growing pile of papers and tweak my lesson plans for next week until dinner."

"Um, yeah, like six o'clock."

"Okay, sleepyhead. I'll see you later!"

Tommy yawns loudly and mistakenly presses some other buttons on the phone. I hear him drop his cell phone. *Que loco!*

The bell rings and signals that my smoke break is up. I take some last few delicious puffs of my Marlboro and flick it into the parking lot, which is pocked with crater-size potholes from many winters and no maintenance. Even the slab of sidewalk I stand on is cracked like shattered glass. I have five more classes to teach and then have to help out with the after-school tutoring program for kids who are new to this country and don't speak much English. I just want to flash forward to El Oriental and talk to Tommy and chow down.

I'm still feeling down from the other night. I know Tommy can cheer me up or figure out what is going on with me. I lean on him a lot because he has been my only true friend in Boston so far. I've become friendly with others here. There's Juanita, my fellow teacher at school who always watches my class when I need to use the bathroom or appease my nicotine craving. There's Marcello, well, scratch that name out. I haven't heard from him since we hooked up. There's Doris, the nice lady at the market who always gives me extra slices of ham at the deli. There's Jim, the straight college student who works at the membership desk at Bally's and gives me free advice on how to work out when we see each other by the weights. He practices his beginning Spanish with me. But can I really count on these friendly faces in case of an emergency? Not really. They are people you say *hola* to and chat with for five minutes on your way to somewhere else. Extremely nice acquaintances.

I've always been a little socially awkward at making friends, which is why I was always with Mami. I did have co-teachers at Braddock High who I was friendly with, but for the most part, I hung out with my ex, Daniel, and his friends. When we broke up, his friends, naturally, remained with him.

Later on in the day, I'm standing outside the restaurant, as usual, waiting for my *loco*. I survived another day of Dorchester High. Before I took the job, I had heard all these stories about the school. Two female students stabbed each other, and one of them was four months pregnant. But I was looking for a challenge, and these incidents weren't the result of teaching or the school itself. They were some bad apples in and outside of school. It's not the students' or principal's fault. These things can happen anywhere.

I see Tommy whiz by, bouncing in his Jeep. After he pulls into a space, he climbs out and saunters toward me. We give each other our warm Latino hugs and do our usual exchange of greetings.

"Great to see you, man!" Tommy says, messing up my hair.

"Same here, *loco!*" I also mess up his hair.

We walk in, take our spot in the corner of the eatery where the young Latina waitress, who looks as if she could be one of my students, hands us the rectangular menus. As I stretch out my legs under the table and settle into my plastic chair, Tommy immediately orders a Diet Coke. I order a Sprite as we eye the menu. I notice that Tommy has a big smile on his face, which is pretty routine, but he seems to be glowing more than usual. There's a certain extra bounce in his curls.

"*Loco, que pasa?* What's going on with you? How's your, ahem, *amiguito* Mikey?" I say, sipping my Sprite with one eyebrow cocked up.

Tommy just smiles.

"Talk! Spill it." I egg him on.

"Well . . ."

Tommy is going to make me drag this out of him. For a gregarious reporter, he can be tight-lipped at times.

"Wait, you and Mikey hooked up, no? Is that what I was interrupting the other night when I text-messaged you? Oh shit!"

"Actually, we had a great dinner and a fun night. But then he got into an accident. Long story short, he's fine. He was shaken up. I met his parents at the scene. They were super sweet, just like Mikey, good people. We all went to the hospital and Mikey had a slight concussion. Nothing too serious. We then kissed outside his house," he says in one breath. I almost spit out my piece of Cuban bread.

"*Que cosa?*"

"Carlos, calm down. It was a kiss. Okay, several kisses just like the ones we shared when we dated."

I grab a napkin to clean up the bread crumbs on my shirt. I've made a mess.

"That is great, *loco!* I knew you guys would get back together. Friends my ass! It was meant to be." I high-five Tommy.

"Thanks, Carlos. It just happened. I just don't want to go too fast, you know. He needs to focus on his recovery, which he's doing a good job at. I don't want to get in the way of that."

"Well, it sounds like you are being supportive. That's wonderful, *chico*. I'm happy for you." I look down and then toward the window where traffic backs up on Centre Street. Plumes of fumes rise from the manholes that line the street's spine. I am truly happy for Tommy, but I secretly wish I had some news like that to brag about as well. Despite my I-will-be-happy declaration in the mirror the other night, I'm still depressed. I can't seem to escape it. The sun setting at four in the afternoon and shortening the day hasn't helped much.

The waitress returns, and we give her our orders and menus. I get a Cuban sandwich although I should order some *tostones* because I can hear the cook frying them or a breaded steak into an addictive sizzle. As we talk, Tommy leans his head against the window and curls a thick strand of his dark brown hair with his index finger, something he does repeatedly without even noticing.

"Carlos, what did you want to talk to me about the other night? I was out with Mikey, and I didn't want to be rude. I hope you understand that. If it's an emergency, you know I'm there, anytime, right? But it didn't sound like it was too important."

"I know. I've just been really down. And it's not just my mother's death. Something inside me feels defeated. I don't know if I should even be here. I was crying the other night at home after Marcello left."

Tommy jumps in. "Did he have a tailpipe between his legs? I hear Brazilians are well-hung."

I roll my eyes.

"Well, yes. I'm not depressed about that, but that's beside the point. I feel like a Latino Eeyore," I softly blurt out, realizing how much of a wet blanket I must sound like now. Luckily, the restaurant isn't too busy, so no one is sitting right next to us and listening. Tommy looks at me with his brown eyes, which always seem to hold some joy and laughter. He leans over and grabs my hand.

"I think I know what's going on. It happened to me too. I speak from experience," Tommy says cryptically. I hate when he teases me like that.

"*Que?* What are you talking about? What is it?"

Tommy takes a deep breath and solemnly looks out the window, snow-caked from the weekend's snowfall. He clicks his tongue against the roof of his mouth and shakes his head.

"Tommy, this isn't funny. What is it?"

He looks at me, and a smirk unfolds.

"I'm surprised it hit you so quickly. You may need to take something." Tommy tilts his head, shakes it side to side again, and frowns.

"Tommy, what is it?"

"I know exactly how you're feeling. When it happened to me, I . . ."

"Tommy! What do I have? Does it rhyme with just-go-on-and-tell-me-already?" I demand.

"*Chico,* relax. You've got SAD."

"SAD? *Que cosa?*"

Tommy grins.

"You're sad because of SAD. It's seasonal affective disorder, the winter blues. A lot of people get it when there's a lack of sunlight and because of gray winter days. It's common. It's the snow. It's the cold. It just magnifies whatever you're down about already. Your body misses the warmth, the sunshine. You will live. Carlos will live!" he declares, speaking to an invisible audience.

"Have you been feeling a lack of energy, Carlos?"

"*Sí.*"

"Have you been feeling down?"

"*Sí.*"

"Have you been wanting to sleep more?"

"*Sí.*"

"Then you got it," Tommy diagnoses me with the confidence of a doctor.

"Okay, so how do I get rid of it?" Lately, I've been thinking about how depressing Boston is during the winter. The trees are naked. No one walks outside much. An eerily cold silence descends over Cambridge at night when I walk the three blocks from the gym to my apartment. Even on the subway, everyone looks as if they just left a funeral.

"I feel so alone at times here, Tommy."

"*Chico,* we'll get you a few things to cheer you up," he says, opening up his jacket as if to reveal an invisible "ST" for Super Tommy. I love *mi amigo,* but I wasn't joking when I thought he was a little weird, even quirky, when we first met.

"But I can only help you with the winter depression. I think there's more to what you're feeling than the cold temperatures," Tommy says with concern.

"What do you mean, *loco?*"

The waitress sets down our plates on the table. As soon as she walks away, Tommy continues.

"Carlos, please don't take this the wrong way, but I think you need to see someone."

"Yeah, tell me about it. I'd love to have a guy to date."

Tommy half smiles and leans closer to me across the table.

"No, I'm not talking about dating. I mean, I think you should see a therapist. I've never lost a parent, so I can't imagine what you're going through or what you've been dealing with. I would probably see a psychologist to deal with the jumble of emotions and to help me find my footing again. I think it would help if you had someone who is objective to sit with you and help you make sense of your feelings and tell you how to get back to the way you were in Miami. When you talk about your mom and how your life was in Miami, you seem so happy. I don't see a lot of that from you in Boston. Sometimes, you laugh and we have fun, but I can sense that you're hiding your sadness."

I feel like I need Prozac right now. Pronto!

"Thanks, Tommy. I appreciate your concern, but I don't think most people see therapists whenever one of their relatives die."

"But this wasn't just any relative. This was your mom, your best friend. I think that's why you keep dreaming about her. There is something else going on that you need to figure out." Tommy gently taps my right hand with his fingers.

"I know. You don't need to remind me. I'm doing my best. I really am. It's just . . ." I grab one of the napkins and blow my nose loudly, which makes the waitress jump a little when she walks by. "It's hard."

"*Chico,* I know. That's why I think you could really benefit from having another perspective, someone else looking out for your best interests. I'm not equipped to help you with this. The best I can do is to listen and be your friend."

"And I appreciate you for that. But who would I see? I don't know anyone here."

"I know the perfect person," Tommy says. His dark brown eyes sparkle at the idea.

"*Quien?*" I slurp the rest of my Sprite.

"Her name is Bella Solis. I wrote a story about her earlier this year. She's a Latina radio show psychologist here in Boston. Think of Julie Andrews with longer dirty blonde hair, green eyes, and a slight Spanish accent, and you've got Bella. She's built up a following with her radio show because she's the only Latina whose show helps people, mostly young women, in New England *en español.* Her show is about to go national.

She's super *buena gente.* She's sort of like a typical Cuban mother but with the tell-it-like-it-is demeanor of a girlfriend. She's tough but tender too. You'd like her."

"And you think she would see me?"

"I can make the call for you. I really bonded with her after my story ran. Her son, a screenwriter in Miami, is gay too, so she would be great to talk to. I bet she'll love you."

"Thanks, Tommy. She sounds really special. Maybe it wouldn't hurt to meet with her at least once."

"Trust me, Carlos, you'll really like her. She's very intuitive and spiritual. I listen to her show sometimes on my lunch break. In the meantime, we're going to Target and CVS to pick up a few things after dinner. Operation SAD-Get-Glad begins," Tommy announces with the determined look of a drill sergeant. Correction, make that a very gay drill sergeant with curly hair.

"Uh oh. What are you thinking of buying? What did I get myself into? *Ay dios mio!* This feels like an intervention."

"Don't worry about it. You're in good hands." Tommy winks with exaggeration.

"I know exactly what we need to do to get you out of this slump. And plus, I need to get you into happier spirits to meet Mikey. I'm planning a dinner so the two of you can finally meet."

"What about your hunky friend Rico? Aren't you going to invite him?"

Tommy grimaces.

"I don't think he's going to want to come. As much as he loves me as a friend, he can't stand Mikey, no matter what I say about him, because of the way Mikey treated me when we dated. Maybe down the road they can hang out but not this soon in our new relationship."

"Relationship, Tommy? Aren't you jumping the gun here with Mikey?" I take another bite of my *media noche*. A piece of pickle dangles from the layers of pork, ham, and melted Swiss cheese, which is stuck on my right molar. I fling it off with my tongue.

"Yeah, I guess we're dating. We seem like a couple, and I'm not interested in anyone else. I can tell Mikey isn't either."

"Well, this calls for another Beantown Cubans toast," I offer, picking up my glass of mostly empty, fizzing Sprite.

"To overcoming the winter blues!" Tommy boasts with his Diet Coke.

"To you and Mikey!" I clink back, already feeling better about my depression.

After a trip to Target in Somerville and then to the CVS in Porter Square where we leave with bags of essentials that Tommy insisted on buying, we head back to my apartment. He replaces my standard bulbs with brighter ones that seem to emulate sunlight. They really brighten up my apartment. Tommy shows me how to take the melatonin supplements just before the sun goes down to keep my levels of serotonin up. He pulls out a box of St. John's Wort tea bags for me to brew before I go to bed.

"See, look at how much brighter and sunnier your apartment is, Carlos," Tommy says, standing by one of my lamps in the living room. It's so bright in here, I might need to wear sunglasses and apply some sunscreen.

"*Ay*, Tommy! Isn't this a bit much? My electric bill is going to go through the roof! You've literally brought the sun into my corner of Cambridge."

"Okay, how about if you just leave the lamp in your living room on when you watch TV and the other lights off. At least you'll get some artificial sunlight exposure. Trust me, this will work. You'll feel better in no time, but you need to take the pills and drink the tea, okay?"

"Alrighty!"

"And there's one more thing I need to get to complete Operation SAD-Get-Glad," Tommy says, with a mischievous look in his eye. He puts two fingers to his chin, scanning the living room as if he's mentally surveying the dimensions. He looks out the window where I have a small space for a hanging flower bed for warmer months.

"Tommy, what are you planning? I can't have any flowers there right now. They'll die outside with the cold if that's what you're thinking." He turns around and looks around my bedroom. I follow him.

"Seriously, what are you going to do? I don't like surprises, and my dad and sister are coming in a few days for Thanksgiving."

"*Bueno,* you'll see. It's the ultimate weapon to help soothe the blues. But I need some time to pick it up, and I'm sure your Papi and Lourdes will love it. In the meantime, I will call Dr. Bella Solis and see when she can meet with you."

Ay, what am I in for? But it's nice being looked after by someone who cares.

14

Tommy

Poor Carlos. My heart goes out to the guy. I'm hoping that my plan will help brighten his spirits, at least until spring arrives. I called Dr. Bella Solis (known to her listeners as *la doctora*) today at work and she gladly agreed to meet with Carlos after the Thanksgiving holiday. If anyone can help him climb out of his current emotional slump, it's Bella. Next up on my list: finding a hibiscus tree for Carlos. Yes, that's my surprise. I sense that Carlos needs something in his home to care for. I gather that he always looked out for his mother. Maybe having a beautiful flowering plant would add something to his home life. I remember thinking of adopting a pet when I moved out of Mami and Papi's house in Miami Beach, but my brain tends to obsess on things. I kept imagining the cat or dog being home alone while I was at *The Miami News* working. I kept picturing myself driving home for lunch to check up on the dog or cat or not taking vacations. My brain was so fixated on the idea of having this imaginary pet that I thought it was better not to have one at all. I can only focus on one thing at a time.

I do remember how lonely I was those first few weeks of living alone, but I was in Coral Gables and not far from the house. I can't imagine adjusting to a new city and coping with the loss of a parent at the same time. That's a tall order. I bet if Carlos had something to give some TLC to, something to nurture, it might fill some of the void he feels. A plant would do the trick because he can watch it grow.

Sometimes when I look at Carlos, I wish I could be a little more like him. He seems like such a simple guy, uncomplicated. He doesn't need to have a brand-new car. He's content with his old Toyota Camry. He doesn't spend a lot of money. He's just as happy staying at home renting a movie with me or grading his papers. His job fulfills him in a way mine doesn't. He makes a difference every day in his classroom. My articles do that but not as often. He's able to stand comfortably in front of a group of people every day and lecture while I work from the confines of an office. Carlos doesn't search for the spotlight the way I do sometimes by having my name on the front page or Features section of the *Daily* or appearing on TV to talk about one of my recent stories. And he's not stuck in the ruts I find myself in: eating the same food, drinking Diet Coke, and constantly repeating myself, which I can't help and sometimes I'm not aware of. One thing I don't envy Carlos for—the loss of a parent.

I'm here at the *Daily* finishing up my latest story on men who wear girdles. (Mirdles, if you will.) It's a new trend. As men grow vain about their appearances, they are resorting to bodywear or support boxers to make them look extra svelte. I can picture the headline: *Don't Call It a Girdle!* After posting an inquiry on the newspaper's Web site, I found several men willing to be interviewed about their bodyshaping underwear. Businessmen, publicists, and some TV anchors wear male girdles although no one would ever know by looking at them. I love these kinds of stories because they are light and fun. They inform our readers about the obscure trends in today's culture. These are the kinds of stories that one can only find in a newspaper's Style or Features section. It gives people a reason to read us, whether online or in print. With all the hard news percolating in various sections of the newspaper and online about the crime in Dorchester or immigrants in East Boston, I believe this is the kind of story that will have people chatting or at least chuckling. I print out a copy of the story, grab my bright blue winter hoodie, and dash outside into the *Daily's* parking lot, which is full of hybrid cars and weathered Toyota Corollas and Honda Civics. Where is my Jeep? I lose my car almost daily. For someone who allegedly has a great memory, even recalling the most minute details, I can't help but keep losing my vehicle. Back in college, I would lose fifteen minutes walking up and down the parking lot searching for my little Honda. So much for being the observant journalist. I'm ambling up and down the lanes of parked cars in the bitter late afternoon cold when I finally see the Wrangler's hardtop. Jeep found. I'm such a goof.

I hop into my Jeep, crank the heater on, and read the story out loud three times, so I can catch any run-on sentences, grammatical errors, or fragments. Spellcheck can only take a writer so far. This is part of my self-editing technique. Two Metro editors walk by and wave to me, probably wondering why I'm talking to myself. *I'm not crazy, people!* I'm just editing my copy. As I continue to narrate the details of the male girdle, my phone vibrates. It's Mikey sending a text message.

> Hey cutie, want to meet up tonight at Barnes & Noble? My car is fixed. I can meet you there. Can't wait to see you!

My heart melts like a mango sorbet on a hot Miami day. I text him back.

> Sure, Mr. Speed Racer. See you there after work. And ditto!

I read my story one more time. On my passenger seat, I notice a printout of an essay I wrote. I took Mikey's advice about writing about my experiences of being a Cuban in Boston. The other night, I wrote an essay called "Dancing En La Cocina" about my mother teaching me how to dance in the kitchen when I was younger. I am reminded of those days whenever I listen to music in my kitchen. The entire essay is a flashback of when I was ten years old and Mami grabbed me in the kitchen and forced me to dance to Celia Cruz. I plan on submitting the essay to a new book of inspirational stories called *A Cup of Cuban Comfort*. A writer friend in Miami sent me a call for submissions. Hopefully, my piece will be accepted and published. Although my articles are in third person, I sometimes want to write in first person to express my emotions, feelings, and perspectives on being a gay Cuban. Perhaps this essay is the beginning of that. I would never be allowed to do that at work.

I grab that printout along with my copy of the male girdle story. I flash my ID card in front of the electronic reader at the parking lot door and head back inside the stuffy, dimly lit newsroom. Rows of business and metro reporters line the newsroom as writers hunch over their desks with phones glued to their ears. Their hands waltz on their keyboards as they file stories for tomorrow's edition or for later online. Back at my desk, some black smut cakes the top of my computer. Sometimes, the air vents spit ink particles from the presses, which I rarely see but can definitely feel vibrating softly like a mechanical purring monster underneath the floor. Sometimes, the fluorescent bulbs above my desk blink like a nightclub.

I make some quick revisions to my article and send the file to my editor. I'm done for the day. I sign off the computer. I glance and smile at the photo of myself with Gloria Estefan after her concert in Boston. I grab my messenger bag and prepare to leave when Paul Harris, our cute arts writer who sits on the other side of the department, walks by and chats with me.

"Hey, Tommy Boy! Heading out?" says Paul, who is a muscular, hunky, black guy. We met here on our first day at the daylong new employee orientation. Although I found him very attractive and sexy, I didn't want to blur my professional and personal lines. We became instant friends. We chat at work and go to lunch and compare our notes as minorities surviving in Boston. Once in a while, he emerges from his cocoon in Central Square in Cambridge and makes an appearance at Club Café. When I see him there, we have a few drinks and gossip about work. Paul and I share a nice kinship. We are the only gay minorities in our department, and we're about the same age. He's one of my few friends from work. The other writers and editors tend to keep to themselves.

"Yeah, Paul. I'm done for the day. I had to file a breaking news story . . . on girdles! What movies are you screening this week?"

"I heard about your girdles story. Some of the editors were laughing about it in the cafeteria earlier. Who knows, maybe some of them wear them! Anyway, I'm screening *Iron Man III*. You know, *Iron Man, Iron Man* . . ." he says, singing the theme song to the old Spider-Man cartoon but with Iron Man as the character. "You'd like this latest installment. In the trailers, Robert Downey Jr. is even more flamboyant than in the other two."

"No way! Did he pump up for this one, or is he just slightly toned like in the first movie?" I ask, noticing how Paul's muscles bulge under his tight gray T-shirt, which he wears backwards for some odd reason. I never understood that fashion statement. What is he trying to say? Did he get dressed in the dark?

"Yeah, he's in better shape. Trust me, you'll like it! Anyway, I'm off to another screening at the Common. Maybe lunch this week?"

"Yeah, definitely. I know the perfect place."

Paul rolls his eyes.

"Oh, God, let me guess! Boston Market, your home away from home?" he says, stretching his arms, making his chest pop out even more. *Yum!* Sometimes, I want to reach out and touch that bulky, smooth chest.

"Yeah, how did you know?"

"Please, Tommy, everyone knows that you go there with coupons. Boston Market is fine. You're driving so I don't have a choice. I'll just have to survive another lunch there with you." Paul waves good-bye and heads toward the escalators while I stroll the other way to our elevated parking lot.

Fifteen minutes later, I pull up to Barnes & Noble. If my Jeep could, it would automatically drive itself here on cruise control because of my regular visits. I head inside, clean my feet on the big green welcome mat, and see Mikey sitting in our corner of the *café*. He smiles when he spots me and rises to give me a kiss and a hug. I embrace him tightly.

"I got your drink and brownie right here, cutie."

"Thanks, Mikey. That was sweet of you."

I peel off my wool coat and settle into my chair. Mikey sips his tea and tells me about work and his car.

"Did you see it when you pulled up?" he says, pointing out the window to his white Rabbit.

"Yeah, the collision center did a nice job. The *wabbit* is healed. It's ready to hop."

Mikey laughs. I tell him about my day and my girdle story.

"You come up with the funniest stuff. Who would have ever thought of doing a story on that."

"It's a different type of essay. As reporters, we have to think out of the box more to stay relevant. The dot-com–ization of newspapers is accelerating so our front page is less focused on breaking news and more on enterprise pieces. But that's not the only thing I've written lately."

"Oh yeah?" Mikey asks, his eyes brimming with interest.

"I wrote an essay."

"Really? What is it about? Can I read it?"

"It's about my mom teaching me how to dance in the kitchen. I'm planning on submitting it to a publisher. I have a copy here. Read it when you get home. I don't like it when people read what I've written in front of me."

Mikey pats my hand as I give him the printout.

"I'm sure it's wonderful, like you."

"Thanks, Mikey. Actually, you gave me the idea after our talk about me writing about being a Hispanic in Boston."

"Well, I'm sure it will be published. Why wouldn't they?

You're talented. I wish I could write like you. I wish I could write! I'm more of a math and numbers guy. I admire how you're able to write and report. I have enough problems writing progress reports for my students."

"Actually, anyone can write. Just imagine you're talking to your friend but put those words onto paper. That's what I do."

"I think you're making it sound easier than it is," Mikey says.

"It's only hard when your mind is focused on one thing and you have to write a story on deadline. Sometimes, I have to force it. It's easier to rewrite than write. As long as you get something—anything—on paper it will be easier to work with."

"Do you get bad cases of writer's block?"

I lean back in my chair and flash a smile.

"Only when I think about you."

Mikey winks at me and says, "See, you have a way with words!"

We slurp the rest of our tasty drinks. We get up and then head outside where Mikey smokes a cigarette under the darkening, early evening sky. The lights of the city add an incandescent aura over the Blue Hills in the distance.

"What are you doing Saturday, Mikey?" We stand under the store's green awning where the indoor heat escapes as people pop in and out of the store. Cars pull in and out consecutively. One would think this place was a fast-food joint with all the traffic flowing through its doors.

"Whatever you're doing, cutie."

"Well, how about if we had dinner with my friend Carlos. I really want him to meet you. You'd like him. He's a teacher. I'm sure you guys would have a lot to talk about."

Mikey takes a few puffs from his cigarette.

"Sure, but I don't want to go a bar or anything, Tommy. I don't want to be around alcohol."

I place my hand on his shoulder.

"No bars. I completely understand. I wouldn't do that to you. I'm thinking we eat in Cambridge near Carlos's. He's heard me talk about you so much that I figure it's time you guys meet. He's been my hang out buddy in Boston these past few months. We're almost like brothers."

"If it's really important to you, I'd be happy to meet him."

"Thanks, Mikey." I plant a soft kiss on his cheek. "I'll let Carlos know and make the arrangements. I think his dad and his sister leave on Saturday after Thanksgiving. He's been pretty down. I think a dinner with us would cheer him up. Maybe we can go somewhere different, some very Boston place that Carlos hasn't been to."

"Anything for you, cutie," Mikey says, nuzzling my neck outside the bookstore. *Que pena!* People are smiling at us as they walk by, including Selena as she heads in to start her shift.

We stand outside in the cold, bitter weather and lean against each other to keep warm. Drivers circle the parking lot like vultures looking for an available spot.

"What are you going to do now?" I ask him.

"Whatever you're doing, cutie. But, I should be headed home soon. I have to work early in the morning."

"Want to come over for a little bit?"

"To your condo?"

"No, to Miami. Of course, my place. I live five minutes away."

"Sure, but I can't stay too long. I'm curious to see your new home. From what you've told me, it's much bigger than your studio in Cambridge."

I explain to Mikey how to get there so he won't get lost. I notice that he's tailing my Jeep. He's been behind me the whole way, waving or making faces whenever I glance in the rear mirror. He does look adorable in his white Volkswagen Rabbit. Mikey is my bunny.

A few minutes later, we're stomping our shoes clean of the old chunky snow that litters my building's parking lot.

"This looks like an old school house," Mikey says, eyeing the four-story, red-brick building from top to bottom.

"Well then, you should feel at home, counselor."

From the main entrance, we walk down about five steps to my unit. Once inside, I take his coat along with mine and hang it up in the hallway closet. I give him the grand tour, which takes about thirty seconds.

Mikey takes it all in and scrutinizes each wall as if he were a tourist in Dorchester.

"This is really nice. And to think you were complaining about your neighborhood. I'm really impressed, Tommy. Big kitchen. Pergo floors. Did you do these yourself?" he asks, standing in the middle of my living room where posters of Cuba, Miami, and Fort Lauderdale decorate the sunny, yellow walls.

"I had the floors done—four Brazilian guys did them for me. I'm not the most handy guy."

"I can tell. You missed some spots with your paint job, cutie," he says, pointing to white spots near the northern wall.

"Ooops. Pretend you didn't see that." I kiss him on the neck.

"Is this the basement level?" he asks, pointing to the windows in my living room which are slightly below street-level. If someone walked by, you'd see their legs scurry along the window.

"Well, it's the A-level, first floor. The street is on a slope so technically, I'm on the lower level."

"So you're on the basement floor then, Tommy?"

"Well . . . I wouldn't say basement level. I would say first floor," I say, feeling slightly embarrassed that my condo is basically an updated version of the apartment where Laverne and Shirley lived in their ABC sitcom.

"Okay, I got it. You don't like to use the B-word. You're sensitive about the base . . . okay. I won't call it that, cutie."

"Hey, it was all I could afford for my first home. It's a fixer-upper. At least it's a two-bedroom. Want to see the rest of the crib?" Mikey nods and bites down on his tongue.

I escort him down the hallway. I point out the small second bedroom which is my office. All I have in there is a desk in front of the lonely window, which has bars on it since I am on street level. Across from it is the bedroom, which is painted a light mint-green and accented with white carpeting.

"I see you have your old sheets from Cambridge." He points to my comforter, which looks as if it were stitched from squares of primary colors.

"You remember that?"

"Of course, I slept on this bed many times with you, especially when I was sick and you took care of me after I drank too much! How could I forget?"

We stand in the middle of the bedroom, face to face. A dim light from the streetlamp filters into the room, highlighting the stack of novels that I have by my bedside.

Mikey then looks at my bookshelf and spots the Red Sox baseball cap he gave me on our first date.

"You still have this?" he says, holding the cap in his hands and marveling at it. He looks up at me with a half smile.

"Yeah, it was one of my favorite gifts from our time together. Whenever I wore it, I thought about you. I know, cheesy, huh?"

"Not at all, Tommy. That's what I've always loved about you. You're so different, funny, sweet, a little goofy. You're just you."

We stand there by the lip of my bed and gaze into each other's eyes. We kiss—open, closed, on the neck, the chin, and wherever our tongues lead us. I gently grab the soft strands of his hair where it falls behind his neck. My fingers brush and massage it. I softly kiss his eyes, and peck his forehead. I smell the remnants of the caramel from his latte. I graze his cheek with the back of my right hand. We hug tightly.

We fall onto the bed and explore each other's bodies like two lost souls who have finally reunited. We slowly remove our clothes. I pull off his T-shirt. He pulls off mine. I lick his freckled shoulders down to his sinewy, lightly hairy arms. I kiss each freckle that I spot. My fingers tickle the small patch of hair on his chest. All of it is familiar and so comfortable, like home. I'm revisiting and reacquainting myself with his body. We roll around on the bed. In the tumble, he swiftly unzips my jeans and yanks them off in one quick motion. I repeat the sequence on him. Naked, we take turns. I'm on top of Mikey, and then he's perched on my waist. Our hands touch every speck of flesh.

"Hey, I want to light a candle to make it more special," I interrupt, rolling over on my side toward the nightstand under the window.

Mikey starts to laugh.

"You're so funny. You always did this, Tommy. Stopping whatever we were doing in bed just so you could light a vanilla candle."

"It just adds to the moment," I say, grabbing the candle, tilting it, and lighting it with a match.

"You add to the moment, cutie."

Once I place the candle back down, it flickers and its soft light outlines our bodies against the wall. It shows Mikey and his beautiful silhouette as he massages my hairy chest. He licks his index finger and traces the outline of my nipples, which unlocks a series of tingles from within me. Our bodies move and flow as one vessel. Over the next hour, we make sweet, tender love.

When we finish, we lie side by side on my bed. Mikey turns to me.

"Tommy, do you think we'll have other nights like this?"

I lean over on my left elbow, smile, and answer, feeling his hot breath on my face.

"Of course! But I think I need to stock up on more candles." We both start to giggle.

15

Carlos

Ay, Papi and Lourdes! Where are they? I'm standing under the blinking blue monitors in Terminal B at Logan waiting for Papi and my sister to come out of the gate. Their plane landed on time. Papi already called me to tell me that the plane was on the ground and heading to the gate. The airport buzzes with activity. It's the day before Thanksgiving. Lines of people with their tickets in hand snake up and down along the terminal as people wait to check in their luggage. Tommy came with me this late afternoon. He offered to drive so I wouldn't get lost at the airport and surrounding East Boston. But right now, he's off looking for something to drink at the newsstand. *Que loco!* He also made a sign for me to hold up. It reads *Los Martins* in case Papi and Lourdes don't spot me first among the crowds of families. I thought the sign was a cute touch.

Papi and Lourdes haven't been back to Boston since early summer when we drove from Miami in my car, towing the U-Haul. I don't know what I have would have done without their help. Lourdes accompanied me to Pier 1 and IKEA where we bought some furniture, dishes, and home furnishings. Papi, ever the handyman, assembled everything. When we weren't unpacking or organizing my belongings, we had dinners and lunches in Cambridge, which I became familiar with quickly due to all these initial outings. Even without Mami, we felt like a family, sort of. When the three of us are together, it's as if a leg to our table is missing. We try to stand as one as best as we can, but we're still a little off somehow. Mami balanced us. After three days, I was settled in, and their jobs were done. They flew back to Miami. I haven't seen them since— until now. Oh, there's Papi! He's waving toward me with one hand while lugging a suitcase with the other. Lourdes spots me, drops her bags, and charges toward me with a big grin.

"Hey, little brother, good to see you," she says warmly, giving me a soft hug. Her floral perfume greets me as well.

"Thanks, Lou," I call her by her nickname. "You look great! You also lost some weight. We're going to fatten you up with some Boston Italian food."

"I lost weight? Why, thank you. That's so sweet of you to say. But it looks like you're the one who really lost a lot of weight, *hermanito*. You're thinner than usual, and I can tell you're still smoking. You smell like a chimney. I don't understand how you smoke and have asthma. You're playing with fire." She twitches her nose to show her disapproval of my habit. I stick my tongue back out at her.

"It's the airport. All the smokers are outside, and when they return to the terminal, the smoke follows them. Blame them!" I lamely explain.

"Yeah, right. You're like a walking Marlboro Light." We exchange closed-mouth grins. *Ay, Lourdes!* The nag has returned.

I almost forget about Papi who finally reaches us after dragging his suitcase. He looks so cute, with his bald head and his husky body hidden under a thick wool coat. He's all bundled up, in anticipation of the Boston winter weather. Mami would be laughing at this scene. Papi looks like he lost a little weight, too. Without Mami at home to cook us our fattening Cuban meals, Papi and Lourdes have had to make do with take-out dinners or Lourdes's subpar cooking—which she thinks is the best. Luckily, Versailles and Miracle Mile aren't far from the house. I guess we've all lost a little weight in the last year.

"Carlito!" Papi announces in his macho deep voice. He hugs me with the embrace of a Cuban bear.

"*Hola,* Papi! Good to see you!" He messes up my wavy hair.

"*Tienes el pelo mas largo!* I used to have hair like that," he says, commenting on my longer hair. In Miami, my hair was short on top and faded on the sides. Now it's wavy and bushier on the sides. I think Boston is growing on me because most guys here have their hair unkept and wind-blown, especially the goth kids who skateboard in the pit at Harvard Square.

"You too!" I say, rubbing Papi's bald head. It's like a bowling ball with stubble.

As we gather their things, Tommy power walks toward us drinking his Diet Coke through a straw.

"*Oye,* did I miss the party?" he says with a warm smile. "I figured you were traveling on Cuban time, so I thought you'd be late."

I introduce everybody.

"This is *mi amigo* Tommy, *el loco* reporter from Miami."

Papi shakes his hand and gives him a manly hug, which catches Tommy by surprise. Lourdes then gives him a hug and a sisterly kiss on the cheek.

"*Mucho gusto,* Tommy! Carlito told us a lot about you. It's always nice to meet another *Cubano* from Miami," Papi tells Tommy, patting his shoulder. Sometimes I forget how well Papi speaks English. He's come a long way. He perfected *you* from *jou.*

"We're trying to create our own Little Havana in Boston. Give us a few years. Boston will be like *la saguesera.*" Tommy explains, referring to the area off Calle Ocho in Little Havana. They all laugh, and Lourdes playfully hits his shoulder.

"Tommy, you're very funny, not!" she sarcastically teases him.

"You kind of remind me of my older sister in a way. Did I mention that we're close, not?"

Tommy helps Papi with his bag, and I grab Lourdes's carry-on. She slowly opens a white box that she has been carrying.

"Is that what I think it is?" I ask, salivating over the succulent aroma.

"Yes, little brother. We brought you *pastelitos* from Gilbert's Bakery. We thought you'd like a taste of home. The last time we were here, we couldn't find any Cuban bakeries."

I immediately grab the box from her hands and delicately take hold of one of the soft, crispy pastries. As soon as I bite into it, the sweet memories of Miami and Mami embrace me like a comforting invisible hug. After my brunches with Mami at Versailles, we would stop by Gilbert's and pick up a box of *pastelitos* for the house.

"You know, those *pastelitos* will be gone by tomorrow," I say.

"I know. That's why we also packed a *media noche* sandwich. It's in my purse," Lourdes says, opening her purse to unveil the wrapped and pressed Cuban sandwich. "See, we've got you covered."

After I wolf down the *pastelito* and try to devise a covert plan to swipe another one without her knowing, we meander through the maze of skywalks and escalators that connect passengers to the various terminals. We finally reach the Central Parking garage smack in the middle of the airport. Ten minutes later, we climb into Tommy's Jeep, and we're off to Cambridge.

The whole way, Papi peppers Tommy with questions about his parents, Boston, and the newspaper. As they chat, Lourdes looks out at the gray sky and at the light snow dotting the downtown skyscrapers and financial buildings in the distance. She's still guarding the box of pastries, which I don't blame her for doing. If I had my way, I'd eat them all right now and smoke a cigarette, but Tommy won't let me smoke in his car. *Ay, pastelitos!*

"Hey, this is like a postcard. Does it always look like this in winter, little brother?"

"Today's a good day, a light snow. But the other day, we had twelve inches fall in one swoop. *Coño!* Right, Tommy?"

"You know it! It's as if Mother Nature was salting the city with a giant dispenser. But you're in luck. We are only having one or two inches today. No big wup," Tommy says, in his writerly way.

"I hope you have a humidifier. The artificial indoor heat is bad for the skin and my sinuses. I don't want to be congested up here. I don't want to get sick," Lourdes says.

"Don't worry. I figured you'd complain about that, so I bought a humidifier. It'll feel like a rain forest in the apartment."

As we talk in the backseat, Tommy and Papi chat in the front, which I find a little funny. I wonder if Papi realizes that Tommy is gay. I wonder if he thinks we're a couple or simply *amigos*. To some people, *amigo* can mean friend or *friend* of the intimate kind.

"*Y tu padres?* What part of Cuba are they from?" Papi asks, holding on for dear life to the Jeep's inner door frame. Tommy's driving has us all bouncing and rocking on the highway as if the truck or SUV or whatever this is was a galloping horse. We just passed the green highway signs directing motorists to Interstate 93, the Mass Pike, and the two tunnels descending below the city.

"My mom is from Havana. My dad is from Matanzas. They live on Miami Beach off Alton Road, by the Fontainebleau hotel. My dad is a waiter at Puerto Sagua. His name is Pepe Perez."

"Ah, I've been to Puerto Sagua. *Super buena comida.* Maybe I have seen him there."

"Well, my dad looks like me, but at sixty and without so much curly hair. What he has left is all gray," says Tommy, pointing to his head of curls.

"*Mis padres* were from Matanzas *tambien,*" Papi says with delight, discovering a sliver of a connection with Tommy. "I think all *Cubanos* are related. *Y te gusta* Boston, Tommy? Do you miss your *padres?*"

"I love it here. I do miss Miami, but I have a good job, and you can't beat the seasons. The last time it snowed in Miami was 1977. I actually remember that. You won't see this pretty picture *en Cuba Norte.* And my parents? Well, they call me every night, so it's hard to miss them. *Mi papa* always calls me to tell when it's snowing, raining, or sunny here whenever he watches the Red Sox or Patriots play on television. It makes him feel like he knows where I am."

"I watch the Red Sox. They're pretty good."

"Yeah, they're the new Yankees!" Tommy says, as Papi high-fives him and laughs in his dry heave.

"So your *padres* have never visited you *aquí?*"

"Not yet, Señor Martin. My mom is scared of flying."

"Call me Aldo. *Un amigo de* Carlos is a friend of the *familia. Verdad,* Lourdes?"

"Yes, Papi. Tommy, you're an unofficial member of the Martin family. Do you realize what you're getting yourself into?" she jokes in her trademark sarcastic tone.

"Tommy, are you going to have *Sanguiven* dinner with us? You are invited," Papi says.

"Sure. *No hay problema.* If there's turkey, I'm there."

I laugh to myself because that's so true about Tommy.

"How much farther are we?" Lourdes whines. "No offense, but it's getting a little claustrophobic and bumpy back here in the Jeep." Lourdes always complains about something. The Martin nag.

"Ten more minutes, and you'll be home!" Tommy winks through the rearview mirror. After he pays the toll (he refused to let me give him the $4), we descend into the pitch darkness of the narrow Ted Williams Tunnel under the Boston Harbor. As Tommy drives and Papi and Lourdes tell us about their flight, I watch Papi, Lourdes, and Tommy talk as if they've known each other for years. Put a group of Cubans together, and they somehow connect, as if they are part of an extended family that is reuniting. I like this scene even though I am squished in the back passenger seat in between Lourdes, those *pastelitos,* and the luggage. Tommy is bonding with Papi and Lourdes. He's taking the edge off of having them here.

The following day, I step out of the bathroom with a towel around my waist and another in my hand. In the kitchen, Lourdes prepares the small turkey I had bought earlier in the week for my first Boston Thanksgiving. From the back, she looks like a younger version of Mami. Lourdes's shoulder-length, light brown hair swings side to side as she ladles some cranberry sauce in one pot and stirs some sweet potato in another.

"Lou, how much food are you cooking? It's just us and Tommy."

"It never hurts to have too much. Besides, you'll have lots of leftovers when we leave on Saturday. You should get a few meals out of this, little brother."

"Hey, if it saves me money, I'm all for it. I can take some to school for lunch."

I begin to dry my hair with the second towel and find that Papi is watching ESPN in the living room. I plunk down next to him on the sofa and try to follow the game. I don't even know who is playing.

"Who's winning, Papi?"

"Carlito, it's the Dolphins."

"Ah, okay. Who is the quarterback, Tom Brady?" Papi shoots me an icy glare. and turns his attention back to the TV. He never liked it when I interrupted his games.

"No, *chico.* That's the Patriots, your team here. Maybe you should help Lourdes in the kitchen," he says, leaning closer to the TV set.

"I was thinking I could show you Fenway Park while Lourdes cooks. It's only forty degrees outside."

"*Bueno,* can we go after the game or after dinner?" It was so much easier when Mami was around. She was our interpreter. She somehow made us understand each other better. Now I'm on my own trying to communicate with Papi. It's as if we speak different languages, and I'm striking out, as usual. I want Papi to have a nice visit so I leave him alone with the Dolphins. I rise from the sofa and return to the kitchen and try to help Lourdes with the food. But her being the control freak that she is, everything remains under control.

"If you want to help, why don't you go and buy us some

desserts. Maybe an apple or pumpkin pie from the market? Go with Tommy. Isn't he coming over soon?" She stuffs the turkey. My kitchen counter looks like a cooking demonstration for one of the morning talk shows. Opened plastic bags of beans, unused pots, and spoons top the counter. That's Lourdes, ever the perfectionist. I do like to cook, but after a long day of teaching, I prefer to stop by Subway or Anna's Taqueria in Porter Square and grab a beef burrito to go.

"Yeah, he should be on his way. I'll just go with him," I say, wrapping the towel around my neck and sniffing the pot of sweet potatoes. Lourdes loves to top them with marshmallows, which makes them even sweeter.

"And maybe you should get dressed in the process. Papi and I don't need to see you standing there half naked," she says, nodding her head in disapproval.

"*Ay, Lourdes!*" I walk away.

As she and Papi disappear into their worlds, I head to my bedroom. I shimmy into my blue jeans, slip on a long-sleeved cotton green shirt, step into my sneakers, and throw on my black wool coat. Facing the mirror, I finger-brush my hair up into brown wisps. It will do for now.

"I'll be back soon!" I say, before closing the door.

"Be careful driving outside," Lourdes shouts. Papi is too immersed in the game to notice that I'm leaving.

I walk down the staircase. My footsteps echo the whole way. At the porch, I light a cigarette and dial Tommy.

"*Loco,* what are you doing?" I sit down on one of the steps to the building's entrance where I have a grand view of the snow-caked street. Most of the cars that line my block are gone though. People, mostly local Harvard and Tufts students, probably went away for the holidays to see their families. I wish I could have gone away. So far, this Thanksgiving isn't how I pictured it would be. It feels like I have two formal guests with me who happen to share my blood, last name, and looks.

"Hey, Carlos! I'm by Harvard Square. I should be there in ten minutes," Tommy says on the other end.

"Okay, I was just wondering where you were. I need you to come with me to buy a pumpkin pie or a dessert. I'll be downstairs when you pull up."

"Sure. No *problema*. How's it going with your family? Are you okay?" Gloria Estefan's music plays in the background.

"Yeah, it's just being with Papi and Lourdes, I feel like I did in Miami after Mami died. I'm the outsider. They're busy doing their own thing, and I'm pretty much on my own wondering what to do." The plants in the flower boxes across the street are covered in snow. The trees that mark the sidewalk look like trunks with empty open palms.

"I wouldn't say that, Carlos. I'm sure they're trying to be as comfortable as they can be in your home. I bet they're also adjusting to the weather change. Just let them do what they want and be a good host. It's not every day that you get to see your family. As long as you spend some quality time with each of them, this will all be worth it. If my mom could magically beam to Boston, she would be here with my dad, but since she's scared to fly, it ain't gonna happen anytime soon. At least you have your family up here. Remember that!"

"I'm planning to take my dad to Fenway after dinner. Want to come with us? At least you can talk to him about sports and stuff. It will be more fun if you're there."

"I think you're overthinking this whole family visit. Just be yourself and relax. It'll all work out. It's your family, not a bunch of strangers. Maybe tomorrow, you can take Lourdes to Copley Square or Quincy Market."

"Okay, Mr. Boston Tourist Guide. So where are you now?" I'm standing in front of my building and blowing smoke upward and toward the other shoulder-to-shoulder tripledeckers and single family homes. Some neighbors have begun to string holiday lights on their homes.

"Carlos, turn around. I'm right here!" Tommy says, waving

from inside of his Jeep with his cell phone. I hop into his Jeep, and we head to the grocery store.

After a scrumptious Thanksgiving dinner and two slices of pumpkin pie, I'm as stuffed as the turkey we ate. My bulging stomach forces me to unbutton my jeans a notch. Lourdes begins to pick up the plates. Papi helps her. Tommy decides to make his exit and head back to Dorchester.

"*Bueno,* this was a great dinner, Lourdes. Thank you for including me in your holiday." Tommy hugs her and then extends his hand out to Papi.

"*Un placer, Aldo.*"

"Thank you for coming over and for picking us up from the airport yesterday. Carlos is going to take me to see Fenway Park in a little while. *Quieres ir?*" Papi says, patting his full stomach.

"Yeah, come with us," I urge and emphasize the point by widening my eyes toward Tommy, but it doesn't work. I can tell Tommy wants to go home because he is gathering his coat and keys. It's six o'clock. He probably wants to meet up with Mikey.

"Nah, you guys go. Carlos knows how to get there. I need to get home and meet up with another friend." *Friend* equals Mikey, who I will meet this weekend after Papi and Lourdes fly back to Miami.

After Tommy says good-bye to everyone, I walk him downstairs. I remember in Coral Gables whenever someone left our house, we stood outside and waved as the person drove off. Some habits stick.

"I guess I'm on my own here. Thanks a lot!"

"You'll be fine, Carlos. You need to spend time with your dad. Just show him Fenway," he says, walking behind me down to the porch.

"Okay, but we're still on for dinner with Mikey on Saturday."

"You got it." We hug outside. Tommy hops into his Jeep and drives away. I stand on the porch and wave good-bye, willing him to return and keep me company but to no avail.

Back upstairs, Lourdes decides to spend the night cleaning up and watching *The Devil Wears Prada* on DVD. It's her favorite movie. She believes Anne Hathaway is her long-lost sister. There is a slight resemblance, but Lourdes has lighter hair, and she's not as tall. They definitely share the same penchant for clothes and shopping. As Lourdes cleans, Papi and I gather our coats and prepare for our drive to Fenway Park.

It's just before 6:30, and Papi and I drive along Massachusetts Avenue, passing the curving old world, crimson streets in Harvard Square. People with coffee cups stroll in the chilly nighttime weather and peek into the shops and merchants' windows. Along the way, we attempt to make conversation. For some reason, our relationship has always been strained, but he is my father, my one and only parent, so I need to do my best to bridge this huge gap between us.

"*Tu amigo* is very nice," he says, sitting in the passenger seat of my Toyota, which he helped me buy when I started studying at FIU eight years ago. Over the years, Papi insisted on changing the oil himself to save me time and money.

"Yeah, he's a good guy." I glance at Papi and then turn back to the road.

"Um . . . is he your, ahem, amigo *amigo*?" Papi asks awkwardly. He's looking out the window as we cross the Harvard bridge over the brackish Charles River to Boston.

"No. Tommy is just a friend, not a boyfriend like Daniel was. We hang out and go out, but we're not dating." I turn left onto Storrow Drive and head towards Fenway. Hardly any cars dot the road. The city looks abandoned, almost shut down in a cold silence.

"Ah, okay. I didn't know, Carlito. You two seem to be *muy buen amigos*."

"I know. We get along really well. I knew you would like him, but no, he's not my boyfriend. It's the same as with you and your friend José. You play baseball together on Sundays in Tropical Park and you drink. You're friends. That's how we are but without the sports. We prefer *Project Runway*." On the right, we pass the elongated campus of Boston University, which is dark and vacant except for the standard nighttime fluorescent office lights. Halos rim the other streetlights, which reflect against the Charles River, illuminating its black murky water.

I drive onto the Storrow Drive overpass to Kenmore Square, and I notice Papi absorbing the city. I point out the large, red, glowing Citgo sign that he always spots on TV when he watches the Red Sox play their home games. I show him the expensive red and beige brick brownstones that dot Commonwealth Avenue as they did three hundred years ago.

"And down the street over there is more of Boston University. This area is full of college students. It's one of their hangouts." I point to Beacon Street and the shoulder-to-shoulder restaurants, pizza shops, and swank hotels. The subway stop sits in the middle of the square. As we drive over the turnpike overpass, the green hulking edge of Fenway Park sits on our left side on Lansdowne Street, which is crowded with more college students and visitors. So this is where everyone is tonight!

"Papi, right there. That's Fenway Park."

He opens the window and a gust of cold air rushes in. Papi's eyes gaze at the green-colored back end of the stadium.

"And that's the green monster, or that's what people here call it," I say with an air of authority. I feel smart that I knew that. Some of my students had told me about Fenway at the start of the school year.

"Can we walk around?"

"Sure, Papi."

I take a loop around the stadium and by luck, I find a parking space near Yawkey Way on the other side of the stadium where the main entrance sits. As we step out of the car, Papi looks up and takes in all the angles. He wears the same enthusiasm as a kid visiting Disney World for the first time. For baseball fans, Fenway is Disney.

We walk along Yawkey Way where flags featuring the Red Sox World Series championships sail along the side of the stadium.

"Carlito, can you take a photo?" With folded hairy arms and a confident smirk, Papi poses along the mural of David Ortiz and Mike Lowell. I snap a photo.

"We need one of us," he suggests.

"*Ay, Papi.* Do we have to? I can take another one of you." I'm embarrassed. I feel like I'm a kid when Papi snapped photos of all of us wherever we traveled on vacation at the end of the school year. It was the annual Martin family trip.

"Just ask someone to take our photo. How often are we here together in front of Fenway, *el famoso* Fenway? This is historic, Carlito."

I feel obliged so I ask a passerby, a young woman with curly red hair and matching freckles. She smiles and agrees to help us out.

"Smile!" she says in a cheerleader tone.

Papi puts his arm around me and leans his head against mine. I stop trying to resist. I start to laugh when Papi quickly messes up my hair again. Flash. Snap. Done.

I call up the image on my camera and show Papi as we stand in front of the stadium's west side across from another pizza eatery and sports bar. He looks funny wearing the ski cap to keep his head warm.

"You look like how I did when I was twenty-eight years old, Carlito. Do you know what that means, *hijo?*"

"*Que, Papi?*"

He points to himself in the image and laughs.

"That is how you will look in thirty years." He puts his arm around my shoulder.

"*Ay, Papi!* Don't scare me like that," I groan.

We stroll around the stadium for twenty minutes. Back at the car, Papi thanks me for bringing him here. Seeing Fenway up close made an impression on him. He is moved. I'm glad he enjoyed something other than watching TV and eating on this trip.

"Now I can tell all my friends that my son, *el profesor en* Boston, took me to Fenway Park, and I will have the photo to prove it!"

"I'll have this printed before you leave, Papi." I store my digital camera in my coat pocket.

As I open his door, Papi puts his hand on my shoulder.

"Carlito, I know I am not your Mami, and I know that you do not have fun taking me to places as you did with her. I know we don't have the best relationship, *hijo*. But one thing I do know is that I love you even though I don't always show it. I hope you know that."

"I know, Papi. I know." I don't know what else to say. He smiles and messes up my hair again. I pull his ski cap over his nose.

"Carlos, enjoy that hair. You are my son in many ways and that includes *la cabeza*."

"*Bueno,* hopefully the bald gene skips a generation." We share a laugh, climb back into the car, and return to Cambridge.

16

Tommy

"Let's meet at the Barnes & Noble at seven tonight and then head to dinner from there. Carlos is excited to meet you. Call me back. Love you!" I leave a message on Mikey's voice mail. I haven't spoken to him since last night when we took a romantic drive along the shore in Scituate and Hingham. We marveled at all the estates that were decorated with Christmas lights. Throughout the drive, we held hands and pointed out the majestic homes that we could imagine ourselves owning one day—if we ever suddenly became as wealthy as the families in these coastal towns.

It's just past noon on Saturday. I'm standing in the parking lot of the Blue Hills and staring at the granite-filled mini-mountain I am about to tackle. I look around and notice only four other cars here. I put on my ski cap, smushing my curly hair. I look like the Michelin man in my blue puffy jacket, jeans, and sneakers. In the distance, snow covers all the trees in a wintery dandruff. The ground resembles a soft, thin layer of vanilla frosting pocked with twigs and dead leaves. To avoid any slip ups, I begin my hike on the paved trail where runners and other hikers hold their children's hands or walk their dogs. It's forty degrees, sunny, and there's barely a breeze. Perfect!

As I trek on the winding road, my heart hammers, pumping harder with each inclined step. Silence fills the woods, and my thoughts drift back to Carlos's Thanksgiving dinner with his family. I think this family visit was good for Carlos. He needed time to bond with his father. I don't share the same awkwardness with my dad as Carlos does with his. My father and I talk about the Red Sox, cars, and my articles, now that he knows how to access them online. Well, with a little help from my sister Mary. Even though my dad knows I'm gay and he's proud of my accomplishments, I still don't detail every aspect of my life to him such as going to Club Café with Rico or hanging out with Mikey again. I did tell my parents about Mikey when we first dated. Whenever they asked me what my plans were for that weekend, they always included Mikey. My conversations were mostly about Mikey and me.

That changed when we stopped dating and my mom noticed the sudden singularity of my weekends, which consisted of running along the Charles River, shopping at Cambridgeside Galleria Mall, or checking out open houses. After two weeks, my mom asked me in her loving, concerned, Spanish-accented voice: "*Y tu amigo,* Mikey? You don't talk about him no more. *Que pasa?*" My throat tightened like a pipe. I simply explained, "Oh, he made some other friends. We don't hang out anymore. That's Boston, Mami." She must have read between the lines because she then said something that acted as a balm to my broken heart.

"*Bueno,* Tommy, that's not the end of the world, right? You won't die from that. You'll make other *amigos.*" I laughed and absorbed her words because they were so true. She made a lot of sense. I would get over this. It's just a guy. I felt better about the situation when I saw it through her logic.

I'm halfway up the hill and working up a sweat. I wipe the sweat off my forehead with the sleeve of my jacket. My calves and thighs tighten. I breathe harder. I glance all around me and I only see bare trees, ice dripping from their branches. I take in the scene and allow Mother Nature to soothe and relax me. Walking through the hills makes me feel that I'm in another world, far from the brick buildings and subways of Boston. When I hike, I have

these desolate woods all to myself. Hiking is my form of medita-
tion, my Blue Hills therapy.

I continue lugging myself up the hill. I wave to a couple and
their young daughter as they pass me. I smile at a built older man
with salt-and-pepper hair walking his chocolate Labrador. My
phone vibrates in my pocket. It's Carlos.

"*Loco,* what are you doing? Are we still on for tonight?"

"Yeah, I left Mikey a message. I'm just here doing my weekly
hike. Gotta work out those buns! Anyway, why don't you come to
my place, and we can leave from there and meet up with Mikey."

"Sounds like a plan."

"And what are you up to? Have you recovered from the
Miami invasion?" I say, approaching the steep incline that provides
an amazing view of colonial homes in Dedham and Westwood
and cars scurrying on Interstate 95.

"I just dropped off my dad and Lourdes at the airport. I think
they had a nice visit. I took Lou shopping yesterday at Copley. Let's
just say she took advantage of the no sales tax on clothing incentive in Massachusetts. She had to buy another suitcase for all her
clothes."

"Ha! What about your dad?"

"He had a nice time, but he wanted to get back to the warm
weather. He's not a big fan of the cold. We had some father-and-
son quality time, if you can believe that, *loco.*"

"No way!"

"Way! The highlight of his trip was Fenway Park."

"See, Carlos, I told you that you guys needed to spend some
time alone. I don't always have to be in the picture."

Carlos sighs on the other end.

"*Ay, loco.* I know. You were right. Tommy Perez knows it all. I
bow down to you, oh holy Cuban one."

"You know it! Anyway, let me get back to my hike. I'm almost
at the observation tower. It's hard to talk and hike. I'm out of
breath. I may need your asthma inhaler."

"Okay, see you tonight."

I reach the observation tower, where other families wearing sweaters and gloves sit on the picnic benches outside the granite tower, which resembles a small fort. I plop myself on one of the ledges and gaze at the view—rolling green hills that seem to go on forever. To the north, I see the John Hancock and Prudential buildings rise into the bright blue sky and dwarf all the small three- and four-story homes and businesses. To the east, a line of planes begin their descent over Quincy and South Boston to land at Logan. The sun warmly kisses my face. My legs swing back and forth like a pendulum. I close my eyes, lean back, and relax. *Ahhh!*

A few hours later, I'm back in Dorchester, standing in front of my refrigerator where I try to decide between drinking a Diet Coke or a lemon-lime Gatorade. I call Mikey again. I'm forwarded to his voice mail. Hmmm. I leave another message.

"Hey, Mikey. I'm here just getting ready. Carlos and I are going to meet you at the bookstore. I can't wait. Love you!" I settle for the Diet Coke. As I walk to my living room and plant myself on my blue sofa, I text him a similar message. I wonder why he hasn't called back. Mikey is usually good about that. Maybe he's at an AA meeting or helping his parents with groceries or something. I'm sure it's nothing. He'll be there tonight.

At five o'clock, Carlos pulls into my parking lot. He looks pretty handsome. He wears an olive-green jacket, dark blue jeans, loafers, and a brown scarf around his neck. His brown hair is gelled and styled back. For a second, he looks like a model because of his lanky, lean frame. He catches me watching him through the slits of my Venetian blinds like a peeping Tommy. He makes a silly face at me.

I buzz him in, and he wipes his shoes on my welcome mat, which is a caricature of a Jeep. (It was a gift from the dealership.)

"What's up, *loco!*" He greets me with a hug. I smell his Dolce cologne.

"Are you ready?" he says. "I can't believe I finally get to meet your man, the famous Mikey."

"Yeah, I'm almost ready. I just need to tame my curls."

"May I? I've wanted to style that head of hair for the longest time, Tommy. It needs an extra touch."

"Sure, but don't flatten it out. I like the curls."

We walk to my bathroom where Carlos rubs some lotion in his hands like a genie about to make a wish come true. His fingers poke through all sides of my hair like Edward Scissorhands. He combs the sides down and the front up.

"Now that's how you should wear your hair." I turn around and look in the mirror. My hair looks more groomed. I kinda like it.

"Thanks. Maybe I should call you the shear genius."

I grab my coat and shoes, and lock the condo doors. We hop into my Jeep and we're on our way. Ten minutes later, we pull into the bookstore's parking lot.

"What car does he have again?" Carlos asks, as he gets out of my Jeep.

"A white Volkswagen Rabbit."

"I don't see it."

"He's probably on his way. I'll call him again."

I dial Mikey. His voice mail kicks in again. Something doesn't feel right.

"Maybe he's running late, Tommy. Let's get some coffee and wait inside by the windows. That's how we can see him when he pulls in."

With our hot chocolate and espresso, Carlos and I grab the latest *Entertainment Weekly* and *Latina* magazines. We settle into a café table by the window that faces the parking lot and incoming traffic. My eyes train on every car that pulls in. A Ford Focus. A Toyota Camry. A Mazda van. No Rabbit. No Mikey.

We wait for twenty minutes. No sign of Mikey. No returned calls either.

"*Oye,* maybe something happened. You spoke to him today, right?" Carlos says, blowing the steam off his cup.

"Actually, I couldn't get through to him. I left him several messages. We agreed during the week that we would have dinner tonight."

"*Bueno,* let's wait a little longer. There could be traffic or something where he lives."

Two cups of hot chocolate later, I begin to grow restless. A mix of anger, concern, and frustration alternate inside me. Where is Mikey? Carlos senses all of this. "How about calling him one more time?"

I agree, and do so, but his voice mail kicks in. I leave another message.

"I'm sorry about this. I don't know what happened," I tell Carlos.

"No worries. It's not your fault, but I think it's kind of lame that Mikey did this to you. You realize he stood us up, don't you? That's not cool."

I hear Carlos's words, but I don't quite believe them. Mikey wouldn't stand me and my friend up. Or would he?

"*Bueno,* let's get out of here and get something to eat," Carlos suggests in a cheery voice. "You can deal with Mikey whenever he calls back. So tonight, it's just a party of two. We can catch a movie after dinner."

As we get up to leave, my eyes continue to lock on to every car that pulls in, but I don't see what I want to see. I wonder what happened to Mikey. More importantly, why would he do this to me? Disappointment crumples my heart. My face reddens with humiliation.

Amazingly, it's a rare sixty degrees today. Mother Nature is teasing us like a seductive temptress. Global warming? Who knows! It was thirty degrees yesterday, and it's double that today. This is cause for celebration before the warm weather vanishes along with the afternoon's light. I decide to take advantage of this with a good run in my neighborhood and Milton. I grab my iPod and step into a pair of black sweatpants, a matching hoodie, and hiking sneakers. I emerge from my dim, lower-level condo into the brightness of the afternoon. *Ahh.* This is more like it. I deeply inhale the nice cool air and walk the five steps down to the street level from the lobby. Once there, I flex my legs up and down to warm up for my run. I still haven't heard back from Mikey about last night's botched dinner plans. Carlos and I had a great dinner at Acapulco's restaurant in Quincy. After stuffing our stomachs to their limits, we then rented *Scarface.* The entire night, Carlos and I impersonated Tony Montana. *Jou cockroach! Say halo to my little friend!* That's another reason for this run: to burn off the quesadillas and the two bowls of tortilla chips that I consistently munched on at the restaurant. But this run will also serve to distract my mind a little bit. I must admit, I've been obsessing about what happened or didn't happen with Mikey. I'm still unclear. *Jerk!*

I begin running along the bike trail that connects Boston to Milton and where the little orange subway trolley centipedes to and from the Ashmont T stop. It's the same trolley that wakes me up whenever it rumbles by early in the morning to ferry the office workers and blue-collar employees from Milton and Mattapan to downtown. Joggers dot the bike trail in full force, enjoying this spring-like anomaly. They wave to me as I pass them. As my heart pumps, so does the music from my iPod. Shania Twain and Dolly Parton sing about broken hearts; Gloria Estefan and some Shakira make my hips want to shake and shimmy. With each beat, I move faster and pick up the pace. A film of sweat beads on my forehead, and I wipe it off with the back of my sleeve. As my hair bounces with each step (I feel like one of *Charlie's Angels* when I run . . . perhaps Sabrina, the smart one), I pass the old red-bricked chocolate factories on my right. Bustling Milton Square sits above me. When a trolley chugs by, I try and race it, but it eventually outruns me. I slow down as I approach the stretch along the Neponset River where it breaks and flows east toward Quincy and Dorchester Bay. My sneakers splash against the puddles of melting snow that flank the trail.

My mind replays the same thoughts the same way a scratched CD abruptly skips. I have two stories to write this week. One focuses on the lack of bilingual Hispanic on-air talent on Boston TV news stations. (There are only two Latinos on English-language news outlets. *Que pasa,* Boston? In Miami, it's the complete opposite.) The other story I am about to embark on involves a behind-the-scenes look at the Make-A-Wish Foundation and how it wields its magic to make wishes come true for sick kids. I'm looking forward to that one. It's one of my feel-good features that everyone will relate to, but more importantly, I am highlighting the work of the unsung heroes, the wish-granters who volunteer their time to give these kids some spiritual medicine. On Saturday, I'll drive to Gillette Stadium and watch a ten-year-old boy with leukemia as his wish comes true—meeting Patriots quarterback Tom Brady after a game. His wish-granter coordinated with the Patriots organization so that the boy can have season tickets to all the home games. Talk about a wish that keeps on scoring! I smile at the mental image of the boy sitting in the stands watching the Patriots play.

As I continue my run, my heart pumps harder, like the pistons in my Jeep. I run up the trolley stop's stairs to Milton Square and head west toward Eliot Street, a quiet idyllic neighborhood street where rows of lovely Victorian, colonial, and clapboard homes sit on perched granite foundations. Mostly Volvo station wagons and expensive brand-name SUVs fill the driveways. When one crosses from my Dorchester neighborhood to these parts, even though it's only two blocks, the housing prices spike thirty percent. Go figure! This neighborhood is out of my reach, like Cambridge was more than a year ago.

My phone vibrates in my pocket. It's a text message from Mikey. I stop in front of a renovated tripledecker that has beautifully decorative pines sculpted in the shape of cones. I catch my breath and read the message.

Cutie, I'm so sorry about last night. I was sick at the hospital. Call me when you get this. Love you!

I reread the message a few times, and questions immediately invade my thoughts. Why didn't he at least call to say he was sick? He seemed fine the other night. Why is he text-messaging me and not calling me? We confirmed these plans all week, and he knew how important this was to me. Why would he blow me off? I delete the message and continue my run. I blow off some more steam and run harder, my feet pounding against the pavement. My legs throb, and my breathing quickens. After I reach Blue Hill Avenue, I turn around on Eliot Street and sprint back toward Milton Square. A few minutes later, I scoot down the stairs on the trolley stop in Milton and run down the bike path at full speed. I pass the colorful mural of butterflies, bees, and frogs painted on the wall that hugs the bike path. I pass my building on the left and continue toward the drawbridge a mile away. With the trolley tracks on my right and the overpass above me, I pass the small rolling fields of sawgrass that ribbons the bike trail before stopping at the rusted red bridge at Granite Avenue. Once there, I'm winded, completely wiped out. I bend over and grab my knees to catch my breath. I trudge toward the wooden benches that local fishermen use during their breaks from casting their lines. I receive another text message. It's Mikey again.

Call me. I'm so sorry. We need to talk. I want to make this up to you. Love you, cutie.

I delete this one too. I decide to slowly stroll back along the dirt trail to my condo. Anger and confusion roil inside me, just as they did the other night.

Fifteen minutes later, I reach my condo, and I'm surprised to find Mikey sitting on the cracked cement steps outside my building. He holds a bouquet of white carnations and a six-pack of Diet Coke. He smiles when he sees me. I'm not that happy to see him though.

"Hey, cutie!" He gets up and gives me a hug. His voice is a little hoarse.

"Hey . . ." is all I can muster. I don't return the hug.

"I'm so sorry about the other night. I was sick. I had strep throat. My parents took me to the hospital because I had a hard time swallowing."

"Oh yeah?" I ask incredulously.

"We spent most of the morning at the hospital and they gave me some strong antibiotics. Well, they knocked me out for the entire day. I woke up this morning. I missed all your calls. I'm so sorry." He widens his big blue eyes in a plea of sympathy.

"You could have at least called or you could have had your mom or dad call. I was worried about you! So was Carlos. What a great first impression!" I fire back. We stand outside my building and then move to the sidewalk to continue talking.

Mikey rubs my shoulder and softly fingers the back of my curly hair, which tickles me. I move away.

"I just felt really sick. It was awful, like swallowing razor blades. I know I should have called, but I didn't and I can't change anything about it. I just feel awful that you were waiting with your friend."

"You should!" I fold my arms and turn my back to him.

"I'm sorry. It won't happen again. Here." He appears before me and hands me the flowers. "I know how much you like flowers, and of course, Diet Coke. This pack should last you, oh, two days or so?" Mikey bites down on his tongue and sticks it out. I'm angry with him, but my internal fury slowly melts away. Mikey always had that effect on me, which is why I lasted so long with him the first time we dated with all his late nights and hangovers.

"Can you forgive me, cutie?" He grabs one of the flowers and tickles my chin. Maybe he is telling the truth. His voice does sound hoarse and he doesn't look as good as he usually does. He looks tired. He has bags under his beautiful blue eyes.

I take a deep breath and exhale.

"Sure . . . but don't let it happen again. If something comes up, at least have the courtesy to call or text message, which you seem to prefer. *Comprende?*"

"*Sí, me comprendo,*" Mikey tries to imitate me.

He kisses me on the cheek, and he walks me inside the building.

"I guess I'll reschedule dinner with Carlos. I know he's having a busy week so I'll figure out when he's available next."

"Sounds good to me. Anything for you, cutie."

I hope so, but a gnawing disappointment waves at me like a red flag in my mind.

17

Carlos

Mami and I walk in a parking lot filled with Christmas trees off Douglas Road in Miami.

"Carlito, how about this one?" she points to a ten-foot tree.

"*Ay, Mami!* That's too big. There's no way I can fit that in my apartment."

"And this one?" She points to another tree that is half the size but twice as fat.

"I don't think that will fit through the door either."

"*Y este? Te gusta?*" Now she's standing in front of a thin tree that is about my height.

"That might do the trick. Wait a minute! What are we doing here? It was Thanksgiving the other night!"

"*Mijo,* this isn't for your apartment. This is for *nuestra casa.* Let's take a walk." We stroll around the Christmas tree lot, which looks like a forest in the middle of bustling Miami. We meander through the aisles of tall and short trees or those wrapped in netting. The pines' fragrance permeates the air. Mami and I traditionally bought the tree for the house every year. It was our tradition, and Papi and Lourdes decorated the tree. As they worked, we secretly wrapped our gifts in her bedroom or we baked holiday cookies in the shape of gingerbread men and reindeer for our family and friends.

"I am proud of you. You did well for *Sanguiven.*" Mami walks by my side, her right hand resting on my upper back. She leans her head against mine and pecks me on the cheek.

"What do you mean?"

"You were good to your Papi. He loved that you took him to the baseball park. *Como se llama?*"

"Fenway Park, Mami. You were there? But how?"

"I'm here right now, no?" She smiles and winks.

"*Tu* papa showed *las fotos* of Fenway to all his friends and customers at the store. *Hiciste bien,* Carlito. *Muy bien.*"

"It was no big deal. We just walked around and stuff."

"Oh, and Lourdes! Did you see how much she spent at the mall with you? *Ay dios mio!* She was never good *con el dinero. Una loquita!* That's why she has eight different credit cards. She thinks she was born to shop. She never took my advice about saving money, and she's been shopping more ever since I left. There goes the inheritance I left her." Mami gestures her hand in a farewell wave to emphasize her point.

"She was on vacation. She had a good time at the mall, but you're right, she does go through money like toilet paper." We both laugh and continue our walk. The trees, propped up against one another, sway with an urban breeze that sends goose bumps along my neck. This place is like a lush maze of trees, something out of Vizcaya Gardens or a mountainside.

"Listen, Carlito, Papi still needs you."

"What are you talking about? He doesn't need me. He's fine in Coral Gables with Lourdes. As long as he has his baseball, work, and more work, he's all set. Can we talk about something else, *por favor?*"

We stop in front of a white plastic tree that seems to glow and mesmerize at the same time. Mami faces me and puts her hands on my shoulders. She cups my face with her right hand and squeezes. She always did so to catch my attention.

"Christmas is coming up, and this will be very hard on the family, especially *tu* papa. He's going to need help with a project. He needs you. I need you there."

"What project?"

"You'll see. Just go to Miami for Christmas. *Comprende?*"

"I was planning to anyway. *Ay,* but what do I need to do down there? What mysterious project?"

"You'll see, Carlito. *Te quiero,* and tell your sister to stop spending her *dinero!* No man will ever marry her with her bad shopping habits. But for now, you need to get up and get going or else you will be *tarde* for your appointment. You don't want to keep *la doctora* waiting." Mami begins to walk away along the path of trees.

"Mami, wait a minute! Don't go. I want to keep talking. I miss you!" Tears drip down my face. I chase her, but she disappears in the distance.

I abruptly wake up. My heart races. I'm out of breath, wheezing as if an invisible hand is clenching my air pipe. From my nightstand drawer, I grab my asthma inhaler and pump two puffs of the cool medicated air into my mouth. It leaves a metallic aftertaste. My lungs slowly begin to expand again, and I feel relieved. My alarm clock reads six o'clock. I lay back, my hands clasped behind my head. I straighten out my legs under my sheet. I try to process the dream and what it may mean. I pull out my journal from the same drawer, and I write everything that I can remember. Maybe I'll bring this to my appointment later this afternoon with Dr. Bella Solis. *How did Mami know about that, too?* I'm curious to hear what she thinks of all these crazy dreams. I'm more intrigued to meet the famous *doctora.* Tommy spoke so highly of her the other day, and he gave me a copy of the article he wrote about her. I've even tuned in to her program on my drives home from work. She receives calls, mostly from women asking advice about their rebellious teenagers or cheating husbands. I wonder what she will have to say to me. I guess I'll find out soon enough, if I can climb out of bed and start my day.

It's four o'clock in the afternoon, and I'm on the Mass Pike heading west from Boston. I finished grading some essays and finalizing my lesson plans for the following week before leaving

Dorchester High twenty minutes ago. I'm driving to Dr. Bella's private office in Newton, the beginning of the western suburbs. As I exit the Mass Pike Newton ramp, I pass clusters of beautiful white, beige, and gray grand Victorian and colonial homes that sit on pudding stone foundations. I drive along the main street where small coffee shops, antique stores, and shops line the thoroughfare. This feels like small town USA in the suburbs. I check the address and MapQuest directions again. I seem to be heading the right way. This also looks like an affluent neighborhood, not an office or medical district.

I finally pull up to the address—a two-story white clapboard Cape house with a Lexus hybrid parked in the driveway. I double-check the directions and the address. I guess this is it. I park in the driveway and walk along the connecting decorative stone tablets that lead to the front door. Wow, this is a lovely home. All the trees are manicured, even in winter. I press the doorbell, and an Asian gong greets me. My nerves ambush me. Suddenly, I'm as nervous as a cat in the rain. *Calmate, you dork!* Why did I agree to this? Maybe I can tip-toe out of here and beat traffic back to Cambridge. As I plan my escape, the door slowly opens. Dr. Bella Solis appears with a warm smile that radiates an immediate calming effect. Maybe this won't be so bad after all.

"Hi there. You must be Carlos. Don't just stand outside in the cold. Come on in." She approaches me with a hug and the casual, familiar ease of an old family friend.

"Hi, Dr. Bella. So nice to meet you. I wasn't sure if I had the right place. I thought I was going to an office."

"I have an office in my home. I find that it makes my patients more comfortable. Would you like something to drink? I just brewed some chamomile tea. It's my own special recipe."

"Sure. *Gracias.*" She takes my wool coat and hangs it up in a hallway closet by the front door. We walk through her living room, which is lined with two large, golden, plush sofas that flank a fireplace where a small fire simmers and crackles. The vibrant colors on the walls, which feature beautiful lush paintings of nature, from sunsets to beach scenes, warmly embrace me, making me forget that it's chilly and wet outside. Lighted gardenia-scented candles perfume the house. She escorts me to yet another room, which I take as her office although it looks more like a cozy reading room. The walls are painted a light blue and lined with shelves of Spanish literary titles and medical journals. Next to a golden brown sofa is a table with one of those Asian fountains where water streams over granite rocks and stones. It's very soothing. I like the sound it makes. It also puts me at ease.

"I'll be right back with your tea. Make yourself comfortable." I settle into the sofa, and it swallows me. My entire body sinks into it, and my feet are elevated off the Berber cream-colored carpeting. The central heat also hums in a mechanical purr. I glance around the room and notice photographs of Bella with the mayor and Spanish television celebrities such as Cristina from Univision, Don Francisco from *Sábado Gigante,* and Padre Alberto, the boyish-looking Miami priest with his own show. There's another photo with Dr. Bella and the Estefans at a fundraiser for children. Framed awards from the city and youth organizations also bedeck the walls. I also notice older photographs of a younger Dr. Bella surrounded by middle school age kids. Maybe students? I wonder if she was a teacher. Behind the love seat across from me is a framed adage: "You have the power to change!" I've heard her repeat that several times on her radio show.

A few minutes later, Dr. Bella returns with a nice yellow mug of steaming tea. She closes the door and then sits down in another loveseat in front of me. She warmly smiles and leans back in her chair. Tommy was right, she really does look like a Latina Julie Andrews but with longer straight hair that falls to the middle of her back. She tucks her hair behind her ears often.

"Are you comfortable, Carlos?"

"Yes, very much. Thank you for the tea and for seeing me on such short notice. This was Tommy's idea. I thought it couldn't hurt."

"You're welcome. Tommy told me that he had a good friend

who needed someone to talk to. He didn't say exactly why, but he did tell me a little about you, that you're a teacher, that you moved here from Miami, and that you've been a little down. That's all I know," she says, crossing her legs. "Tell me a little about yourself. What brought you to Boston?"

"Were you a teacher, Dr. Bella?" I sip my tea.

"Yes, I was. I was a middle school teacher for a few years." She points to some of the photos of her former students. "My principal noticed that I had a line of students waiting to speak with me after school on Fridays about their problems, and he encouraged me to leave the classroom and try counseling. So I eventually followed his advice. And that led me to the radio work. Everything that has come my way, I did not ask for," she says, in a soothing, how-can-I-help you voice. "If you believe in what you do, if you do it with passion, things will come your way. I understand you're a teacher, too, and a new job brought you to Boston. That is wonderful, Carlos. We can always use good teachers here." She grins and leans in closer from her chair.

I tell her about the job fair I attended in Miami for Boston school teachers. I tell her how I became a teacher and how it gave me a sense of purpose in life. I start rambling. I'm suddenly hyper and nervous, and I'm speaking a mile a minute.

"Carlos, calm down. Take a few deep, slow breaths. You're okay. You're in a safe place. I'm just here to listen. I am here to help you. I am your psychologist, your friend." Dr. Bella reaches out and holds my hands in hers. A calming energy invades me.

"Now tell me, why are you really here? It's okay. You can trust me. Whatever you feel like discussing is fine with me. This is your time, your space."

My eyes well up. I start talking about my mother and how she died over a year ago and how Miami was never the same, how I've never been the same.

"She loved to garden. She had this beautiful garden at our house in Coral Gables. She thought of it as her other child." I glance down at the pristine carpeting, and I remember Mami's face.

"The loss of a parent is a very difficult experience. I can tell you loved her, that you still love her very much. And you moved here to start over on your own?"

"Yeah, I thought if I could get away from Miami and from all my memories there that I would be okay. Don't get me wrong, I love Boston and the great job I have, and I have Tommy as my buddy here. But for some reason, being here has also been very difficult because Mami keeps appearing in my dreams and it feels like she is still very much alive, telling me what to do."

"Your dreams? What happens in these dreams?"

I describe the most recent ones. I pull out my journal, and I show Dr. Bella how I write them down before I forget.

"Do you mind if I read some of them?"

"Sure, go ahead." I hand her the journal. Dr. Bella then sits back and reads the book as I study the rest of the photos and plaques on her wall. Dr. Bella is apparently well regarded in the professional medical community as well as the civic one. She smiles and laughs as she reads. As she closes the journal, Dr. Bella looks up at me with her big soulful green eyes and tilts her head.

"Your mother sounded like quite a lady. By reading your journal, I can tell how much you love her and miss her. From what you are telling me and from what I've read, I sense there is some unfinished business that your mother wants you to take care of. Tell me about your father. What is your relationship with him? You haven't talked about him. Are you close?"

"Well, that has always been a weird relationship. He's closer to my sister Lourdes. I always felt more comfortable with Mami."

"Did your father ever do something to you when you were younger? I hear a little resentment in your voice. Your shoulders tensed when you mentioned him. When you talk about your mother, you light up and your body is relaxed. When I mention your father, you seem agitated and somewhat uncomfortable. What is that relationship like?"

"It's just always been weird with him. We are nothing alike. He likes sports. I don't. He loves to talk about money. I don't. He is a

very simple man who came from Cuba and opened his own convenience mart in Miami Springs. He works very hard, and he did
that a lot when I was growing up. It was always about the store."

"Ahh, I see. And your mother was always around to spend
time with you and tried to fill that void? Did you want to spend
time with your father when you were little?"

"Um, not a lot. He was up here a few days ago for Thanksgiving.
I took him to Fenway. He's a big baseball fan."

"And what was that like? Did you have fun?"

"He loved it. He was like a little kid. We took some photos so
he could show his friends in Miami."

"So you enjoyed that time with him? I get the feeling that you
and your father never spent much time together. I take it that this
was a special day, no?"

"Yeah, after the park, he told me how much he loved me and
how proud he was of me even though we don't have the same
relationship as I did with Mami."

"And that moved you. You were surprised by his revelation.
Your father doesn't open up like that a lot, right? "

"Ah, no! He's one of those Cuban macho guys with the iron
exterior. He barely cried at the funeral. It's as if by not showing
emotion, he is showing the world how strong and indestructible he
is. His wife died. He should have showed more emotion."

"Carlos, I think when you moved to Boston, it wasn't solely
about getting away from Miami. I believe you were trying to get
away from your father. And I believe that you are not just mourning the loss of your mother but that you miss your Papi very
deeply. In fact, I think you've yearned for your father's love and attention longer than you realize or care to acknowledge."

My throat constricts and my eyes tear up.

"You think I miss Papi? In Miami, he was never around."

"Exactly!"

Dr. Bella hands me a tissue.

"Here," she offers with a closed grin. "Think about your
relationship with your father. What have you always wanted from

him? Why did you gravitate to your mom so much? Your mother is trying to tell you something very important in these dreams. In the last one, you wrote how she mentioned a project that she wants you to assist your father with. Pay attention to that, Carlos. Spend time with your father for the holidays. I believe something very important will come out of this."

"I'll take what you've said into consideration, Dr. Bella. Thank you." I grab another tissue and blow my nose.

"Now, I want you to come with me for a second. We are going to practice an exercise." She motions for me to get up. She leads me to a large mirror above the red brick fireplace. Dr. Bella then stands behind me.

"What do you see, Carlos, when you look at yourself?" She places her hands on my shoulders in a comforting manner, like Mami would when I would arrange a dress tie.

"I see a good person. I see a lonely person. I see a sad man." I wipe away a tear with the wadded tissue from earlier.

"What else do you see? Look closely and focus."

I zero in on my face. My light brown eyes stare back at me.

"I see my father. I have his nose, his eyes, his wavy brown hair when he had some." I shrug and laugh.

"Do you know what I see, Carlos? I see a handsome, intelligent, good guy with a big heart that he wants to share with his students, his friends, and most of all, his father. I also see a little boy who wants to love and be loved by his father. Can you see that?"

"Yeah, a little."

"We want to take care of that little boy, reassure him that it's okay to miss a parent, that it is okay to want the love and the attention of a father. Now I want you to repeat after me: 'I am a complete man with a good heart who deserves the best in this world and nothing less. I am a resilient man who loves his father but most of all, loves himself.'"

I repeat what Dr. Bella says.

"You're going to be fine." She pats me on the back and turns to face me. "Until we meet next time, I want you to think of a way to honor your mother. What would she appreciate more than anything? What was something she enjoyed doing for you, your sister, and your father, or for herself? The answer will come to you in time. How about if we meet again after your Christmas vacation? I want to hear about your holiday with your father and sister. I'll be back in Boston after the New Year. I'm going to the Bahamas with my family. I'm as pale as the snow outside."

"Okay. Maybe I'll have more to share when I come back."

Dr. Bella loops her arm around my elbow and walks me to her front door where she gives me a hug. I catch a trace of her perfume, which carries a sweet, powdery, lavender scent.

"Take care of yourself. And if you need to talk to someone in case of an emergency, here's my cell phone number." She hands me her business card with her cell phone number scribbled on the back.

"I'm here for you, Carlos. I'm your friend. I'm only here to help."

I wave good-bye as I venture back outside into the frigid cold weather with a heavy heart filled with questions.

18

Tommy

Mikey and I stroll the wide corridors of South Shore Plaza for an early Christmas shopping spree. The mall bustles with shoppers who are dashing from one sale to the next. White Christmas lights bedeck the trees that line the mall's center. Reindeer, Santa hats, and stockings hang like ornaments above the stores. Holiday music from "Jingle Bells" to Mariah Carey's Christmas CD plays overhead on hidden speakers. I love this time of year because Boston bounces back to life for Christmas, despite the frigid temperatures. The city embraces the holiday spirit and wears it like an old favorite coat too comfortable to take off. Down the street from the mall, gingerbread men and elf figurines pose on the front lawns of snow-caked homes while sparkling twinkling lights adorn windows and front doors. Christmas in Boston feels more authentic than it does in Miami because of the weather. Santa might suffer a heat stroke from South Florida's rampant tropical humidity. Something magical and breathtaking happens in Boston when December arrives. Cold weather becomes an afterthought because of the warmth of the holiday spirit. A Boston Christmas is a Norman Rockwell painting that morphs to life, and I am glad to be a small character in that scene.

It's Saturday afternoon, and Mikey and I decide not to buy each other's gifts today. Instead, we shop for everyone else. We al-

ways have fun at the mall. Somehow, no matter what we do, it's always an adventure. We each carry two bags filled with gifts. Mikey
bought his mom and sister gift cards to Macy's and his father a shirt
from Sears. I bought Carlos a gift card to Banana Republic. For
Rico, I got a gift card to Hollister. He loves wearing the store's
ribbed, body-defining shirts. For Mami and Papi, I bought a nice
card with holiday wishes in Spanish. I also plan to enclose a check
for $500. They need the money, and I know they would rather
have this than some artificial gift card that they would probably
give away to someone else. They are simple people who don't
need or want for much, except that I call them each night. Besides,
I plan to be there for the holidays so that's my other gift. And for
my sister Mary, I bought a gift card to Talbot's, one of her favorite
stores. If I were to buy her a blouse or a shirt from that store or any
other, she would return it right away. I haven't bought anything for
Mikey yet. I'm stumped on what to purchase. Maybe when I visit
Miami for the holidays, I'll get him something there.

"Let's get some cheesecake, cutie," Mikey says when we pass
the crowds circling outside The Cheesecake Factory.

"Ugh. I don't want to ruin my dinner. That stuff is really fattening."

"You need to gain some weight, cutie. I want you to be a bear,
my bear."

He rubs my stomach like a genie. I stop walking.

"A bear?" I blurt out.

"Yeah, you would make a cute sexy bear with your hairy chest.
You're too thin."

"I don't want to be a bear. Bears are fat, gay, old men with
chests and backs as hairy as carpets, the guys you see roaming
around Provincetown like polar bears in the summer. How about a
cub? They're younger and thinner."

"Okay, you're my Cuban cub. I'll call you Boo Boo."

"Thanks, Yogi. Remember, you're older than me by two years."

Mikey sticks out his tongue at me and bites down. I mimic
him and twitch my nose. We share a quiet laugh.

"What are you doing for Christmas? My family is having our annual dinner at the Marriott Hotel. I was thinking you could come over," Mikey suggests as we eye the rows of cheesecakes in the cool and brightly lit dessert case at the restaurant, which swarms with couples, children, and parked empty baby strollers. I surrender to the Cheesecake Gods and decide to order a slice to go.

"I'm headed to Miami. Since I didn't go home for Thanksgiving, I must go for Christmas. It's usually one or the other, or I won't hear the end of it from my parents. The Latin guilt trip!"

"Oh."

"But I'll be back for New Year's."

"So I'll have you all to myself on the last day of this year and the first day of the next."

"You got it!"

We order our obscenely fattening desserts. I get the Linda's Fudge Cake, which is flanked by sprinkles and swirls of fudge. Mikey orders a slice of the colossal carrot cake. We pay the cashier and carry our plastic boxes and utensils back to the mall's main corridor. Under the mall's skylights, we sit on one of the benches across from the CVS. We feed each other the desserts.

"So what do you want for Christmas, cutie?"

"You don't have to buy me anything. Really. I rather you spend your money on something else." I suck a clump of chocolate and fudge off my spoon.

"But I want to get you something." He scoops some of his carrot cake onto his fork and shoves it in his mouth. A crust of frosting smears his upper lip. I lean in closer and lick it off.

"How about making a donation to an organization in my name? Maybe Fenway Community Center or the Make-A-Wish folks. There are people in need of gifts and toys. I'm happy with my Jeep, Diet Coke, and *Providence* reruns. Seriously, I really don't need anything."

Mikey moves closer and kisses me on the cheek.

"That's why I love you. You always think of other people."

As we sit and wolf down our desserts, I study Mikey's face and feel his sweet energy. What is it about Mikey that endears him to my heart? Something connects me to him, and I can't put my finger on exactly what. There's an indescribable pull when we're together, and yet, I feel his presence when we're apart. I use my index finger to tickle the light brown scruff on his face. He fires back by threatening to shove some cake in my face.

"You wouldn't!" I say.

"Try me!" He dangles his fork near my hair.

"Okay, okay! I believe you. Now just back up and step away from the hair! Step away from the hair," I say, like a police commander might negotiate a crime scene.

As we finish our cakes, my phone vibrates. The caller ID displays Carlos's name.

I excuse myself from Mikey for a moment and turn around to talk.

"*Loco,* what are you doing?"

"Hey, Carlos. I'm here at the mall with Mikey. We're shopping. What's up?"

"I just worked out. What are you doing later? Want to get some dinner?"

"Yeah, that sounds good. I'll invite Mikey to come with us. Is that cool?"

"Of course. I still want to meet him even though he was a no show the other night. I guess . . ." Carlos sighs, "I can give him another chance. *Ay, loco!*"

"Thanks, *amigo.* I want to see what you think of him. I'll come over with Mikey at eight o'clock. That way, he can see your cute apartment."

"*Bueno,* see you later, *loco.*"

I flip my phone shut and whirl around back to Mikey. He looks like he wants to say something.

"Did you hear that? I thought it would be nice if we had dinner with Carlos like we planned last week."

Mikey grimaces and shoves more carrot cake into his mouth. He then looks at his watch and checks his phone.

"I'd love to, cutie, but I told my sister I'd drop by her place and visit my nieces. I thought we were shopping today and just having lunch."

Hmm. I'm not sure whether to believe him or not. He didn't mention this at all earlier when we met at the mall. Where is this coming from? More Mikey doubts, just as when he didn't show up for Carlos's dinner.

"Can't you cancel this one time? I'm sure your sister would be okay with it. I really would like you to meet Carlos. He's like family."

"I know, Tommy, and I will, but I was looking forward to seeing my family. Maybe next week?" He begins to tickle the back of my hair.

"Umm . . . sure, I guess," I deadpan, but I'm really not sure. As we finish shopping, concerns linger inside my head and my heart. It seems that whenever I make plans for Mikey to meet a friend, specifically Carlos, Mikey (*poof!*) disappears. He wasn't like this when we first dated. In fact, he was always drinking and hanging out with his friends. He was the social butterfly with the bright blue eyes. He met Rico a few times. Although they didn't care for each other, Mikey at least met him.

I decide, against my better judgment (it must be the holiday spirit), to let Mikey off the hook this time. Eventually, he'll meet Carlos and any other friend I have. How could he not? My patience is beginning to wear thin.

It's eight o'clock on the dot, and I'm walking the three flights of wooden creaking stairs to Carlos's apartment. When I arrive at his door, he appears with a big smile on his face, which is quickly replaced with a pensive, confused look.

"Hey . . . where's your guy?" Carlos says, looking behind me and down the stairs for Mikey.

I wipe my shoes on his welcome mat, which is in the shape of Cuba.

"He had plans to see his family tonight. I'm sorry."

I walk in, and Carlos takes my coat and hangs it on his coatrack by the front door.

"*Loco,* that is so lame, again! That's two strikes in my book. What's his deal anyway? How hard is it for him to meet a friend of yours?"

"I know. The first time he was sick. This time, it's his family."

Carlos raises his left eyebrow and tilts his head in disbelief. I bet he does this with his students when they give him a bullshit story for skipping class. We walk to his bar table in his kitchen and plop ourselves on stools that face one another. A depressing pile of essays and homework sits next to us and blocks the view of the living room.

"And what will the excuse be next time?"

"Carlos, you will meet him. I promise. But I have to agree, I find this all so strange. He knows we're close, so he should *want* to meet you."

"Well, I am beginning to take offense to it. I haven't done anything to him. I think there's more going on here than you realize. Is he shy?"

I lean forward on the table and twirl a piece of a paper towel around my finger.

"He's not shy, at least not the first time we dated. With me, he's very outgoing and chatty. He's a lot of fun in his own way."

"I see. And he's a guidance counselor, so he deals with students one-on-one?"

"Yeah!"

As he talks, Carlos gets up from the table and grabs a plastic bottle of water for himself and a Diet Coke for me. He keeps a stash handy for my frequent visits.

"I may be going out on a limb here, but do you think he's socially uncomfortable without having alcohol around? Maybe he's shy without the liquor. That would explain these sudden disappearing acts when you want him to interact with you and another person, especially *un amigo*."

"Hmm. I hadn't thought of it that way." I open my drink, which oozes carbonated fizz. I take a long pull.

"When it's just you and Mikey, it's great, right? But if you try to expand your social circle with him, he has something else to do. Why else wouldn't he meet me or anyone else you know?"

"Well, last year he met Rico a few times."

"Yeah, but he was drinking like a fish then. From what I know about alcoholics, liquor acts as a social lubricant. It puts them at ease in social settings. Without it, they can feel naked and awkward. Maybe you need to talk to Dr. Bella, too. I had a great session with her the other day. She helped me see things a little differently."

"I knew Dr. Bella would offer some insight. She's really great, like a cool and understanding aunt you can confide in."

Carlos nods his head and takes a swig from his bottled water. His light brown eyes suddenly become animated.

"*Oye,* I have an idea. I know how I can finally meet Mikey. Let's ambush him!"

"*Que cosa?*" I almost spit out my drink.

"Trust me on this. The next time you have plans to have Mikey over at your place or if you guys meet at the bookstore, I'll suddenly show up and make it look like an accident. He won't be able to run away. He'll have to say hi and talk a little. I am loving this idea, *loco.*"

I cringe.

"Don't you think that's kind of rude? Would you want that to happen to you if you were in his shoes?"

"Tommy, rude is not meeting your boyfriend's really nice and smart friend who is new to Boston and wants to make friends." Carlos's eyes widen to make his point, and he tilts his head again in his teacher mode.

"I can make it look completely natural, an accident, a meeting by chance. I can be shopping for books for my class."

I digest the idea. It can't hurt, right?

"What if he gets up to go the bathroom and escapes through a back window? Then what?"

"Well, then you know that he might not be as comfortable as he says he is with his alcoholism. Recovery is a lifetime process, and if you guys are seriously dating, wouldn't you rather know now than later whether or not he can socialize with your friends and family? It can't always be just the two of you, especially with me around here and your family and friends in Miami. You can't escape a Cuban family. I'm learning that the hard way."

"Okay, it's a deal. We'll do this your way. Carlito's way," I humor him. "The next time we meet up, I'll call you ahead of time and you can, ahem, *accidentally* find us there. When did you suddenly become a smart and sneaky teacher?"

Carlos caps the top of his water bottle and feigns offense.

"I learned it from you, *loco!* So we're all set for Project MA— Mikey Ambush. I can't wait. Now let's get out of here and get something to eat. I want to tell you all about my visit with Dr. Bella." Carlos clears the table of our drinks, and grabs our coats from the rack. "You won't believe what she told me. I actually feel good about this therapy thing."

"You should, Carlos. She's one of the best around."

19

Carlos

I stroll up and down the rows of desks and collect my students' essays on *The Gift of the Magi*. It's the last day of class before Christmas break, and the students are rowdy and distracted. I don't blame them. I want to get out of here and head to Miami and relax in the warmer weather.

"So class, does anyone have any big plans for Christmas break?" My students chatter and rummage through their bags. Their chairs screech against the black tile floor as they wait for the last bell to ring. In the back of the classroom, the radiator clanks and hisses.

"I'm going to Puerto Rico to see *mi abuelo,*" shouts Pedro, in his Latino Boston accent, which I never knew existed until I moved here. He's a C student, but I give him an A for conduct because he's mostly well-behaved.

"That's great, Pedro. You can escape this horrible cold and bring us back some of the warm weather. I'll have your paper graded by the time you come back with a tan."

Sue, one of my chattier students, turns around in her desk and looks up at me.

"My family is going skiing in Vermont. Do ya ski, Mr. Martin?"

"Ah, no. I haven't gotten around to taking lessons. I think I might scare away the deer if I were to tumble and scream down a mountain. I don't think Cubans and snow mix all that well, especially in the mountains."

I pass Leroy's desk. He sketches in his art pad.

"Yo, Mr. M! I'm gonna play video games with my cousins. I have eight of them. My family comes over for Christmas, and we have this enormous dinner with turkey, rice, cranberry sauce, sweet potato pie, pumpkin pie, and . . ."

"That sounds delicious," I interrupt before he rattles off the entire menu at Boston Market. "Maybe you can save me a plate."

"What are you going to do for Christmas, Mr. M?" Leroy asks, followed by similar inquiries from other students. Everyone leans in and suddenly focuses on me. I never thought I was that interesting, but my students always seem more intrigued with my personal life than English literature. I don't think they know I'm gay. I don't share that part of my life with them.

"Well, I'm going to Miami to visit my family. It'll just be my sister, my dad, and me. Nothing too big or fancy. We're low-key."

"And what about your mom?" asks Blanca, one of my Dominican students who has a hard time focusing in class. I suspect she has ADHD.

"My mom passed away a little over a year ago. So, it's just the three of us."

"I'm sorry, Mr. Martin," Christa pipes in.

The rest of the class *awws.*

"That sucks," Pedro says. "Sorry about that."

"It's okay. Really. Our holiday will be simple. Probably not much different than your typical gathering."

After collecting the papers, I stand in front of the class and announce my Christmas gift to them.

"Now that I have your complete attention, we need to discuss your next assignment." The entire class groans and I hear, "What?" and "Huh?" and "Another assignment?" and "Dang!"

"Yes! I have a homework assignment for you for winter break, and you absolutely must complete it. I don't want to hear any excuses. Got it?"

"Ah, c'mon, Mr. Martin, give us a break!" Leroy pleads.

"But you're going to enjoy this and thank me later."

"But, Mr. Martin, it's Christmas!" Sue says, combing her long strands of blonde hair.

"Now listen, class!"

More groans. I better get to my point before I have a mutiny in Dorchester.

"Your assignment is . . ." I tease them. More groans and grunts. I love making them squirm.

"To have a great holiday and to enjoy yourselves. I was just kidding. There's no assignment. That's my gift."

The class exhales in relief. Some students laugh.

"That wasn't very funny, Mr. Martin," Pedro scolds me.

"I had you guys going, didn't I?"

The bell rings, and everyone scatters to head home. I lean against the edge of my desk where some students drop off gifts for me. I thank them and smile. I open some of the gift bags, and I find envelopes with $5 and $10 gift cards to Dunkin' Donuts and Starbucks. I'm moved. Many of my kids come from low-income homes. Their parents would have better use for this money than buying me gifts. One of the gift cards is for Boston Market. I bet Tommy would like that. The gifts are nice gestures, but what matters most is the thought behind them. A simple "Happy New Year" would have been good enough. My students show their appreciation for me when I least expect it.

I wave good-bye to everyone and wish them a happy holiday. By the time the students have vacated, a small mound of cards pile on my desk. As much as my job feels like never-ending work, I know I'll miss these kids over the next two weeks. I'll miss how Leroy doodles or how Pedro is always the first to raise his hand. I also enjoy hearing their stories about their weekend outings and their families. Grading their papers allows me to peek into their little lives. Whenever I say good-bye to them at the end of the week, I imagine what kind of adults and professionals they'll grow up to be.

This was my last class of the day, so I gather some of the essays and paperwork and shove them into my brown backpack. I clear the blackboard, pull down the window shades, and arrange my desk in order. Before I lock the door, I stare at the empty classroom for a few seconds. I grin and then flick off the lights.

Juanita, my colleague, spots me outside my door.

"Well, Carlos, you survived your first half of the school year. You're still coming back after the new year, right?" She tilts her head and gives me a quizzical glance with a half smirk.

"Of course! Where else would I go? Besides, imagine what my kids will give me at the end of the school year. Look at all these gift cards!" I hold up the bag of cards. We're standing in front of my door, down from the rows of abused and slightly rusted school lockers. The students are long gone. Only the voices of fellow teachers and custodians fill the corridors.

"In the past we've had new teachers disappear right after the winter break. I don't want that to happen with you, you hear?" she scolds me in her sassy but well-meaning tone.

"Oh, I'll be back, for sure. If not, who will watch my class when I need a cigarette break five times a day?" She playfully smacks my shoulder.

"Now don't get me started on that bad habit of yours. Now go on and have a nice time in Miami with your family. I'm sure they miss you. As for me, I'm off to Jamaica to visit my sisters and brother. I need to get my color back," she says, her fingers grazing her beautiful chocolate skin.

We hug and wish each other a Merry Christmas.

"See you next year, Carlos! Bring me back some of that Miami sun and get back some of your Cuban color. I know Cubans aren't that white." Juanita walks away with bags of student gifts.

"Happy New Year to you, too!"

With my backpack flung on my right shoulder and my bag of gifts in hand, I walk down the cracked steps of the school and saunter two blocks to the subway stop in Fields Corner. I normally drive, but my car was literally frozen in the street this morning. My tires were wedged into blocks of ice from the recent freezing weather and snowfall. I didn't have time to de-ice all four of my tires. And even if I did, I wouldn't have known how to do that, something to add to my *Things To Learn In Boston* list. So I rode the subway, a direct trip from Porter Square on the Red Line. I need to do this more often because when I ride the "T," I feel more integrated into Boston city life. I'm surrounded by the colorful cast of characters who make up this town. I enjoy watching people flow in and out of the subway on their way to who knows where.

Twenty minutes later, I'm sitting on the hard plastic seating of the inbound Red Line car. High above the other passengers are display ads for beer. Along the paneled walls, posters offer cash for anyone brave and desperate enough to volunteer to take part in obscure medical experiment studies. More ads promise quick classes to learn to speak English, Spanish, or Chinese. The fluorescent lights flicker whenever the subway picks up speed. An electronic voice announces that we're approaching South Station. I sit back. My feet are flat against the black linoleum floor. I grab the *Daily* that someone left on the seat next to me, and I begin to read it when a loud feminine voice with a lisp booms overhead and interrupts me.

"Excuse me, but aren't you Tommy Perez's *amigo,* Carlos? I'm absolutely positive it's you because I *never ever* forget a cute new face." I crane my neck up and see this giant of a man with short, loose, dirty blonde curls and a face that resembles a male version of actress Rebecca Romijn. *Ay no!* I recognize the guy. It's Kyle, the guy Tommy wrote about a few months ago for being the model on *The Real World* Boston season. He's the guy who now uses his fifteen minutes of fame for good by being a spokesman for HIV awareness. He's the guy who stands out in a crowd because he is so tall and *muy* loud, as he's being now. He's the guy everyone knows as "K-Y" because of a messy threesome episode with K-Y Jelly on the TV show. He's also the guy sucking my space right now. I have nowhere to run.

"*Hola,* K-Y, ah I mean, Kyle! Yes, I'm Carlos. We met briefly at Club Café one night. Good memory! How's it going?" Kyle takes my inquiry as an invitation to sit down next to me and chat. His lean model figure squishes into the seat and me. He folds his long, lanky right leg over his left and places his hands on top of his knees like a proper lady.

"Well, things are *fabulous!* I have some fun events coming up. I'll be the host of the White Fiesta fund-raiser in Miami later this month. Second time in a row! You must go! But right now, I'm on my way to my next project at the Make-A-Wish Foundation offices."

"Make-A-Wish? Is that a catering company?"

Kyle laughs loudly, which makes his head bob back and his loose curls shake. Other passengers, plugged into their white iPod headphones, immediately shoot annoyed looks our way when Kyle laughs. *Ay, que pena!* How soon can I get off this train?

"No, darling. It's a nonprofit group that makes wishes come true for sick children. I'm going to be a volunteer. I have a training session this afternoon. I thought I could lend some of my celebrity to the organization, you know, so they can raise more money."

"*Oye,* that's great. Anything to help sick kids. It sounds like you have a lot going on since your reality TV days. I read Tommy's story on you." I hold onto the metal support bar to my left as the subway car rocks and rattles to a halt at South Station.

"I remember Tommy mentioned you were a teacher. Have you ever thought about volunteering? I bet you'd be good at it." He blinks at me, a flirtatious Minnie Mouse in the flesh.

Kyle leans in closer and stares at me with his big blue eyes as if he's trying to put me into a trance with his looks. But it doesn't work. Although he's cute in a pretty-boy model sort of way, he's also a giant ham, which I don't like. I also don't believe in reality television or the wannabe celebrity of the contestants. Why would anyone put their dirty laundry on national television, especially in a threesome episode that involved gobs of lube? *Ay no!* It's not my thing. I don't like the spotlight or attention. What I do is about my students, not about me. I believe people should help others simply to help them, not to boost their careers or public profile. Tommy can be a little like this at times, but he also has a goofy charm, which I find endearing. And besides, his stories do inform the public about what Hispanics are doing in Boston, so I don't hold his ham factor against him when he starts to brag about his latest article. Tommy is proud and passionate about his writing. It's who he is, and I accept that about *mi amigo*.

"I'm so busy with school and mentoring that I never really thought about volunteering. I have a lot on my plate as it is."

"Well, we could always use cute *Cubanos* like yourself with Make-A-Wish or with the AIDE AIDS organization here in the city. We need to do more outreach with the Boston Hispanic community. Here's my card. Think about it. If you want to help make a difference in the community, just call me. Or, ahem, if you want to volunteer your time one on one with moi, then definitely call me and you can teach me a lesson or two. My cell is scribbled on the back of the card." He winks in an exaggerated way and hands me his card, which has a photo of himself with a big smile and wearing a tight blue shirt with three buttons open. Kyle's contact information fills the card's backside.

"Um, okay. I'll think about it. Maybe when things slow down in the spring or summer when I'm on break. But right now, I have too much going on."

"Fabulous, *papi chulo!* Just consider it. That's all I ask," says Kyle, three inches from my face. I smell his cherry Chapstick. He's so girly.

The subway screeches to a stop and its doors slide open. *Gracias a dios!* Passengers scramble in and out like an urban herd. Another minute and Kyle would have slipped me his tongue, and I would have had my face and hands plastered against the glass windows screaming for help.

"This is my stop, Carlos. Call me! Buh-bye," he says before giving me a double air kiss. He waves and begins to step off the subway. "Oh, and tell your *amigo* Tommy to call me. I think I have a story idea for him."

I softly grin and wave back. Kyle disappears into the crowd of riders moseying on the platform.

The train slowly starts to rumble again toward Cambridge. When it crosses over the Charles River, I stand up, lean against the metal support pole, and take in the majestic scene. Brownstones rise in Beacon Hill like small brick dollhouses. Small boats dot the river. I pull out some of the gift cards that my students gave me and I smile. Leroy, Christa, Sue, Pedro, Blanca, and almost all my students gave me something. They are small gifts that mean so much. My heart bursts with pride. Boston continues to grow on me. The more time I spend here, the more I feel this is *mi hogar*. I have my students, my job, a good friend and a decent apartment. I think about what Kyle said about volunteering, and I start to wonder what I can do to help the community, my community. I think of Dr. Bella's words from the other day. "You should find a way to honor your mother's spirit," she said. As the train forges ahead, so do my thoughts.

20

Tommy

Project MA (Mikey Ambush) is about to begin, and it's going down at the Barnes & Noble tonight. He's meeting me here for our usual latte/hot chocolate. I dial Carlos on my cell and fill him in on the plan.

"Hey! Mikey is on his way to the bookstore. Can you stop by? He'll be here in twenty minutes."

"*Ay dios mio!* I'm on my way. I can't wait to finally meet this guy. I'll make it look completely natural."

"You better!"

"I promise, *loco.*"

I flip my cell phone closed and sit by the window that faces the parking lot where the fumes from the idling cars curl into the air. It's about seven o'clock so Mikey should be here any minute. The after-work rush of professional suburban yuppies descends on the café for coffee, desserts, and newspapers.

To pass time, I roam around the magazine stands and browse *Consumer Reports* and look up my Jeep Wrangler's model. It ranks below average on reliability. Hmmm. I look up Mikey's Volkswagen Rabbit and it gets a big check mark for "recommended." As I study the car's specs and features, which have grown on me since Mikey showed me his car, I hear a friendly, familiar, Boston accent that makes the hairs on my forearms rise in a good way.

"Hey, cutie!"

I turn around and see Mikey standing behind me. We hug and pop kiss. His light scruff on his face rubs and tickles my cheek.

"Good to see you, bunny!"

"Bunny?" he asks with a tight-lipped grin.

"Well, if I am going to be your Cuban bear, you can be my bunny. Got that, Roger Rabbit?"

"You're so cute, Tommy. I'm going to get some coffee. Can I get you something, like a bowl of honey since you're a bear?"

"Nah. Just the usual."

"But there's no Diet Coke here."

"I meant what I usually get here. A hot chocolate. Low fat."

Mikey heads to the café counter, and I grab our usual table by the window. I keep an eye out for Carlos's beat-up Toyota Camry. I hope he doesn't get lost. The guy is horrible with directions. I can't imagine how he got around in Miami. He still confuses Dorchester with Roxbury and Mattapan, and Back Bay with the South End. They all look alike to a degree, but still. When I first moved to Boston, I got lost so many times that whenever I got lost, I recognized the street from a previous lost encounter. I learned Boston by getting lost. I should write a story about that.

A few minutes later, Mikey returns, cradling our drinks and carefully walking toward me as if he were carrying a tray of fine china. He sets down the two cups, and our eyes lock throughout the entire process. I look away momentarily and grin and I catch my reflection in the glass window. Mikey then takes off his bulky North Face green hoodie and wraps it around the back of his chair. We chat about our day.

"We had a holiday party for the kids at school. Rick, our physical education coach, dressed up as Santa. I came as an elf," Mikey says, blowing the steam off his coffee. He pulls out his elf hat from his jacket and wears it for me.

"Aww. You were an elf? I bet you were the cutest one there!" I reach over and wrap my fingers around his.

"Well, I definitely wasn't the shortest one. Our librarian and two teacher's aides, who are in their early twenties, also played elves. You'd think we were extras from *Lord of the Rings* or something. I think we looked more like hobbits than elves."

"I'm sure you guys looked great and the kids appreciated it. We don't do anything like that at the *Daily*. I'm not really close to anyone there. Everyone is in their own world. It's not like when I worked at *The Miami News* when we had a potluck lunch and Secret Santa. It's a different work environment, more conservative than Miami. To each his own. Boston!"

"So no one gave you anything at work?" Mikey's bright blue eyes bore into mine. He still has the elf hat on, which pushes his brown straight hair down into bangs.

"Just professional holiday cards from business associates and publicists whose clients I've written stories about. It's no big deal. It's work, not family or friends."

"Well, I bet Santa will make up for that with lots of gifts when you go home. Your family is probably really excited that you're coming."

"They are! It's *Noche Buena,* a big party with a pig. We call him Pepe."

Mikey sticks out his tongue and bites down.

"Carlos is also headed to Miami. I feel bad for him. It'll be the first Christmas without his mom."

"Poor guy. That can't be easy. Maybe I'll meet him when you guys get back and we can go out to dinner or something."

"Actually, that might happen sooner than you think."

"What do you mean?"

"You can meet him right now. I think he just walked in through the door, which is strange because he doesn't live around here," I say, squinting my eyes to focus on Carlos who is standing by the store's entrance and scanning the place.

"He's here?" Mikey asks. His face is full of panic and discomfort. Maybe he's constipated or the coffee hit him in the wrong spot.

"Yeah, he just walked in. What a surprise!" I improvise.

I get up and wave to Carlos. He spots me and walks gingerly toward us.

I look back at Mikey who resembles a bird that wants to fly away but whose wings are clipped. Sweat begins to form on his forehead, and his thin, light brown eyebrows furrow. What's going on with him?

"Carlos! Hey! What are you doing around here?" We hug, and there's a smirk plastered on Carlos's face.

"I went to the mall to buy some gifts. This mall is much bigger than the one in Cambridge, and for once, I didn't get lost in Boston. Can you believe that?"

"Bravo!" I clap and laugh.

I turn toward Mikey and introduce them. Mikey rises and shakes Carlos's hand.

"So good to meet you, Mikey."

"Yeah, same here," he deadpans. Something's not right here. Mikey isn't happy to meet Carlos, who is now taking off his coat.

"Sit down with us, if you have time."

"Thanks. I have a few minutes before heading back to Cambridge. I stopped by to get some coffee," Carlos says casually.

I grab a chair from another table and drag it over to ours. Carlos settles in, and I offer to buy him a double espresso, which he gladly accepts. I leave them alone for a few minutes while I fetch the drink.

From the café counter, I glance over at the table and notice that Mikey is warming up to Carlos. They chat and exchange a laugh here and there. It looks like they're bonding. I wonder why Mikey seemed so disturbed when I mentioned that Carlos was here?

I fumble for some bills and pay Selena for the drink. I return to the table where I walk into a conversation about education.

"We only have two guidance counselors at my school, and there are 1,500 students. Can you imagine?" Carlos says.

"Tell me about it. I'm pretty much it at the elementary school. I think I need a counselor myself to deal with all my kids."

I give Carlos his double espresso and scoot back into my chair. I sit between these two important guys in my life in Boston. My two worlds collide, but in a good way.

We talk about our plans for Christmas. I invite Carlos to my parents' house for *Noche Buena* or at least on Christmas Day, if he wants to get out of his house.

"I want you to meet the wacky Perez family. If you met my mom, then you'd know why I have all my weird quirks. I'm really my mother's son. She also loves Diet Coke and eating turkey sandwiches all the time."

"So there are two of you? You're not weird. Your quirks are cute, just like you. It's who you are. Don't ever change yourself for anyone," Mikey says.

"Yeah, we love you, Tommy, and all your ticks, even though they limit us to certain restaurants," Carlos says sarcastically.

"My mom will love you. She has a soft spot for young Cuban teachers. If you were straight, she would try and set you up with my sister Mary. And hopefully one day, Mikey, you can meet Pepe and Gladys Perez. You'd really like Miami, if you can handle the muggy weather in the spring, summer, and fall. Come to think of it, it's year round."

"How hot is it down there?" Mikey asks, sipping his coffee.

"As hot as your coffee. Right now, it's eighty degrees and it's December. Wait 'til June, when the humidity tacks your clothes to your skin and inspires everyone in Miami to start blow-drying their hair straight."

Mikey shakes his head.

"That's too much. I'd melt. I'd be a puddle."

"You get used to it after a while. If I'm surviving my first winter in Boston, you can definitely handle T-shirt weather," Carlos chides Mikey.

We sit there for the next hour chatting, and I watch with pride as Carlos and Mikey bond. I knew they would hit it off. They work in education, and they're good guys. I wouldn't call just anyone my friend or boyfriend.

Two cups of hot chocolate later, it's eight o'clock. A very caffeinated Carlos decides to head back home.

"*Bueno,* Mikey, it was a pleasure to finally meet you. Maybe we can all hang out again sometime soon." Carlos gets up and embraces Mikey with a warm hug. Carlos does the same with me.

"Yeah, that would be cool. Maybe we can see your apartment in Cambridge. Tommy and I always hang out here in Braintree or the South Shore. It's time for my boy to take me somewhere else." Mikey playfully hits me on the shoulder.

Carlos grabs his drink to go.

"Call me tomorrow, *loco.* We can figure out our plans for Christmas."

When Mikey turns away, Carlos gives me a quick thumbs-up and silently mouths, "He's super cute!"

I nod and smile back.

As Carlos leaves, Mikey and I stroll around the bookstore and browse the music section.

"Your friend is very nice," he says, as he browses the new Keith Urban CD.

"I know. I knew you guys would get along."

"Oh, and by the way, you're a horrible actor, Tommy."

"What are you talking about?" We flip through the stack of CDs of holiday music in the next aisle.

"I'm not stupid. That wasn't an accident or chance meeting. You called him and told him we'd be here and don't deny it. You're a very bad liar. You're a liar!" His voice rises and he faces me.

"*Que cosa?*" I say, trying to sound sincere.

"Tommy, puh-lease. That was an ambush, and I don't appreciate being surprised like that. I told you I'd meet your friend, but I don't like surprises. That wasn't cool. You couldn't just let things be and happen on their own." Mikey's tone is accusatory. He's angry. An inner light switch has flipped inside him. Who is this talking to me?

"I just thought it would be easier if Carlos stopped by. Every time I make plans for you guys to meet, something always came up. I just wanted you guys to meet, that's all. No harm was done." I rub Mikey's shoulder. He moves away, treating my touch as if it were radioactive.

"I don't have a problem being social. I can be social when I want to. I don't need someone setting things up behind my back." His voice is tinged with more anger, and I can sense it raging inside him like a cresting wave.

"Mikey, calm down. You're making more of this than it really is." He leans in and jabs his index finger into my chest.

"That's it. You don't understand. You don't ambush someone you supposedly care about like that. You don't understand how it's weird being social without having a drink. I don't need this crap, especially from you." Mikey storms out of the bookstore. I quietly power walk behind him and call out his name without causing a scene or raising my voice. Fellow customers stare at us. I'm embarrassed. When we reach his car, he hops in and rolls down his window.

"Just leave me alone. I'll talk to you later, you stupid jerk!"

"But . . . I . . ." The words disappear from my mouth. I'm stunned. What did I do wrong? Mikey backs up and pulls away. His Volkswagen Rabbit speeds down Granite Street, and the car's red, circular, rear lights fade in the distance.

I stand there alone in the parking lot with my mouth wide open and my heart stomped on. I try to make sense of what just happened. This is not how I had envisioned the night. All I wanted was for Mikey to meet my friend, and while that part went well, the rest of the night blew up in my face. What's going on?

Mikey acted the way he did whenever he drank too much over a year ago. The blue-eyed Dr. Jekyll and Mr. Hyde has returned but without alcohol as his elixir. And perhaps that's the problem. He misses his liquor, his social lubricant. How am I going to fix this before Christmas? Maybe I can't. With my hands in my pocket and my head down, I slowly walk to my Jeep. Tears stream down my face. As I drive home, I wonder why this is happening again.

21

Carlos

"Carlito, I'm so happy that you are coming home for *la Navidad*. Remember how we baked gingerbread cookies, *nuestra tradicion?*" Mami says, her back turned to me as she pulls a pan of warm, baked cookies out of the oven. She wears her favorite red apron that reads "Welcome to my *cocina!*" I sit at our small wooden table in the corner of the kitchen and watch her work her holiday magic. Mami's hibiscus plants sway outside along the kitchen window, which offers a lovely view of her backyard garden. Mami always enjoyed washing dishes or cooking food while keeping a watchful eye on her flowers.

"I loved those cookies. They were the best. You never told me the recipe. What did you put in them?" Mami plops the pan on the kitchen counter and lets the army of gingerbread cookies rest and cool. The aroma of freshly baked, succulent cookies fills the room as if this were a small bakery on Calle Ocho. Mami wipes her hands clean on her apron, unfastens it, and sits with me. She leaves the apron on the table.

"*Bueno,* I put sugar, flour, *y* ginger." She points to her fingers as she names each ingredient. She goes on to explain the recipe. I write it down on a paper towel.

"But you know what the most important ingredient is, *hijo?*"

"More sugar?"

"Ah no!"

"Evaporated milk?"

"No, *niño!* These are cookies, not a flan!"

"So what's your secret ingredient, Mami?"

"Love. You need to make the cookies with love. That's why they taste so good, because I love you and your *hermana* and your Papi very much."

Mami gets up, stands behind me, and brushes the back of my wavy hair with her hand. She then kisses the top of my head. When I was little, she always did that as I sat down at the kitchen table to write my essays and solve my math equations. Behind me on the wall are framed images of various types of coffee mugs.

"So write this recipe down. I want you to make cookies, the Martin way, for *la Navidad.* Lourdes is not very good in the kitchen. She takes after *tu papa.*" I laugh because Lourdes isn't the best cook, but she tries. The food is edible and so far, no one has suffered massive food poisoning.

"You will continue this tradition from now on. *Comprende?* Just because I am not there doesn't mean that *nuestra familia* can't have our holiday cookies. I need you to do this for me and for the whole family. Make me proud, *hijo,* but you always do whether you realize it or not." She hugs me from behind my chair again.

Mami walks away from the table, slips on her apron, and checks on the gingerbread men. They've cooled down. She takes a bite from one of the golden brown cookies and she says "Mmm" the whole time. The feeling is mutual, and I decapitate a gingerbread man with my teeth. These cookies are to die for.

I scarf down the rest of the cookie in one big bite. Mami carries the tray and starts walking toward the dining room. She looks back at me and wipes her hand against her apron.

"You will do fine. Just follow my recipe and follow your heart. I love you, *hijo.*"

"I love you too, Mami."

As she walks into the dining room, I scoot my wooden chair back against the red tile and get up to follow her. I want to keep talking. I miss these moments. They calm and soothe me despite their fleeting nature. But when I open the door, I suddenly wake up. I'm lying in my bed in Cambridge and feeling disoriented. I rub circles around my eyes with my knuckles and let out a couple of long yawns. My mouth is so dry, and I suddenly have an urge for Mami's cookies. My stomach growls, performing its own symphony. I prop myself on my left side, grab my journal and scribble down Mami's recipe before it escapes me. On the last line I write: **Make the cookies with love.** And I will, on Thursday, as soon as I land in Miami.

Christmas was very important to Mami. It was time to bond as a family besides our end-of-the-school-year trips. Without her to anchor the holiday, I don't know what to expect this year. Mami was like the star that shines and completes the top of a Christmas tree. Without her guiding presence, I'm not sure we should even honor Christmas, but I know she would want us to. I climb out of bed, drag myself to the kitchen and brew some *café* to wake me up. My house phone rings. It's Tommy.

"Hey. Just calling to see how you were doing. Are you ready for your flight?"

I add some coffee to the filter. I lean against the kitchen counter and face the living room.

"I just need to pack and I'll be all set. What about you? Did Mikey sleep over last night?" I yawn like a lion.

Tommy takes a deep breath.

"Nope. He took off after you left the bookstore. He was pissed at me. Wicked mad!"

"Why?"

"Because of Project Mikey Ambush. He saw right through it. He didn't appreciate it. He thought you were nice though."

"*Ay,* Tommy . . . I'm sorry to hear that. This is all my fault."

"It's okay. You were trying to help. I'm just stumped. I don't know why he's so upset. It was pretty innocent."

The coffee machine hisses and fills the apartment with its delicious aroma. My stomach continues to rumble from the dream.

"I think there's more going on with Mikey than he's letting on. It's his first year of recovery. That's the hardest part in the process."

"Yeah, I know that, but it's not like I got drunk in front of him. If anything, I've been there to listen to him, and I don't drink or go out to bars, out of respect for him. Geez, what else am I doing wrong?"

"Listen to me, *chico.* It's not you. It's him. It might be too much for him to handle you and staying sober. He's probably stressed out."

"Well, I didn't deserve the way he treated me at the bookstore. I've been so supportive."

"I know you have, but you can't fix everything that is wrong with Mikey. He's dealing with a lot. Let him be for now. *Bueno,* we'll have fun in Miami. I leave this afternoon and you leave to-morrow, right?"

"Yeah, Miami. I can't wait!" says Tommy, his voice suddenly lifting.

"Okay, *loco,* I need to get ready. I'll call you when I land."

"Thanks, Carlos. Talk to you soon."

"Adios!"

My coffee's ready, so I pour myself a large cup and add some milk. I hold the mug to my lips and savor the warm, fresh taste. I imagine drinking it with Mami's cookies. I'll do my best to repli-cate her sweet creations the way she would want me to. Miami, here I come.

22

Tommy

It's been two days since my clash with Mikey at the bookstore, and I still haven't heard from him. I decided to leave him alone. Work has been a great distraction. I wrote a story on how holiday shoppers use online wish lists more often to buy gifts for friends. It's another fun holiday feature, my last for the year. I won't return to work until after the New Year.

When I get stressed or upset, I clean relentlessly, which is what I'm doing now. I take my Swiffer and wipe my Pergo floors clean in a rhythmic motion while Gloria Estefan sings on my laptop. I vacuum my condo, and wipe down the bathroom mirror and TV monitor with a cloth. I'm a robot in motion. I want to leave my place neat before I take off to Miami later this afternoon. A light snow has fallen over the city, and as much as I like the snow, I've grown tired of it already. I've been mentally traveling to Miami and imagining the warm tropical air and thick heat, which can feel like steam rising from an iron. *Ahh,* home! As I stand and daydream in the middle of my living room, surrounded by posters of Miami and Fort Lauderdale, my buzzer sounds. I press the intercom. "Tommy, it's Mikey. I'm outside." My mental mirage suddenly collapses like a falling stage curtain. He better be here to apologize. I won't let Mikey ruin my feel-good Miami vibe.

"I'll come outside. Stay there." I adjust my shirt, and put on a baseball cap because my hair is messy and resembles a Chia Pet more than a human head. I slip on my blue puffy jacket and climb the five steps up to the lobby where Mikey greets me with a tight grin that says he knows he messed up. He bites down on his tongue and sticks it out. I've grown immune to it.

"Hey, cutie!" He moves in to hug me.

"Hey, yourself."

"Can we talk?"

"Sure. Let's go outside." With my right foot, I clear one of the cement steps of old leaves. We sit down.

"What's on your mind?" I ask, turning away.

"Look, I just wanted to apologize for my behavior the other night. That wasn't me. I don't know what got into me. I should have never said those things to you."

"But you did, and they hurt. I was trying to do something nice, introduce you to a good friend, and you become a total jerk."

Mikey puts his arm over my shoulder. I face the street ahead.

"I've been having some trouble dealing with the alcoholism lately. I thought if I didn't go to a bar that I would be okay, but it's not that simple, cutie. I'm having flashbacks to last year and all the gay holiday parties and the drinking. I hear about people going out and drinking and having fun. I just feel frustrated and isolated. I guess I took that out on you."

"You think?" I interrupt, facing him.

"Let me finish. I miss drinking. I miss my friends, who don't want to meet up with me unless it's at a bar, and I can't do that. I'm adjusting to this new sober life. It's been a little hard." He looks down and flicks a leaf with his finger.

"But you have your AA meetings. That's what they're there for." The small orange commuter trolley rumbles by across the street.

"Well . . ." Mikey says, his eyes on the leaf. "I have to tell you something. I haven't been completely honest with you, Tommy."

Now, I don't know what to think. What else hasn't he been truthful about?

"I stopped going to the meetings," Mikey reveals in a soft voice. He still looks down and then away. Embarrassment is scrawled all over his face.

"But why? You need them." Confusion and shock crest inside me.

"I don't like sitting in a circle with a bunch of strangers talking about my feelings. It's just not me, cutie. I haven't been to a meeting in a month. Instead, I've been reading books about Buddhism and spirituality."

I stand up and take a deep breath. This is crazy. I try to process what he has said, but I'm still in shock.

"Mikey, you need those AA meetings or you should at least see a therapist. I can do only so much for you. I'm your boyfriend, not a therapist. I'm not equipped for this. You need some professional help in dealing with this."

Mikey gets up, and I follow him to the building's steel railing that faces the parking lot. We position ourselves to lean over the railing. Down the street, cars speed by and a lone jogger runs and breathes heavily.

"I know. I know. I'll get some help. I'm a counselor. I know all this stuff. It's just different when you're on the other side of it. There's something else you don't know about me."

I brace myself against the railing. What other bomb can Mikey drop on me this afternoon? Where is this all coming from? How did I miss the signs?

"Out with it," I say, my puffs of breath marked by the forty-degree weather.

"Last year, I was really social because of the alcohol. When I don't drink, I can be very shy, painfully shy."

"You?" I say incredulously.

"Yeah, cutie. I feel very awkward in social settings or gatherings. The beer would take care of that. And now that I don't drink, I don't feel comfortable being around new people."

Mikey smiles downward.

"But with me, you're very chatty and gregarious. You're not shy at all."

"That's the thing. I already knew you, and I feel I can be myself around you. When you ambushed me with your friend, I had all this anxiety inside me. I was panicky. I took out it on you, and I regret that. You were trying to be nice and introduce me to another nice person. I'm so sorry, Tommy. I'll never do that again."

I've heard those words before, a soundtrack that replays in my mind. The first time was last year when he swore he wouldn't drink. Now he's swearing he won't disappoint me, but he always does. He deflates my spirit with his empty promises.

"This is a lot to absorb all at once. I don't know what else to say. I can be there for you, but not if you keep disappointing me like this. I don't deserve this. No one does. My life should be free of strife. I deserve to be happy, in a stable relationship."

Mikey gently grabs me by the waist and turns me toward him. We face one another, brown eyes to blue eyes gazing at each other.

"All I know is that I love you very much, Tommy Perez, and I want you in my life, and I will do whatever it takes to control my moods and actions."

"I love you too, but you need to work on yourself a bit more. Why don't we use this time during the holidays as way of taking a break? I'm not talking about a break-up or anything but as a time to figure out what's going on and where things stand. I need this time away."

"I can still call you while you're in Miami, right?" Mikey fingers the back of my bushy curls.

"Of course. I want to hear your voice on Christmas Day. But seriously, Mikey, please take this time to really reflect on your alcoholism and your shyness. You should find someone to talk to, maybe your sponsor. You need a different kind of support than I can offer."

"I know, and I'll get it."

We hug in a strong embrace and kiss outside my building.

"I promise I'll get better."

"I know, but you have to do that on your own. I've run out of second chances. Got it?"

"Yeah, cutie."

"While you're here, I could use another kind of support. Can you take me to the airport? My flight is in a few hours."

"Sure, cutie. Anything for you."

Mikey wraps his arm around me. We venture back inside my building into the warmth of my condo. But his revelation stays with me. I rode this rollercoaster relationship once with Mikey. I don't want the drama and emotional turmoil that Mikey manages to import into my life. Something has emotionally shifted within me. A brick wall has begun to ribbon my heart. A few days in Miami with my family is exactly what I need right now. No matter what happens in my life, being back home helps me put things in perspective. Maybe there, I'll realize what I should do about Mikey, but I think I already know.

23

Carlos

Ay, Miami! How did I ever live in this thick heat? It envelopes me like the suffocating steam from a sauna as I stand and wait outside Miami International Airport in Arrivals for Papi and Lourdes. I immediately peel off my coat and baseball cap to cool off. I leave on my *Made In America With Cuban Parts* T-shirt and blue jeans. The city's hot breath causes my clothes to stick to my body. Even at the airport, the tropical vapor ruffles my hair. I definitely don't miss this uncomfortable heat at all. I need another shower.

One by one, cabs slowly pull up toward me and then drive off when I don't acknowledge them. Idling rental cars and vans wait for customers. With the back of my hand, I wipe off a film of sweat from my forehead. *Que calor!* Just when I think I am going to dissolve into a Latino puddle of sweat, I spot Papi's light blue Chevrolet Impala approaching. He always loved that car, and he treats it as though it were a Cadillac. It's ten years old and in mint condition. Papi and Lourdes wave from the front seats. As Papi turns on his hazard lights, Lourdes steps out and hugs me. Papi follows and pats me hard on the back.

"Did you have a good trip, Carlito?" Papi greets me. He loads my luggage into the trunk as the soundtrack of the beeping cars and revving engines plays in the background.

"Yeah, it was a smooth flight. Very packed. But no food. I had to drink a Sprite to hold me over. *Tengo hambre!*"

"Well, some Versailles take-out will take care of that," Lourdes says, grabbing my coat. "We picked up some food on the way. We got your favorite, chicken steak with plantains."

"Yum! I can't wait. Thanks, Lou. I'll eat it on the way to the house." Papi shuts the trunk, and we all hop into the cool, air-conditioned car.

"No problem, little brother. It's nice to have you back home," she says, as Papi pulls away from the airport and toward Coral Gables . . . home.

Fifteen minutes later, we pull into the driveway of our butter-yellow house (Mami's favorite color). The image disturbs me. Mami's flowers wilt as if they're depressed, missing her presence. The grass lacks its verdant sheen. The tablet stones, which mark a trail from the sidewalk to the front door, are overgrown with weeds. The stones mix in with the grass. Mami would be so upset that her lawn and garden have been left unattended. It's not a complete mess, but it's definitely not the way it was.

As I step out of the car, I lean against its door and stare at our house. This house is me and all of me, and I've abandoned it. A cloud of guilt hovers over me for leaving this behind for Boston. So many layered memories float to the surface, and I remember them as if they happened yesterday. I remember how Mami squatted down and tended to her garden. She snipped some of her best blooms, wrapped them in newspaper, and offered them to guests. I recall how Lourdes confused the drive and reverse gears and almost crashed Mami's Toyota into the garage door when she learned to drive. The warm memory of shirtless Papi sitting in his beach chair and listening to a baseball game on his A.M. handheld radio flashes before me. I remember how Gata Linda, our fluffy gray outdoor cat, loved to lounge on the front door welcome mat that read *Casa Martin,* but guests could only read *Martin* because Linda's big furry butt blocked the first word. The mat was her special place. It was next to the sprouting potted fern, which she chewed on to get our attention, much to Mami's dismay. Gata Linda perked up and meowed whenever one of us dashed in and out of the house. I bet Linda keeps Mami company in heaven—or at the very least, in her dreams.

We stroll into the house and a familiar scent of home embraces me. The air of my childhood. It's a mix of old wood, lavender air freshener, and a hint of Mami's perfume. Even though it's been a year since she died, the fragrance remains, and in a way, so does Mami.

With my carry-on bag on my shoulder, I hang a left from the tiled hallway and head toward my bedroom. The door creaks open, and the sight of my room makes me feel like a kid. But the room feels and looks much smaller than I remember. Inside, I notice Lourdes has cleaned up. The smell of Lysol mountain scent permeates the room. My twin bed continues to wear my light-blue comforter and yellow sheets. My graduation diplomas from elementary school through high school bedeck the space above my wooden desk, which is strewn with my old literature books from high school and college. On the second shelf sits a photo of Mami and me kneeling in front of her garden with Gata Linda at our feet. A smile appears on my face.

As I look around, I realize that these walls don't contain much of me anymore. Lourdes has slowly taken it over as an extended office for her real estate business. She gathered some of my belongings, from my high school yearbook to my notebooks and essays, and stacked them inside a white plastic bin in the corner. At least my pair of tennis rackets, which I used to play with Mami when I was ten years old, leans against the corner of the closet door. Lourdes also took down some of my posters of Spain, Cuba, and France, places I would like to visit one day. I can't be too upset with my sister because, technically, I no longer live here. When I moved, I packed everything I could and exported it to Cambridge. What's left behind are items that I didn't want to take with me such as my old clothes and old student papers. Sleepy from my morning flight (or the Miami heat), I decide to take a nap in my old bed, the one Papi and Mami surprised me with when I turned seven years old. It squeaks whenever I sit on it, but it's the most comfortable bed I've ever had. I slip out of my sneakers, stretch, lay down, and pass out. *Que rico!*

Later that afternoon, I lazily climb out of bed, stretch like a cat, and head into the kitchen for something to drink. After grabbing a glass of milk, I bound into the living room and notice there's no Christmas tree by the chimney. None of our stockings, each with our names sewn on the rims, hang along the mantle. Each wall features a framed large picture of the family. There's a photograph of Lourdes's tenth birthday party. We are sandwiched between our parents and a princess-themed cake. Another framed photograph captures the four of us standing in front of the garden before we drove to Marco Island for vacation. I was eighteen at the time. The most recent photograph was taken two years ago before Mami got sick. It shows Mami with a big smile on her face. She wears a pink blouse and white pants as she embraces all three of us with her head leaning against my shoulder. After I take a personal inventory of the frames, I notice Lourdes lying on the rattan sofa with the floral print. She is reading *Latina* magazine.

"You're finally up, little brother! We thought you were going to sleep through your vacation." She perks up on the sofa. I sit down next to her.

"It was the flight. I'm just tired." I yawn and sip some milk. "How come there's no Christmas tree?"

"Because Papi didn't want one. We shouldn't be celebrating Christmas, Carlos. Not with Mom gone."

"I know, but shouldn't we respect Mom's wishes? You know she would have wanted us to at least have a tree." I leaf through the fashion and sports magazines on the coffee table. My feet press against the cold beige Mexican tile that lines most of the house's floors. The central air quietly hums in the background, and the afternoon's natural light slants through the window blinds, casting shadows on the tile.

"Then you talk to Papi! He snapped at me when I brought it up, but that was before we knew you were coming. We thought you were going to stay in Boston for Christmas with your friend Tommy." As she talks, her eyes remain fixed on the magazine.

"Maybe we can buy a tree. It's not too late. Christmas is the day after tomorrow."

"Then talk to Papi! Besides, picking out the tree was something you and Mami did together. Papi also thought it would be too hard on you to do that this year without her."

"Lou, what hasn't been hard without Mami around? I think in her honor, we should find a big, beautiful tree. Speaking of Papi, where is he?"

"He's at the store, checking up on his employees. You know he can't stay away from the business too long. It's in his blood. It's almost an obsession."

"Yeah, I remember. While he was always working, we were here with Mami. When he was here, he was calling the store. Anyway, how about if we surprise him with a tree? We can go to the lot on LeJeune Road, buy a tree, and have it decorated before he gets back."

"What if he gets mad?" Lourdes says, now looking up at me over the rim of the magazine.

"Well, you can deal with him. You're closer to him than I am."

"Don't say that. He loves us both. Equally."

"Yeah, but he's more comfortable with you, Lou." She puts down the magazine, and her eyebrows narrow. She leans in closer to me.

"What makes you think that?"

"I was always with Mami, and you were always with Papi. That's how it always was. I don't know why, but it was."

Lourdes tilts her head and frowns.

"Not exactly. That's how you saw things, Carlos. I loved Mami and Papi equally. It didn't matter which one I was with. I was happy either way, but you never wanted to hang out with Papi, and I always noticed that. So I did my best to be there when you weren't, to show him that at least one of his kids wanted to spend time with him."

Que cosa? I'm confused. I was always with Mami because I got along better with her. Papi was always with Lourdes. We each clung to a different parent. It happens.

"You're wrong, Lou. I hung out with Mami more because Papi was always working. If he wanted to spend time with me, he could have," I say, in an accusatory tone.

Lourdes shakes her head and sighs.

"You've got it all wrong, little brother. Papi sensed that you never wanted to hang out with him, so he gravitated toward me. Mami tried to fill that void by always being with you and by doing things together as a family. For a teacher, you can be pretty dense sometimes."

"But we don't really get along," I blurt out, leaning back against the soft rattan sofa. My right leg folds across my left knee. I look away.

"Because you guys never really tried, or at least you didn't. It's this stupid Latin macho thing. Instead of dealing with your issues, you go to someone else and run away. Jesus! He's okay with you being gay. He had trouble with it at first, but Mami helped him deal with it. So you don't have any excuses for not having hung out with him more when you were younger."

I evaluate Lourdes's words: *"Papi sensed that you never wanted to hang out with him, so he gravitated toward me."* I would never intentionally hurt Papi like that. Did I really push him aside all these years? *Ay no!* It can't be.

"But Lou, he never made any time for me. He never seemed cool with the gay thing."

"*Ay,* Carlos! He worked so hard so we could have a nice life, this beautiful house, an education. You always seemed jealous of his hours at the business. He tried to make time for you, but you always pushed him away. And he was cool with you being gay, after a while. Didn't he meet and get along with your friend Tommy? Papi knew he was gay, but he also sensed he was your friend, the platonic kind. Papi has come a long way. Think about it. If Papi spent more time with you when you were younger and if you had let him, I bet you guys would be closer.

"Look at what happened in Boston during Thanksgiving. Papi kept talking about how *his son* took him to Fenway Park. He showed his store employees your photos. He's very proud of you, little brother, even though he might not always show it."

"He did?" I rub my fingers against my temples and try to process everything Lourdes is sharing with me. My eyes begin to glisten at the thought of Papi flashing our photos to his customers and employees. It really was a fun night, exploring Fenway. It's a recent memory that we made that makes me smile.

"He framed one of the photographs and hung it in his office. The top of the frame reads: *Having a ball!* Listen, little brother, I know we've never been super close, mostly because you thought you knew everything when you clearly did not, but we have only one parent left. We need to make the best of our relationship with Papi. I'm close to Papi, but he needs both his children, now more than ever that Mami is gone. I can't do it all by myself here."

When did Lourdes become so wise? Here, I thought I was her pesky little brother. It's not that I thought she didn't care for me. We never seemed to have a lot in common, but we did. We both loved our mother and father, in different ways. Shouldn't that be enough of a commonality?

"So how about if we go shopping for a tree? My treat. And we can decorate it before Papi gets home from work? It would be fun, Lou."

"I think Papi might like that. We need to make this house festive again, give it some life. Sometimes I think I'm going to see Mom in the kitchen when I wake up in the morning. It's been a hard adjustment. Having you here helps take the edge off, little brother, especially now during the holidays."

"I know the feeling. Everywhere I look, I think I see or hear Mami. I guess it takes time. Let me get changed, and we'll go to the tree lot. Later on, we can bake some of Mami's gingerbread cookies."

"But we don't have the recipe. She always did it from memory, and we forgot to get it from her," Lourdes says. She gets up and leaves the magazine on the glass coffee table. She begins to walk to her bedroom to change clothes.

"Actually, I do have the recipe. It's a long story," I call out to her.

As Lourdes gets ready, I scrutinize the framed photos on the walls again. In Lourdes's birthday photo, it's the four of us. I study it. Papi looks as if he's trying to show affection toward me. His eyes look downward, and he smiles in my direction. But my body language—my shoulders lean in the opposite direction—suggests that I was pulling away. Mami, with her tender grin, stood between us as a bridge. In the other photo, we stand as four in front of the house. The poses are similar. Papi stands behind me with his hands on my shoulder, and he smiles down at me. I scrutinize the photo some more, and I notice that my body shifted more toward Lourdes and Mami. I cast a similar pose in the other group photos. Could Lourdes be right? All this time, Papi tried to connect with me, but I passively kept him at bay and sought Mami for comfort. I blink back some tears at the realization. I have acted selfishly and hurtful toward my dad, Papi. A pang of shame overtakes me.

24

Tommy

Ahhh, Miami. The heat. The humidity. The traffic at the airport. The brightness of the South Florida sunlight. The swaying coconut palms on every median and block. Miami. I'm ready for the beach. I can't wait to bike along the boardwalk and Ocean Drive or run in mid-Beach.

Standing in my flip-flops, shorts, and Boston Red Sox T-shirt, I'm giddy at the airport waiting for the Perez cavalry. A flush of excitement fills me. Oh, I see them now, pulling up in Mary's champagne BMW. What a diva! What school teacher drives a BMW? She wears her Christian Dior sunglasses. To get my attention, she flashes the high beams of her lease (she cannot afford to own the car on her teacher's salary in Miami-Dade county). She pops the trunk, and I scurry around the car and dump my carry-on bag inside. I hop into the backseat where my mom scoots to make room.

"*Hola,* Tommy!" She plants a kiss on my cheek and squeezes it.

"*Niño,* I am going to cut your hair. It's longer than mine," my mother says, using her index and middle fingers to gesture scissors cutting.

"Please, Ma! You know you want this bush of curls for yourself instead of your flat, straight hair. By the way, you need to revisit Sami's salon. Your grays are showing."

"Ay, de verdad?" she says with concern, touching the top of her auburn hair.

"Just kidding, Ma."

She playfully squeezes my knee.

Papi, wearing his favorite Florida Marlins baseball cap, turns around from the front seat and pats me on the head and quietly smiles. With a look of sheer terror, he braces himself on the interior frame of the car as Mary prepares to pull away. She's an aggressive driver à la *Speed Racer.*

"Hi, Tomas! Did you have a good flight?" Mary greets me from the rearview mirror. She always calls me by my real name. I hate that.

"Yes, Mary. It was great."

"Well, that's good," Mary says in her monotone voice. That's all she ever says. *That's good.* She's in teacher-mode 24-7.

She pulls out of the airport, and we're on our way to *la playa,* Miami Beach. Home. As Mary treats the highway like her personal Indy 500, I tell them about Boston. I don't have much to say since we speak every night. Mami starts to rattle off all her imaginary illnesses.

"My arthritis is acting up. The pain travels from my head to my neck to my back and to my knees. This humidity is awful for my joints."

Mary lifts up her glasses and rolls her eyes at me through the rearview mirror as our mother, the hypochrondriac, complains once again about the humidity even though she grew up in Cuba and has lived in Miami Beach for forty years. She knows nothing but humidity. Papi turns around, gestures with his hand to his head that she's *loca,* and says, "What doesn't your mother have? The pharmacists at Walgreens know her by first name. They see her coming, and they close down because they know your mama will be there for hours." My mother playfully hits him on the wrist, and he laughs to himself in the front seat.

"Ya, Pepe!" my mother scolds him with a glare that could probably replicate Superman's heat vision.

We're climbing the first bridge of the Julia Tuttle Causeway heading east. Mary plays her Enya CD. In the distance, a canyon of pink, white, and light blue condos and hotels rise along Collins Avenue against the Atlantic Ocean. The sunlight shimmers against Biscayne Bay like aqua crystals. Grand colorful cruise ships sit in their berths waiting to embark on their fun voyages. Whenever I visit, I find it hard to leave. I call this condition the Miami blues. I get used to Miami all over again and pick up where I left off before I moved away. This place is so beautiful, a tropical wonderland. I've learned to appreciate it more now that I live 1,600 miles north. Maybe one day, I'll move back. For now, my life and career is in Boston. I have too many good things happening for me there. If I could cut myself in half and leave a part of myself in Miami and a part in Boston, I would. When that is a remote possibility, I'll keep flying back and forth until I decide where to permanently pot myself like one of these coconut palms we just passed.

"*Oye,* do you guys think I can invite my friend Carlos for Christmas?" I lean in through the arm rest from the back seat.

"*Ese es tu amiguito de* Boston, the teacher?" Ma asks.

"The one whose mother died?" Mary follows.

"Yeah, that's the one. I thought it would be nice if he could hang out at our house for a bit."

"Of course, Tomasito. *Invitalo,*" Dad says.

"I can make him some of my flan, but I can't eat too much. It gives me gas, *tu sabes,*" my mother announces, rubbing her stomach to emphasize her point.

Papi turns around and repeats the *she's-una-loca* look. I raise my eyebrows in loving agreement.

"Uh, thanks, Ma. We'll keep you away from the flan."

As Mary guns the BMW over the second Julia Tuttle bridge toward Miami Beach and our early grave, I think to myself that it's good to be back in Miami.

25

Carlos

It's *Noche Buena,* the first without Mami. Papi decided that we should have a quiet evening at home. We ordered pork, yucca, black beans, and rice from Versailles' take-out. Lourdes popped in a CD of Christmas carols in Spanish by Jon Secada and Christina Aguilera. As we sit around the table, we reminisce over some of our funniest Christmas stories, like the time Papi dressed up as Santa Claus with sunglasses for my kindergarten class.

"Papi, I knew something was strange that day. Since when did Santa wear sunglasses?" I sip some red wine.

"*Oye,* it was sunny that day in the North Pole. The reindeer had sunglasses too. You and your friends believed me."

"Well, not completely. When you left, we saw you changing out of your suit. Your old Impala was parked near the classroom window and I remember thinking, 'Is Papi Santa Claus?'"

"Actually, I thought you looked cool, Papi. The photos were hysterical," Lou pipes in from across the table. "Mami sent them out that year as our holiday card."

We all laugh at the memory. The story always made Mami laugh hysterically because she was in the classroom that day. She had baked her gingerbread cookies for the class.

"Remember when *tu mama* bought the fake big snowman and put him outside the house to stand in the garden?"

"*Ay, Papi!* Who could forget that? She put a scarf on him and a bunch of hibiscus flowers in his hands," Lourdes recalls. "And all the little kids in the neighborhood would stop by and take pictures with him. What did Mami call him?"

"Salvadore!" I blurt out.

"Yeah, Salvadore the Snowman," Lourdes says fondly.

"Why don't we do a toast to Mami? She really made Christmas so special every year. I wish she was here. This was her favorite time of year."

Papi's eyes sadden. Lourdes looks downward and takes another sip from her wine. Jon Secada croons "The First Noel" in the background.

"Okay, I'll begin. On this night of family and faith, I want to wish you a very Merry Christmas, Mami. We love you, wherever you are. You're not here physically, but you're in our hearts. *Te quiero,* and Salvadore the Snowman misses you too!" A comforting feeling of warmth suddenly embraces me. I look up at the framed photo of all of us on the mantle. A smile flickers across my face.

Papi and Lourdes clink my glass.

"To Mami!" they say in unison.

We drain our flutes.

After dinner, we continue with tradition. We gather in the living room by the Christmas tree. Yesterday after work, Papi walked into the living room, and he was pleasantly surprised to see the tree. He stood before it, studied the ornaments, and quietly grinned. The tree stands eight-feet tall, and the bright white star on top barely touches the ceiling. Since we brought the tree home, an evergreen fragrance has scented the entire house like a holiday perfume. It's almost like Christmas of years past. *Almost.* To help recreate the scene from last year, I bring out a plate topped with gingerbread cookies. I baked them yesterday with Lourdes before she went for her daily one-hour jog. I baked a batch of twenty, and these little men taste pretty good.

As we settle into our sofa, Lourdes suddenly gets up with a

smirk on her face and announces, "I'll be right back." She disappears down the hallway to her bedroom.

Papi then turns to me.

"Carlito, tomorrow I need your help with a project."

"Sure, what is it?"

"We can talk about that tomorrow. Are you going to be around in the afternoon?"

"Of course. Tommy invited me to his parents' house, but that's later. Whatever you need, I'm here for you, Papi." He puts his hand on my shoulder and gently squeezes. I munch on one of the cookies, which rains crumbs on my shirt.

A few seconds later, Lourdes returns with two gift boxes. I dash to my bedroom and grab their gifts. Papi does the same. We meet again in the living room, where we exchange gifts. I furiously rip off the holiday wrapping, which litters the tile floor along with some cookie crumbs. As we open the boxes, we devour gingerbread men. I'm on my third one. They're delicious. I think I nailed Mami's recipe.

"Carlito, these taste like your Mami's."

"Really?"

"Yeah, little brother, you managed to replicate her cookies. How did you do that?"

"I did it the way Mami baked them, with love and lots of sugar and dabs of ginger." I wink at my sister.

Lourdes's gift to me: a green cardigan and a $100 gift card to Wal-Mart, in case I need to buy groceries or knickknacks for the apartment.

Papi's gift to me: a new leather wallet and a gift card to Barnes & Noble, in case I need to buy new books for school or for pleasure.

I gave Lourdes some gift cards to her favorite stores. I gave Papi a special Red Sox World Series photo book and a DVD produced by *The Boston Daily*, which Tommy ordered for me with his employee discount.

"*Gracias,* Carlito. This is a great gift. I am going to show it to my baseball team at Tropical Park Sunday."

"Great, Papi. What's the name of your team again?"

"The Cuban Cigars!"

I start to laugh.

"I guess you guys are smoking," I say.

"More like gasping," Papi interrupts. "*Somos viejos!*"

We stack our gifts into individual piles, and Papi informs us that there are two more gifts. He heads back to his bedroom and returns with two small jewelry boxes. One for me and one for Lourdes. Papi watches with a tender expression as we carefully open our gifts.

"These are from your Mami. She bought these for you last year and wanted you to have them this Christmas. She didn't want you to think she forgot about you this year."

Ay dios mio! I am completely caught off guard. My emotions, like an incoming tide, overwhelm me. Tears creep down my face. Lourdes looks up and blinks back her tears. We look at each other in amazement of our mother. She always thought of everything. She always thought of us. How did she have time to buy these during the last few months she was in hospice care?

I open the box. Inside is a new silver watch. It catches the glint of the tree's blinking lights. I turn it over and an inscription reads: *Carlito, I am always with you, every minute, every hour, every day. Te quiero, Mami.* I wear it on my right wrist, and I caress this beautiful gift with my index finger. Silently, I thank Mami.

Lourdes holds up her gift, which is a pearl necklace. She smiles, snaps it on and pulls out her long hair from under it. She fingers each pearl like it's the finest gem in the world. Lourdes reads the note that came in the box.

For my beautiful daughter, the pearl in my heart. Te quiero!

I scoot over and admire Lou's necklace as she gushes over my watch. Papi grabs his digital camera and photographs us with our new gifts. I hold up my watch, and Lou poses, pointing to her necklace.

"*Feliz Navidad, familia,*" Papi says. The camera flashes and electronically snaps. "Merry Christmas, Mami," we say in unison.

I spend most of Christmas morning in the pantry, answering phone calls from my aunts, uncles, and distant cousins I haven't seen in months. I constantly have to click from one line to the other on the house phone because of the flurry of incoming calls. Since I haven't been to Miami since I moved, I have a lot of people to catch up with. At noon, Tommy's name pops up on my cell phone. When I answer, he immediately greets me with, "*Feliz Navidad,* dude!" in his usual chipper tone.

"Merry Christmas, *loco!* What are you up to? Are you in Miami?"

"Of course. I arrived yesterday afternoon. *Ahhh.* I love it here. How was your *Noche Buena?*"

As I talk, my eyes roam out the window to the wilting hibiscus flowers and gardenia tree. Before I head back to Boston, I am going to try and revive them.

"It was pretty nice. I got a gift from my mother."

"*Que cosa?*" A loud clack follows. I think Tommy dropped his phone.

"Are you there, *loco?*"

"Yeah, I just dropped my cell. What did you mean you got something from your mother?" I rest my face against my right fist and explain.

"Mami left Lourdes and me gifts. She knew this Christmas would be hard without her, and she wanted us to know that she was thinking of us."

"Carlos, that is, wow, amazing. I don't know what to say. What did she give you?"

"A beautiful watch with an inscription. I'm wearing it now."

"I can't wait to see it. I wish I could have met your mother, *chico*. She sounds like she was an incredibly sweet woman."

"I know, *loco*. Anyway, how's your Christmas going?"

"We just exchanged gifts, and we're about to have our holiday brunch. It's one big meal for the entire day. You're still coming over later, right?"

"Yeah. I have to do something later with my father, but I should be free in the afternoon. I can't wait to meet your parents and sister."

"Cool. See you later."

"Merry Christmas, *loco.*"

"You too, Carlos."

Two hours and fifteen phone calls later, I've succeeded in catching up with the entire Martin family. Some neighbors also called and said they would drop by and see me before I leave for Boston. I stretch and rise from the small wooden coffee table in the pantry when Papi enters the kitchen. He grabs a Materva soda can and pulls the lid open, unleashing an oozing, fizzing sound. He approaches me with a gentle expression on his face.

"Can you help me with something?" He takes a swig from the sweet golden soda.

"Yeah, Papi. What do you want me to do? You've been so mysterious."

"*Bueno,* come with me to the bedroom, and I'll show you. I think it's time that we do this."

I follow Papi down the hallway to his bedroom. I haven't been in here since Mami passed away. When I walk in, I gasp. Mami's jewelry, keepsakes, and clothing are displayed on the bed. I wasn't expecting this. He wants to give away some of Mami's belongings, and in a way, I understand why. I can't imagine what it must be like for my father to have these constant reminders in their bedroom.

"*Ay, Papi.* Do we have to? Are you sure?" My eyes start to well up.

"It's time, Carlito. *Tu hermana* has already picked out what she wants. Now it's your turn. She would want you to have some of her favorite things, in case you have children in the future, perhaps a daughter. I didn't want to wait until your next trip. It's too . . ." Papi sighs sorrowfully and continues, "hard to have these things here."

It's bittersweet for me to see what is displayed on the bed. Mami's favorite blouses and pants. A neat row of bracelets, necklaces, and brooches. Some are gifts that I gave her over the years. They include ceramic mugs, earrings, and Mother's Day and birthday cards. Several of her weathered gardening books sit on the corner of the bed. Mami's presence is very strong in this room because all her favorite things are here. They carry her essence. One by one, I hold the various pieces of jewelry and immediately picture them on her. I smell her blouses and pants and they exude her scent, a mix of lavender and an Estée Lauder floral perfume. A shawl that she would wear out to family dinners and functions still has some of her light brown strands of hair.

"Papi, I can't do this. We should leave her things here." I stand at the edge of the bed. Papi puts his right arm around me.

"These are my gifts to you and Lourdes. Your sister took your mami's wedding ring because she wants to wear it the day she gets married. She also took some of her gold earrings to give to her future children. She wants to keep some of the dresses that your mother wore and adored. I'm keeping some of the jewelry, the gifts I have given to your mama from over the years. I want to keep those forever, *hijo*."

Papi and I sit at the edge of the bed, and I caress each item. Seeing these familiar pieces of clothing and jewels before me only underscores that Mami is gone forever and that Papi, Lourdes, and I are really on our own. All we have is each other. As much as I miss her, I can't imagine what these last few months must have been like for Papi. He has been constantly surrounded by Mami's spirit. I can't blame him for wanting to part with some of these items. I realize this was a loving gesture, allowing Lourdes and me to take the items that will always remind us of the things she enjoyed. I do my best to be strong for Papi. I agree to take the gardening books and Mami's shawl, because it also carries her scent. I tell Papi that I would like some of her brooches. Not that I would wear them but to store in a jewelry box for safekeeping in Boston. It means so much to possess and care for these things. She always taught us to be compassionate and generous. In that spirit, I suggest that we donate whatever is left over of her clothing to the Salvation Army so that the gifts may continue giving.

"Papi, let's do some good with Mami's belongings. Her clothing can benefit a needy mother or family. Mami would like that. I can handle this for you."

"Okay, Carlito." I carefully gather my keepsakes and place them on Papi's nightstand table where their wedding photo sits under a lamp. He then helps me fold and pack some of the clothing into boxes for donation. After an hour, the bed is clear. We're done.

"*Gracias, hijo.* I couldn't have done this without you."

I hug my father as if I were hugging both my parents.

"I love you, Papi. I know I haven't always shown it, but I do. I have missed you more than you know. I'm so sorry for not being of more help around here and for pushing you away all these years. I should have stayed in Coral Gables with you and Lourdes."

Papi gently pulls away from the embrace and firmly plants his hands on my shoulders.

"You left to find a new life. Don't ever apologize for that," he says sternly. "You made a new home and found a new job. You did what you had to do, and I am very proud of you, Carlito, especially now, more than ever. I know your Mami is very proud of you too."

We stand here in the bedroom, the place where we lost Mami, but where my father and I found our way back to each other.

26

Tommy

"Welcome to *Casa* Perez!" I greet Carlos, as he walks up to my parents' house in mid-Miami Beach.

"*Loco,* this is a beautiful neighborhood. I passed all these mansions off Pine Tree Drive to get here." We hug at the front door.

"That's why my dad bought this little house . . . the neighborhood! Ricky Martin lives three blocks away. Jennifer Lopez's waterfront estate is not far either. This was a little fixer-upper that he bought with all the tips from his years of working at the restaurant. This is my dad's castle."

Once inside, I give Carlos a quick tour of the house. We cross into the dining room where Mary sits at the dinner table. She's online looking up real estate foreclosures. She wants to buy her own condo. I introduce them.

"So nice to meet you, Carlos. Tomas tells me that you teach high school, too," she says, getting up from the dining chair and hugging him.

"Yeah, one of the urban schools in Boston."

"How do you like it?" Mary says, settling back into her chair.

"It's been an adjustment from teaching at Braddock High in Kendall, but the kids are pretty good. Not too many behavorial problems."

"Yeah, tell me about it." Mary turns around from her chair and tucks her short, dark brown strands of straight hair behind her ears. She has a pixie cut. "One of my students was suspended for writing on the board that I like—well, I won't use such foul, disgusting language, but it wasn't very appropriate. Once I find myself a rich husband, I'm quitting my teaching job and traveling the world," Mary says, with an air of Latin royalty. My sister believes she's a lost princess, waiting for a prince to come and rescue her from this ordinary life. She lets out a big sigh. I stand behind her chair and gesture to Carlos that my sister resides in la-la land with Snow White and friends.

"Sorry to hear that, Mary. At least they arrested your student," Carlos says, looking at the framed pictures of fruits in our dining room.

"Thank God, they did. I gave him an F. Anyhoo, welcome to our little house." Her eyes return to her laptop and real estate search. Carlos tightly grins as I lead him to room number two: the kitchen. We catch my mother swaying and swirling by herself to the music of Shakira. Her back is turned, and she doesn't notice us right away.

"Ahem, Ma. This is my amigo Carlos, from Boston. Carlos, this is my mother, Gladys."

Mami turns around and flashes her big smile and says *"Hola."* She then rushes toward Carlos, grabs his hand, and starts dancing with him. Carlos looks at me, unsure of what to do.

"Very nice to meet you. Now *baila, chico, baila!"* she commands Carlos, who looks surprised. He lets my mom lead the way as if he had a choice. They stomp two steps forward, then two steps back. They swish to the left and sashay to the right. Carlos looks like he is trying to kill invisible roaches instead of dance. He starts giggling. I like seeing him like this.

"You go, Carlos! Kill those *cucarachas* even though you can't see them," I humor him. "Okay, Ma. Leave him alone. He just got here."

"Now I know who inspired your essay for 'A Cup of Cuban

Comfort,'" Carlos says, his eyebrows perking up. Shakira continues singing, rolling her Rs like she has a speech impediment.

My mom twirls him one more time toward me and releases him. She continues to dance with an invisible partner.

"*Quieres Coca Cola de dieta,* Carlos? We have plenty," she says, opening the refrigerator and unveiling rows of the soda's silver cans. She maintains her beat the whole time.

"No *gracias.* Maybe later but thank you Señora Perez."

"*Y* flan? You will like my flan!" From the refrigerator, she pulls out a plate topped with the large, sweet, golden dome of a flan. She holds it up to Carlos's face so he can smell it.

"I'm not that hungry right now. How about in a little while?" Carlos says, doing his best to be polite. In Latin households, it's hard to say no to food when the host insists on sharing.

"Okay. I will save you a slice. *Nuestra casa es tu casa. Feliz Navidad!*" My mother closes the refrigerator door and continues dancing, clapping her hands to each beat of the conga rhythm.

As we leave the kitchen, I softly tell Carlos, "Okay, so that's my mom. Let's go before she drags us into a conga line." We pass Mary in the dining room again as I lead Carlos to our A-shaped roofed living room, which opens to our sun-filled Florida room. My father is there watching an old John Wayne western on AMC.

"Pa, this is *mi amigo* Carlos, *de* Boston." My father slowly gets up from his brown leather recliner and shakes Carlos's hand. The room has two recliners and a small sofa that faces a large television. Each wall has a group shot of our family.

"*Bienvenido,* Carlos! How do you like Boston? Very cold, no?" Papi sits back down and adjusts his Florida Marlins baseball cap, which hides his thick, gray, curly hair.

"*Ay,* very cold but not too bad. I'm surviving."

"Do you live near Tommy?"

"Ah no. I live in Cambridge."

"Oh, Tommy used to live there. You are in his old *barrio.*"

"Yeah, something like that."

"Want to watch a western? They are my favorite movies. John Wayne. Clint Eastwood." My dad points to his DVD collection of classic westerns that line the top of the TV set.

I interrupt and save Carlos.

"Pa, we're gonna go to Lincoln Road soon, so maybe we'll watch a Western later." Carlos thanks me with his eyes. They shake hands again, and Papi returns to his John Wayne marathon. As we walk toward my bedroom, the sound of gunfire thunders from the Florida room TV set.

"Your parents are so cute, Tommy. You look just like your father, but you act like your mother. I can see where you get your ticks from. You have a sweet family, *chico,*" Carlos says as we walk on the creaking wooden floors that line the entire house. When we arrive at my bedroom, I sit at my desk, and Carlos lies down on my twin bed. He props his head with a pillow.

"And your sister reminds me of Lourdes. Not in looks but in personality. I bet they would get along. Maybe Lou can help your sister find a condo or something. She could use the extra business."

"That's a good idea, Carlos." As we talk about our *Noche Buenas,* Ceci, my white cat, pokes her head through an opening in the door and meows. She prances in. She looks up at me with her big brown eyes and then leaps onto my bed. She licks Carlos's arm.

"She's so beautiful!"

"And she knows it. She's a big whore. She goes with anyone who pets her." As Ceci's white bushy tail curls up in front of Carlo's face and tickles him, he laughs.

"So what's new with Mikey? Have you heard from him?"

"He sent me a text message wishing me a Merry Christmas and telling me how much he loves and misses me."

"And how do you feel about that, *loco?*"

I lean back in my chair and prop my feet on the edge of the bed near Ceci. I exhale sharply.

"I miss him too, but it's nice being home. I needed this break from him. I'll figure out what to do about Mikey when I get to Boston. Right now, I just want to disconnect from Boston, work, and him. Actually, the whole experience inspired me to write a short story."

Carlos massages Ceci's thick coat. Her tail sails in his face.

"Yeah? About what?"

"On the plane, I wrote a story about three guys who meet up every Thursday at Club Café, kind of like a same *Sex and the City* but in Boston. One of the guys is a Cuban writer from Miami who has a hot Italian friend. The Cuban guy ends up falling for a blue-eyed teacher who has drinking issues."

"Hmm. Sounds familiar, Tommy. Where do you get your material from?" he taunts.

"I don't know. It just comes to me. Anyway, I wrote a continuation of the story this morning, like another chapter but through the point of view of the Italian stud character. The story is writing itself."

"Is there a nice Cuban teacher from Miami in this story?" Carlos asks, sitting up with Ceci in his lap. He rubs her stomach, and she purrs like the feline slut that she is.

"Um, no. That could be another story. Actually, I think I can make this story into a book."

"That's a great idea, Tommy. There aren't a lot of gay novels about Hispanics. You'd do a great job. What would you call this?"

I lean in closer to Carlos and whisper, "*Boys of Boston!*"

"I love it! Hit it!" Carlos taps me on the arm like a little kid. "I'd read it! I think this could be very good for you, like therapy. Writing my thoughts down in a journal has helped me deal with my mother's loss and my issues with my father."

"Thanks, *chico*. I'm just seeing where the writing takes me. So how was your day with your father?"

Carlos takes in a deep breath before he recounts his day. He looks down at Ceci as he speaks. Behind him and above my bed is one of my front page stories from *The Miami News* that Papi framed for me.

"We spent the afternoon going through Mami's things. We're donating her clothing to charity. It was so hard doing that. I hope you and your sister never have to do that, but we got through it. We did it together. I've been feeling a lot closer to my dad lately. I think this is the project my mother told me about in a recent dream." Carlos then looks up with a half grin.

I grab Ceci from him and coddle her in my arms like a baby. She continues her loud purring. Carlos sits up on my bed.

"It's great that you guys are bonding. He's your only parent. You guys should be much closer than you've been."

"I know and we're getting there. From now on, I'm going to do my best to spend more quality time with Papi. I believe that is what Mami has been telling me all along. Even Dr. Solis suggested that."

As we talk, I hear a gentle knock on my door. It's my mother, and I tell her to come in.

She opens the door, and the bang bang bang of Western gunfire spills into my room from the TV. My mother appears with a sweet smile, holding two plates with slices of flan. She also brought two cans of Diet Coke.

"You cannot leave Miami until you eat my flan, Carlos." She hands him his plate, a spoon, and a Diet Coke.

"*Gracias, Señora Perez.*"

"*Ay niño,* call me Gladys!"

She then hands me my plate and kisses the top of my head.

"Enjoy!" she says, waving goodbye and strutting back into the hallway to her own beat.

Carlos folds his legs like a human pretzel. We dive into our flans.

"Thanks for having me over, Tommy. I feel like I'm home here," he says, taking a pull from the soda.

"You're welcome anytime," I say, watching Ceci leap out of my lap and onto the bed where she tries to lick Carlos's flan.

"Hey, want to go out later? I bet there'll be a lot of people on Lincoln Road tonight," I say with the pitch of a salesman. I take a sip from my soda.

"But it's Christmas. Who goes out on Christmas? Isn't that like blasphemous or something?"

I lean in closer to Carlos.

"Dude, this is Miami. After everyone eats and exchanges gifts, they go out and party. What better way to celebrate the holiday than by getting dressed up and hitting the town? I can lend you some clothes so you won't have to drive back to your dad's house in Coral Gables."

"Ah, you mean, your Costco brand of jeans and shirts? I think I'd rather drive back to the house and change clothes."

I glare at Carlos and feign offense. I then hold up Ceci in front of my face as if she were speaking for me.

"Don't knock it until you try it. Seriously, we'll go out and have fun. I know exactly what you should wear."

"Okay, okay. I'll wear your clothes. Want to go in my Papi's car? He let me take his beloved Chevy Impala, which is a gift in it-self," Carlos offers, taking Ceci back and holding her in his arms.

"I've got a better idea. We'll go in my ride."

"Your ride? What are you talking about, *loco?*"

"You'll see. It's how I get around in Miami Beach when I visit."

27

Carlos

It's 10 o'clock, or I think it is. I can't tell because my watch is shaking so much from the ride. Wearing matching black helmets, Tommy and I are bouncing along Pine Tree Drive on his Vespa. Yes, a Vespa.

"Isn't this fun?" Tommy shouts from the front seat of the scooter, which sounds like a buzzing chainsaw gone wild.

"Yeah, if you like to eat bugs," I shout back, bugs splattering the front of my helmet.

"This is the best way to get around South Beach. You always find parking in a Vespa."

"Um, I'll take your word for it. Just focus on the driving!" I yell, as sports cars and SUVs whoosh by us on Dade Boulevard. We pass the convention center on the left and Miami Beach High School on the right. As we approach the Holocaust Memorial, Tommy hangs a sharp left by the giant green hand that extends into the sky. I remember when I went on a field trip there with my students and they got to meet real Holocaust survivors who were there for a special presentation. Straight ahead is Meridian Avenue and Lincoln Road. A few minutes later, he pulls into a spot in front of David's Café. We dismount the white Vespa. We made it in one piece.

"See, wasn't that fun? We got here in less than ten minutes."

"Yeah . . . fun!" I say sarcastically. I remove my helmet, which has flattened my wavy hair. In the reflection of the restaurant's windows, I fix my hair and spike it up.

With our helmets in hand, we stroll on Lincoln Road, passing the Starbucks, boutiques, and outdoor café tables. Tommy was right. The strip is packed with tanned, sculpted men who seem to secretly want to be international models. Women and their artificial bulging cleavages bounce by as if they just left an open casting call for the Pussycat Dolls or a Spanish *telenovela*. We stop at Score bar and grab one of the smaller outdoor tables. We set our Vespa helmets on the chairs across from us.

A manboy bartender takes our drink orders and then disappears into the club with its pounding dance music.

"Isn't this great? The warm tropical air. The swaying coconut palms. If we were in Boston right now, we'd be bundled up in our coats buried in snow," Tommy says, leaning back in his chair and taking in the scene.

"Yeah, this is kind of nice, Tommy. Good job, *loco!* Who knew so many people went out on Christmas. I'm still surprised there are so many people."

When the manboy bartender returns with our drinks, Tommy leans in closer and points to a table of three guys who sit two tables down from us.

"Psst. Look at those guys. Two are pretty cute. One is okay. Actually, isn't that Ted Williams, the Channel 7 news reporter?" Tommy says nonchalantly as he points to the Portuguese-looking guy with short black hair and extremely white teeth. The guy signs some autographs from admiring fans from nearby tables.

"Yeah, you're right. I remember watching him on the news when I lived here. He's such a ham, Tommy. His face is splashed on all the billboards and buses here."

"Oh my gosh, look who he's with!" Tommy's voice rises with sudden enthusiasm. He taps my right arm like a little kid.

"Quien?"

"The guy with the short black hair, blue eyes, skinny physique. He looks pretty Anglo."

"Oye, I can see the guy, but who is he?"

"That's Ray Martinez, the super cute Cuban movie critic at my old newspaper, *The Miami News.* I never got to meet him when I worked there because I was based in the Fort Lauderdale bureau. I always had a little crush on him. I read all his reviews."

"Chico, go and say hi. You have the perfect excuse. You're Cuban gay journalists. Introduce yourself. I bet he'd be interested in talking to you about your experiences at *The Boston Daily."*

"I can't. That would be awkward, Carlos," Tommy says, biting the rim of his index finger. He has been excited and nervous since he noticed Ray Martinez a few feet away.

"Besides, there's another guy at the table, the American-looking one with a goatee and light-brown, spiked hair and a platinum necklace. He kind of looks like a former boy band member."

"Yeah, but that could be a friend. Actually, he's pretty handsome. I've noticed Mr. Backstreet Boy keeps looking at all the Latin hotties, so I don't think they're on a date or anything. Uh oh, I think you missed your chance to meet the one and only Ray Martinez. Look who just arrived."

A thin college-age guy, who looks like a younger John Stamos, sits next to Mr. Martinez and plops a big wet kiss on his lips. Now they're holding hands at the table. They look pretty happy together. A couple.

"Oh well. I guess that's his boyfriend," Tommy says, probably shooting invisible daggers at the kid.

"Yeah, and it looks like the other two are on some sort of Miami manhunt," I offer, taking a swig from my Cuba Libre.

"Yeah, but Ray Martinez is more my type. The other two, not so much."

"Speaking of types, what's going to happen with you and Mike? Inquiring Cuban teachers from Miami want to know."

"Carlos, I don't want to talk about Mikey tonight. We're here to have fun and celebrate Christmas and our families. Let's focus on tonight and us," Tommy demurs, deflecting from the subject at hand. I notice every now and then, he checks his cell phone for new text messages. I bet he'll stay with Mikey, which is fine, but part of me believes that we should date people who balance and nurture us. With Mikey, Tommy plays the rescuer. It's a lot of work. Tommy doesn't need that. No one does.

As we sit back and watch the flowing herd of beautiful muscled Latin men, Tommy and I savor the moment.

I offer our traditional toast.

"To us, the Beantown Cubans in Miami."

"To good friends!" Tommy returns the toast with his Diet Coke and vodka. "And may Ray Martinez and his little boyfriend break up!" Tommy announces a little too loudly. Ray Martinez and the guys at his table glance our way. Embarrassed, I shyly grin and wave.

Ay, que loco.

28

Carlos

SPRING

"Wake up, wake up, Carlito. Today is the big day!" I open my eyes and catch Mami standing by the edge of my bed. She's wearing her favorite sage green dress that she only wore on special occasions. A white gardenia flower is tucked behind her left ear.

"*Ay, Mami!* Five more minutes. I just need five more minutes of sleep." I pull the covers over my face. I hear her high-heeled shoes echo against my wooden floors as she walks toward me. She yanks my comforter and whispers, "You don't want to be late. The school is waiting."

"I know, but I'm nervous." I lift myself and sit upright on my bed.

"But why? You talk in front of your students all the time. Why is this any different? You will just have the entire school there."

I let myself collapse back on my bed. My hands cover my eyes.

"*Ay, Mami*, don't remind me." She tilts her head and smiles. She grabs my hands and pulls me up. Mami gently drags me to the stand-up mirror near my window that overlooks the other Cambridge triple-deckers. As I stand before the mirror, Mami scoots to my closet and grabs my navy blue suit and tie. She hands them to me while she sits down on the corner of the bed.

I start to slip on my slacks.

"Mami, why are you all dressed up? You look different from the other times." Through the mirror's reflection, I see her sitting on the edge of the bed and watching me get ready.

"You don't need me anymore."

"Mami, of course I need you. You're my mother. I love you. I don't know what I would have done this first year in Boston without you." I button up my white dress shirt and tuck it into my slacks.

"But your life is on track again. You and your Papi have found each other. You're happy again. You love your work and your life in Boston. It's time for me to move on."

I turn around and face her. She stands up and adjusts my tie.

"Does this mean that I'll never see you again?"

"I don't know, Carlito, but I promise you this: You will have a great life. You have done so much more than I or your father have ever done. You have become a man I admire.'' She tightens my tie and smooths out my collar.

She grabs my jacket and helps me put it on. We both face the mirror. She stands behind me and rests her beautiful face against my left shoulder.

"Where will you go, Mami?"

"I don't know, but whatever happens, always remember that I love you and I am with you."

I touch the top of her left hand as it rests against my shoulder. I lean my head against hers. We match the pose in the framed photograph that sits on my nightstand.

My radio alarm clock buzzes and jolts me awake. I glance around my room. Mami is gone. A gentle spring breeze blows through my bedroom window. Shafts of morning sunlight drill through the window and cast dancing shadows on my floor. A chorus of birds sing. A lavender fragrance perfumes the room. I look to my bedroom door and notice my suit hangs against it. I lift myself out of bed and begin my day.

★   ★   ★

It is after school. The final bell has rung and I'm ready for my presentation. Dozens of students and faculty have gathered in front of Dorchester High's main entrance along the patch of land that has been long abandoned but is not anymore.

Twirling one of his curly hairs, Tommy stands in the front row and gives me a thumbs-up. He mouths, "You look great, *chico!*" He beams his trademark happy-go-lucky smile. I like seeing him like this again. Although he broke up with Mikey after the New Year, Tommy has slowly bounced back to his old self. He still misses Mikey, but he realized that he can only do so much for the guy. Mikey had to take care of himself and so did Tommy. I respect Tommy even more for walking away from someone he loved so dearly. I guess that old saying is true: When you love someone enough, you let them go and set them free. Tommy loved himself more. Tommy tapped into an inner well of strength and courage to walk away from Mikey this second time around. He has healed slowly but surely from the split. These last few months, Tommy has rechanneled all that energy into his creative writing. He just finished writing his book, and I look forward to reading the rough draft. Another positive note, now I get Tommy all to myself.

Next to Tommy is Papi and Lourdes, who flew up for this special event. Papi looks so cute in his brown slacks and white dress shirt. The sun gleams against his bald head. It's not too warm, a cool 65 degrees. Perfect. The earthy smell of fresh mulch scents the immediate air.

Papi and I have come a long way this past year. We have gradually developed a more solid relationship. When I visit Coral Gables, I do my best to spend time with him even if it involves baseball. At times, I catch myself feeling down. I don't think I will ever be the same since Mami died, and I have accepted that. I don't think anyone really gets over the loss of a loved one. But at least I know that I have one parent I can count on and the love of my sister and friends. This school project has also helped soothe that current of sadness that has weighed on me this past year, but I will get to that momentarily.

I'm trying to make up for all those times Papi wanted to spend quality time with me when I was younger. Three weeks ago, I attended a Florida Marlins game with him in Miami. I still don't know what happens on the field, but I make the most of it. At the house, I've recruited him to help restore the garden. I made him promise to speak to the plants—just as Mami did—when he waters them. At first, he resisted, but he eventually surrendered. The concept seems to be working because Nena, the gardenia tree, has sprung back to life with white bulbous flowers. This weekend, we're planning to attend a Red Sox game, my first. Tommy plans to come with us, which will make it more fun. He will also help me surprise Papi by introducing him to Cuban player Mike Lowell after the game. Tommy is writing a profile on the baseball player and has access to him in the locker room. Papi will be so excited. I can't wait to see the look on his face.

Back at the front of my four-story school, Lou stands and chats with Papi. She wears a light peach dress that complements her light brown straight hair, which falls to her shoulders, the way Mami's did. They both wave to me, and I nod and smile back. Also in the crowd is Dr. Bella Solis, beaming with pride even though she sports a pair of large and oval-shaped Jackie O sunglasses. I'm glad Dr. Bella is here because she was the one who gave me the idea to honor Mami this way. Behind her stands a tall figure with blonde curly hair. I am puzzled to recognize reality TV star Kyle. He waves his right arm and shouts "Yoo hoo!" and flashes his signature Joker's smile. I fake a smile back and wonder, why is he here? *Ay, Kyle!* Oh well, the more the merrier.

I stand in front of this new lush garden that bursts with prime roses, petunias, lilies, hibiscus flowers, and hydraganeas. The flowers' radiant colors brighten the front of the plain brick school and make it more welcoming to students, fellow teachers, and our neighbors. A circle of bricks rings the garden, which is near our flag pole. A yellow butterfly flutters over the petunias and then to the lilies. With everyone gathered, I step up to the podium, unclench my fists, and speak into the microphone.

"Hi, and welcome to Dorchester High. My name is Carlos Martin, and I'm a teacher here. I want to thank you all for being here on this beautiful April day. We are gathered today to honor the work of the inaugural Dorchester High Garden Club. I started this club earlier this year so that our students could take pride in contributing to our school's community. I wanted to show them that if they put their heart and hard work into a project, their efforts would blossom in other ways. I wanted them to be proud of where they are from. But more importantly, I wanted them to be productive members of the community. I wanted them to know that they could make a difference with something as small as this seed that I hold in my hand. Each spring, a new group of students will pick up where the previous group left off so that the garden remains as an ongoing gift to the school and the neighborhood." I pause for a moment and point to the garden. Everyone claps. A thin film of sweat forms around my neck. Across the street, neighbors step out onto their triple-decker front porches. They watch and listen as I continue. Their window sills are also packed with pink and white tulips.

"Before we cut the ribbon, I want to dedicate this garden to my late mother, Maria Martin. She wasn't just a fantastic mother but was also a beautiful and loving wife, neighbor, and friend who believed that we all are special in our own way. My mother is not here with us now, but her spirit is alive in all our hearts and in this garden. I got the idea to start this garden club because of my mother's great love for flowers and nature. Gardening was one of her favorite hobbies, and it brought her great joy and peace. I hope that this garden does the same for our students, faculty, and community."

My eyes well up, and I wipe away a tear that crawls down my cheek. With help from my students, Leroy, Blanca, and Sue, we cut the green ribbon with a giant, plastic pair of scissors. The crowd erupts with more clapping. Tommy whistles and shouts, "You go,

Carlos! *Whoo-hoo!*" With a smirk, I glare at him to quiet down but then laugh.

"I now present to you the Dorchester High Garden Club. Welcome to our garden, your garden." All my students line up in front of the garden and take a bow. Everyone claps in a round of thunderous applause. I know that somewhere, Mami is clapping, too.